# fallen

Also by David Maine

*The Flood*

# fallen David Maine

CANONGATE
Edinburgh · New York · Melbourne

First published in Great Britain in 2006 by
Canongate Books Ltd, 14 High Street,
Edinburgh EH1 1TE

First published in America by St Martin's Press, New York, 2005

1

Copyright © David Maine, 2005

The moral right of the author has been asserted

*British Library Cataloguing-in-Publication Data*
A catalogue record for this book is available on
request from the British Library

1 84195 684 8 (10 Digit ISBN)
978 184195 684 8 (13 Digit ISBN)

Printed and bound in Great Britain by
Creative Print & Design, Ebbw Vale, Wales

www.canongate.net

for my family

# Contents

## Book Three
The Family

## Book Four
The Fall

**book one** *the murder*

# 40 *the old man*

The mark burns upon him all the time now. Its hurt is open and shameful like a scab picked until it bleeds. In years past he could find ways to forget it or at least misplace his awareness for a while; it was never easy but he managed. These days he cannot. There is nothing to fill Cain's time so the mark does this for him.

It stains his flesh like a parasite.

Countless people have witnessed it over the years, but even those who have not don't lack for an opinion. Some say it is a letter—the first letter of his name, reversed to show God's displeasure. Others say it carries the shape of a stillborn child, or a wolf's skull, or a coiled serpent. Still others, less fanciful perhaps or just duller, claim it is no picture at all. Merely a smear unreadable, the Devil's thumbprint or God's. What does the shape matter? The point is, it is there, plainly visible, crying out to be seen.

But the miracle lies in the seeing. For all those who look upon the mark see it differently. Like the Tower of Babel reflected mirrorwise, everyone who lays eyes upon Cain's face beholds something different from all the others, sees the message spelled in a different tongue, though the message is always the same.

And what message is thus conveyed? A simple one: Don't touch. Stay away. Leave this one alone.

The others in this house, Cain's in-laws and grandchildren, heed this advice and give him a wide berth. Only his son remains stubbornly loyal. And recently, his dead brother as well.

But now Cain is convinced that Abel has left him forever: tonight's visit was his last. So with nothing more to do, he waits to die.

He is not being dramatic. Among his many faults, this is not one. He expects to be dead by morning.

The old man shifts and wheezes. The wet climate he finds himself banished to torments his breathing. Deserts are tough but at least the air is clean. Not that he expects sympathy: impetuous he may be, hot-tempered and violent, resentful and self-pitying, any number of undesirable qualities. But he has never been stupid.

So then. He shifts his weight in the crepuscular gloom of the hut and allows his gaze to drift past the low open entryway, outside to where the fading crimson sky has clotted into dusk. From outside float children's laughter and the calmer voice of his son. Cain knows he is not welcome out there. Nor unwelcome exactly; but if he ventured from his hut the voices would quickly fade, glances would be cast down, the children would drift off, and the women's mouths would tighten.

No. He will stay inside this night. At least it will be his last such.

Cain settles onto the earth, arms folded behind his head. A sigh ripples through his nose and musses the yellowing whiskers of his beard. So the matter of his mortality has been decided. In a strange way a burden has been lifted. If he were carefree he might start whistling, but he is not. He is a man who dwells upon serious thoughts. As a boy he dwelt upon serious thoughts. As a fetus in his mother's womb he was prone, quite likely, to serious ruminations, while his lighthearted brother simply enjoyed spinning and kicking in the watery gloom. People change in some ways as they grow; in other ways they don't.

Maybe that's the nub of it, he thinks. Maybe that's where all the problems started between himself and his brother—himself and his mother—himself and his father. With two unborn souls, spinning or brooding in the watery wet, waiting for the unforgiving light of their first morning.

There is something in that, some truth waiting to be grasped like a teat in an infant's hand. But like that teat, the truth is too large and unwieldy for the old man's grip, and when he clutches at it, it bounces to one side, slipping heavily from his fingers. And whatever lies beyond Cain's vague sense of disquiet slips away as well.

He is old and gets distracted easily. When the idea is gone he doesn't bother to follow it, and soon forgets it altogether.

•

This evening Cain appears calm but he his not. His terror is that of a tiny boy dropped from a great height during a thunderstorm while vultures pluck his flesh. His stomach feels slightly out of kilter, down where his intestines should be. This makes his midriff hurt. It makes his back and his loins and his molars hurt. Was this how his brother felt as the life hurtled from his body, or did he feel something else entirely? Rage for example or bewilderment, or perhaps an overwhelming grief that blotted out all else with enormous reptilian wings?

Cain tucks his chin against his clavicle, shuts his eyes tight, and tries to keep the world at bay. Outside, his grandson Irad cackles as the children play some game involving rocks and noise. He is, he thinks, almost ready to leave this place behind forever. Almost eager, in fact.

Almost.

So behold him there: Cain lying alone in the hut, thinking back on his life, tallying it up. Waiting to die.

# 39 *the brother*

Lately something strange has been happening to Cain: he has been having conversations with his dead brother. In the early morning, during the rift between sleep and consciousness, Abel appears in the hut, squatting at the foot of Cain's sleeping mat, cracking his knuckles or picking his teeth.—And how is it with you lately? he likes to ask. His voice is colorless, like the air.

Abel has been gone fifty years now, and Cain is a jumpy, scared old man.

These visitations terrify him, but the terror precludes any violent outcry. He does not command Spirit begone! or Out with you, shade! or any of a dozen other entreaties that cram into his mouth. Fear commands that he lie half-groggy on his mat and converse civilly with his long-murdered brother. So he replies, I am well enough.

—That's good to hear, nods Abel. He says this every time, with the same bland sincerity that used to so curdle Cain's nerves when they were both younger. Just boys really. And alive.

Abel says this every time too:—Soon we'll be reunited. I'm looking forward to it.

Cain says nothing but wonders if this is true. Hopes it is. Fears it is.

Abel's fingers brush against the floor of the hut, leaving no furrows in the sand. He looks no older than the day when Cain pummeled him with a stone and pitched him off a cliff. For that matter there is no sign of the violence of his death. Green eyes flicker from a broad, open face, and a tangle of brown curls caresses his shoulders. He had always been a pretty youth, olive-skinned and dimpled: five decades of extinction has not changed this. Cain grimaces. He is

crippled and riven with pain, and sometimes his eyes water with un-
fairness of it: that Abel should remain eternally young, while Cain
must suffer rancid teeth and creaking joints and incontinence and all
the rest.

He is fully aware of the absurdity of this.

•

Tonight Abel appears for one final visit.—Father appears well, he
says, as if Cain has asked. But he hasn't: Cain never asks. He left
that family behind long ago, and if he is startled by the longevity of
his parents, he doesn't let it show.

—Mother too, Abel continues.—Everyone settled now, with
grandchildren, except for the twins who died some time ago.

—I didn't know that.

—Oh yes. Epon and Epna. By the plague, within days of each
other. Also Kerod, in childbirth, and the infant as well. A boy.

Cain digests this. The names echo in his memory like rusted bells.
He can barely recall their faces, but hadn't Kerod been special to
him, once?

—Everyone else is all right, Abel continues.—The other children
and that, that—His hand flutters.—Seth. The one who—took my
place.

—Yes, I remember your speaking of him, says Cain. The puzzle-
ment in his brother's voice when he mentions Seth is one of Cain's
few pleasures these days.—Our parents didn't waste much time in
mourning, did they?

Petulant, Abel frowns.

Cain impassively ponders his parents' advanced years. If age
weighs so heavily on him, how must they feel? Spent indeed by all
accounts. Ready to find a comfortable grave and stretch out. Well,
good luck to them. Or perhaps not—perhaps their days are lightened by grandchildren who do not fear to kiss them, by in-laws who
do not spurn them, by neighbors who speak their names aloud and
not in whispered invocations used to frighten wayward children.

Cain can only imagine such an existence.

Then Abel says, You should go see them.

Anger wells up at that, oozes through Cain like pus. The intensity of it catches him off guard. Those two little words—*you should*—are like the memory of a slap.—I'm not long for this world, as you well know. And why would I go anyway? Besides to kill *him*, perhaps. Finish the job I started.

Abel is already starting to vanish.—Don't talk like that.

—Piss off. I'll say what I like.

—For now, brother. For now . . .

—Piss off I said!

He is cursing an empty room.

The encounter leaves him trembling, but whether with rage or fear he can't say. Not for the first time he wonders bitterly: Why does it have to be his brother who so visits? Why can't it be his wife? He would give much for a few moments with Zoru again.

Though perhaps—just perhaps—it is better this way.

•

No great revelation ever comes from these appearances, no warnings of damnation or promises of redemption. Just a few words, an implicit reminder. A notification as it were.

In a way Cain is grateful for this. There are many damning things his brother could tell him that would bring no joy whatsoever.

•

Another memory dogs him lately:

A boy's flickering face, a lupine stranger lit by firelight, leaning eagerly forward. A certain glitter to the eyes as he says, If it wasn't for you, he'd still be alive right now.

Decades ago, this was. The boy had not been speaking of Abel.

—Sitting here talking to you, the wolflike boy had said.—Instead of me.

Recently Cain has grown preoccupied with that conversation and all it implies. This might be why he calls out in his sleep from time to time, Do you forgive me?

8

**fallen**

There is never any answer, of course—there is no one around to hear him, and even if there were, who would take the responsibility of answering? Maybe this is why Cain always wakes, morning after morning, with a heavy feeling of unutterable sadness in his gut. Heavy and painful, as if he long ago swallowed something unhealthy, and is only now starting to properly digest it.

# 38 *the son*

The morning before Cain's last night on earth—the morning before Abel's final appearance—Cain is visited by his son, Henoch. This is expected. This happens every day.

For many years Henoch has been famous as a builder. He is known as the architect of the city in which his family now lives. Stories tell of how he would dream palaces by night and then construct them by day, hard against the wide straight boulevards from his dreams, interspersed with public plazas and watercourses and covered bazaars and temples and a harbor and plenty of plain ordinary homes for the plain ordinary people of his city. Fishermen and traders and husbandmen and so forth. This grand project had taken many years, starting in virtual obscurity but, as he labored and word of his glorious city spread, attracting all manner of men like gnats to a campfire. Some of these men brought their families and settled in the city and added their skills and industry to its glory. Some of them, predictably, were rabble who added nothing but had much to say.

Henoch was not a boastful man or a proud one but apparently he saw little point in hiding his light under a bushel. So when he completed building his city, he retired from the sight of men for many days to think on its proper name, before finally deciding on: Henoch.

This caused no small amount of glee among the rabble.

—Henoch? they cried.—He's named the city after himself? What, are all his children named Henoch too?

—And his wife! giggled one.

—And his goats! snickered another.

—And his mother! brayed a third.—And his father too!

At this they fell silent. Everyone knew who Henoch's father was. No city, regardless of its charm and wonder, could outshine the shadows of *that* notoriety. No boulevards, no matter how flawless, could make straight a lineage *that* crooked. No city need ever be named Cain to ensure *that* name's preservation for posterity.

—Well anyway, snorted the rabble after it took a moment to collect itself.—Naming it Henoch, there's presumption for you.

The mystery was: Where was Henoch's father, anyway? Henoch himself was visible everywhere during those years, sweating through the long humid days, planing boards and firing bricks and carving stone and laying cobbles. A big man with arms as wide as most men are tall. Muscles rippling under his shoulders like angry snakes. He would have intimidated people but for his laugh, which set other men at ease and caused women to wonder why their husbands were not so. Henoch laughed often and liked to remark that this lifted more burdens than his shoulders ever could.

His mother Zoru had died years before, taken off by the plague. People well remembered his grief at that: it had been epic, and all construction had halted for the better part of a year. During that time Henoch's booming laugh went unheard.

But the old man? No one knew where he'd gone, though rumors abounded that he'd long ago been banished east, east. But east was *here,* where Henoch had built his city. And so the mystery remained.

What neither the rabble nor the upright citizens knew was that Henoch the man had not designed Henoch the city. Cain had done so, from his hidden lair. Henoch had merely carried out his instructions. The boulevards and bazaars and palaces and plazas were all Cain's doing. His motivation for this he kept to himself, though Henoch enjoyed the work well enough and could not deny that it had brought him prosperity as well as an unexpected closeness to his moody, difficult father.

The project lasted many years, until one morning Henoch was informed by Cain:—Enough. I am done. Let them finish the rest without me.

—All right, said the son.

Cain went on, There remains only the matter of a name for this place. I have thought long on the subject and have decided it will be named for you.

Henoch's braying laughter was reminiscent of a kid goat.—Eh?

—The city, his father explained gravely, shall be named Henoch.

Henoch laughed even harder.—What rubbish.

Cain's expression was that of a man in middling discomfort.—Nonetheless.

—Father, you can't expect me to go out there and announce to the whole city that they're to be named after me. What will people think?

Cain met Henoch's grinning face with a severe look of his own.—I have long since stopped caring what others think, he said.—Of me, or of anything else.

●

This morning Henoch visits his father in his hut in the family compound. Henoch tried for years to convince his father to quit his self-imposed exile and move into the family rooms, but the old man is stubborn as a tortoise and half as expressive. Finally the boy gave up.

Cain refuses the breakfast Henoch brings this morning, saying, I may die tonight.

—So may we all, laughs his son. His expression suggests that the idea does not trouble him greatly—that he would, in fact, take it as something of a lark.

Cain furrows his brows. This glibness of his son has always puzzled him, but a voice in his ear whispers, Let it go.

Henoch is a busy man and Cain knows this. Even with construction ended, there are many demands on his time as first citizen. Crops must be sowed and woodland cleared; merchants approaching from the west must be met and assessed. Disputes over property and marriage and inheritance need settling. There is much assuaging of tempers and coddling of egos. Some days there is time for his father's indulgent grimness, but this is not one of those days.

Cain does not judge Henoch harshly. Hundreds of times over the years, father has greeted son by mumbling: I may die tonight. There is no way for the boy to know that, this morning of all mornings, the words are true.

Now Henoch says, A caravan approaches from the west.

Cain shrugs as if this gossip is of no concern. The whiskers of his beard nearest his mouth and chin have yellowed with age. As a younger man his hair and beard were yellow as sunlight: it looks almost as if Cain's younger self has returned after a long absence.

—Perhaps they bring that strange fiber with them, says Henoch.—What do they call it? Cotton.

Cain grunts something noncommittal.

—It's good for clothes, Henoch continues breezily. When Cain has no answer, he tries again.—This dry spell continues undiminished. The farmers grow concerned about the sowing.

Cain responds as a piece of stone might. Or not so much: even quartz glitters and opal changes as light falls upon them. But his eyes remain pale blue and static as he gazes past the entryway into the morning sky, also pale blue and static. There is no moisture in the air, no promise of rain later. For this time of year, such weather is unusual.

Henoch's good cheer falters. He stops talking and instead pokes at his teeth with a piece of straw.

Cain's calm demeanor masks turbulent memories. He is reminded of a similar springtime morning thirty years earlier, equally sunny, equally pale and dry. He wonders if his son would remember as well. Henoch had been little more than a skinny youth when Cain beckoned him to the family's hut. Already in those days Cain rarely ventured out. The family scratched crops from the ground, netted fish in the bay and drew water from the spring, with thrushes and larks and a few miserable wild pigs for company. There was no city at all, no boulevards or bazaars or grand houses, and few enough people happened by: it was the edge of the world. But Cain carried the mark on him and disliked even chance encounters with strangers.

On that morning Cain talked to his son and noted that Henoch was distracted by a pair of cooing doves and a small tumult of finches playing in the field nearby. It was only when his father paused that Henoch looked at him, sheepish, and Cain realized he'd not been listening at all.

—I'm sorry, Father?

Cain sighed.—Attend. I have visions of a city rising up in this desolate place. We shall build it together, but you must be my public face.

—A city? frowned Henoch.—But there is nothing here.

—All the more reason, his father answered with a logic that appeared to quite stymie the son.—If there were a city here already, we could not build another.

The son frowned but made no argument.

Cain put his hand on Henoch's shoulder, a gesture that elicited a violent start from the boy: they were not a family much given to displays of physical affection, and Cain suspected that—son or no son—Henoch was perfectly aware of what his sire's hands were reputed to have done. To blood kin, no less.

And a man who could kill his own brother . . .

—Look, Cain said, a bit louder than necessary. As if drowning out the startled wail of his own unpleasant thoughts. He guided Henoch to the little clearing that fronted the hut, and with a sweep of his arm illustrated his tour of the surrounding country.—To the east, the ocean's natural bay is ideal for the traders from across the water. We shall build some piers there. The grassland to the south is perfect to grow whatever crops we want.

Henoch protested, We already have all we need.

—Not for us. For the people who come to live in the city.

—I see, said Henoch, though it was obvious he didn't.

—To the west run the caravan routes, continued Cain. A flicker of something cut across his eyes, and for a moment he looked— wistful? Nostalgic? Bitter?—There is much we'll barter for, once we have workshops of our own.

—What will the workshops make?

Cain pointed to the forest in the north.—Furniture and carvings. Ceramics from the river clay. Copper, if we can find it, for kitchen items. We'll need workshops in that area, and a wide avenue to the harbor, and a bazaar, and over there—he gestured vaguely—some sort of caravanserai.

Henoch nodded thoughtfully.—And people, he said at length.

—Indeed. People with the skill to make all this happen.

—Weavers, suggested Henoch.—Leatherworkers.

—Fine idea, Cain nodded.—Weavers it is. We'll need to grow flax then, and raise goats if you're serious about the leather.

—Sure I am.

—We have much labor to look forward to then. Cain risked another pat on the boy's shoulder, and this time he didn't jump.—But together we'll make light work of it. When we're through, a proper home is what we'll have.

Henoch stood frowning, taking it all in, and Cain wondered if he could give it shape in his head. He hoped so. Henoch was a practical youth, good with his hands, precise in his eye, and if not strong for his age, then at least willing to work; but visualizing things he'd never actually witnessed was not a habit in him. Cain on the other hand imagined things all the time: his brother's thoughts as he flew to his doom; his father's expression upon receiving the news . . .

Suddenly Henoch turned to him, smiling broadly as if those famous, violent hands had been forgotten.

But never—Cain knew this—for long.

—You've given much thought to this project.

Cain nodded: it was true. But as if his day's quota of truth had been exhausted, a lie then skated off his tongue.—For some time now, I've thought of little else.

•

Nearly thirty years later, Henoch slaps his knees, rises with a grunt.—I must go. If we truly are to die tonight, there's much to finish beforehand.

His son's odd humor again. Cain forces a thin smile and bestows his standard farewell.—Be productive.

Henoch stands in the doorway hesitantly. There's an air of concern on his face and Cain wonders if he looks especially awful today. He certainly feels especially awful.

Henoch asks, Is there anything you need?

For a moment Cain considers the answers that spring to mind: *There is much I need, but you can't get it for me.* Or more simply, *I need your mother.* But he is not prone to such maudlin and says only, You are busy, go and don't mind me.

A moment longer Henoch lingers. Then he is out the door. Cain hears him exhale loudly, as if sighing in relief, but knows too that he is an old man and his ears may be playing tricks on him.

# 37  *thirty years previous*

Finally one afternoon, indiscernible from countless other afternoons since his exile began, Cain stops and looks about him. He breathes deep, eyeballs the cove and beach, surveys the grassland with a critical eye. Squints at the forest as if calculating something. The wife and child wait.

—This is far enough, he announces at length.—We'll stop here.

Zoru glances about her but seems too dazed to take in much of her surroundings. In a voice as gray and washed out as her eyes she asks, For how long?

—For good.

Even this pronouncement fails to stir her. Zoru stops and turns to wait for Henoch, who shambles along two dozen paces behind them. The boy is overcoming a fever and rash, and has lost his customary energy and spirit. Zoru fusses over him, placing her hands on his cheeks while he grumpily protests being treated like a child.

Cain unloads the bags draped across the donkey's back. They have with them a small tent, a few rough tools of stone and wood and a narrow copper blade for skinning game, some kitchen utensils and blankets. This plus a few lengths of net and twine make up their possessions in this life. The donkey was old when they got it and has traveled hundreds of leagues with them. It is good for perhaps another few months.

They had brought some chickens but they died. They had brought goats that ran off one night when Henoch failed to properly tether them. Cain shuts his eyes at the memory and calms his hands. It was years ago but the episode still rankles.

A voice in his ear whispers, It is long past. Don't dwell on it.

The family has made camp countless times before, and each knows what is expected. Cain explores the beach, which as he had hoped slopes gently into water so clear as to be nearly colorless. An abundance of fish flutters through it like sedate butterflies, finger-length and brightly colored; a few are large enough to eat. Cain twirls in the sand, his footprints describing little arcs behind him as he casts the net. He hauls the catch ashore and lets the fry wriggle back into the waves, keeping only a pair of silvery-gray grouper longer than his feet. These he tosses onto the sand to spasm and die while he unfurls the net again. Before long he has more than enough for tonight's supper and tomorrow's breakfast as well.

He enjoys the work so much he goes on with it, releasing the net and hauling it in, setting the creatures free. His movements are practiced and smooth yet minutely different each time. It might be, Cain reflects, the thing that he has learned how to do best in his entire life.

Zoru has built a fire by the time he returns, while Henoch scavenges more firewood. Henoch had pleaded fatigue and sickness, but Zoru told him to get on with it anyway. Cain approves: fever or no, everybody does his part. But Henoch has passed from the childhood stage of unfettered adoration for his father, and has moved to a difficult point of feeling that every demand on his person is a deeply rooted injustice.

Cain grimaces at the remembered familiarity of *that.*

He squats and drops the fish at Zoru's feet. She switches without pause from feeding the fire to gutting the animals. She is a dark-skinned woman designed with little excess flesh, but a great deal of energy. Masses of black hair fling themselves from her head in all directions.

—I think we could prosper here, Cain says.

—It's a good sign that we caught these fish so easily.

He smiles at that—*we* caught?—but nods.—Plenty of fertile land. And the spring of course.

The spring bubbles up from the ground a few hundred cubits to the east, and runs in a tinkling brook to the sea.

Zoru uses a forearm to wipe a strand of hair from her eye.—I'm glad we're stopping, she says in a low voice.—The boy's tired. And so am I.

—I know.

—We can't keep on forever.

—I know.

It is a conversation they have held many times over the years. Given the circumstances, it seems now to have run its course, like the spring emptying onto the beach.

Henoch returns, dragging a small lightning-struck sapling. It is too green to burn well: it will smoke and sputter and provide little heat. Cain sighs through his nose. Doubtless the boy grew tired of looking for something appropriate, and simply dragged back the first fallen tree that came to hand. He's old enough to know good wood from bad.

Or is he? Perhaps not. Perhaps Cain has not taught him, or not in a way that the child can understand.

Cain wonders, not for the first time, whether a child is born with the man already inside him waiting to emerge; or if there is only a blankness, a void inside ready to be filled with whatever might be placed there. It is a question that has nagged for much of his life, and he has never yet found a satisfying answer.

Henoch wrestles the resilient gray branches off the sapling and feeds them to the fire. His father watches and his mother burns the fish in a flat copper pan. As expected, the new wood is smoky. Parents and child engage in an elaborate dance to avoid choking, by bobbing and weaving their heads whenever the wispy gray fingers clutch at them.

Cain wonders what his father had made of him at this age. The idea is startling, that he and his father might have such things in common as the pleasures and annoyances of parenthood. Seldom has he let himself consider the world through his father's eyes.

What *had* he been like, at age fourteen? Surly and sullen, no question. Silent much of the time. A child much given to brooding and calculation and tallying up the day's unfairnesses. Admittedly, there had been unfairnesses to tally. And whose fault, ultimately, was that?

The picture comes back to his mind then: his father standing over him, quaking in fury, his brown face even darker than usual. Black eyes glittering like comets. White threads coursing through the kinky mass of his beard. *Never have I beheld such an abomination.* . . . 

Cain on the ground, mortified, the image of his mother's naked backside still fresh in his mind.

His blood still sang at the memory. And at his brother's voice, later that night, in his ear.—You've nobody to blame but yourself, you know.

The words settled around his heart like an infection.

That might have been the turning point, Cain thinks now. As he has thought many times over the years. That might have been the moment when he decided, at age fourteen, that one day he was going to have to kill his brother. Not for humiliating him, no. His father had done that. But for saying he deserved it.

•

He hadn't always hated his brother. What child did? The feeling had grown up like a weed, sprouting on soil too harsh to support any more useful fruit. In time it thickened, its stems growing woody and tough. When at last it flowered, its blooms were brilliant red and its perfume carried an acrid tang.

His father, a fair enough man by most standards, had tried his best with the youngster. But as the years passed and the family accumulated children one after another, even Adam had proved unequal to the task of adequately loving his firstborn.

As for Cain's mother, well. Cain can barely remember her face.

So then: maybe he is the original misanthrope. The thought does not exactly warm him, but it doesn't scare him either. He has many reasons to scorn the bulk of humanity, and feels no shame for it. But what about his son? Will he scorn Henoch as much as he has scorned nearly everyone else? Does he *want* to?

The thought pains his stomach. It's not true . . . he doesn't think.

The boy adds another handful of green twigs to the fire. He catches Cain watching him and demands, What?

Cain blinks.—Sorry?

—You're staring at me again.

—Just thinking.

—Think someplace else then.

—That's enough! snaps Zoru.

Such cheek! And it can't all be blamed on the boy's illness. Had Cain ever dared to speak so disrespectfully to his own father?

Well, yes. Often in fact.

Cain looks away, grinning in spite of himself. Better that the boy has spirit than be a toadying foot-licker, like *some* he could mention.

He sets aside his worries. How could he ever scorn Henoch? It's normal enough to grow a bit impatient with the boy from time to time. Or so he hopes. But to banish Henoch from his sight, the way his own father banished him—the very idea causes his insides to clench up. He could never do such a thing.

But an insistent voice nags: Had Adam felt the same? Cain remembers their conversation on the night Adam revealed his origins.—I would never send you away, he had said. And Cain had urged, But just suppose.

—Never, repeated Adam.

Now another gust of smoke tightens Cain's throat. Liar, he thinks bitterly. Lying son of a bitch.

*Never have I beheld such an abomination. . . .*

Zoru slides a fat-bellied fish onto each of their plates.—Your father says we'll stay here and wander no longer.

The boy turns moss-green eyes on him.—It's true?

Cain nods.

They eat for a time in silence. Cain steals glances at his son, who appears distracted and flushed. Small pink spots prickle his arms and cheeks and Cain has a sudden vision of his boy as one of those thin, bandy-legged men who never grow into any vitality. Something like Cain's own father in fact. He fervently hopes this isn't true.

Picking at his food without interest, Henoch gazes about in a constant review of his surroundings. He so resembles a sparrow guarding its nest that Cain smiles again.

The boy overlooks nothing: he remarks this too.—What?

—You seem most interested in your new home, Cain tells him.
His face is grave.—It's my first.

—True enough, Cain nods.

—It'll be different to stay in one place, says Zoru.—But you'll get used to it.

The boy nods eagerly.—I'm tired of wandering.

Zoru's eyes hook Cain's for a moment before pulling away. Momentarily he feels the sadness of never having asked Henoch: So, what would you like to do? Nor his wife for that matter.

He bends into the fish, and bones crackle under his teeth. Hot oil slickens his lips.

No point in regret. If he needed to wander this far, so be it. Nothing to be done about it now. What could be done, though—what he *could* do—

Cain lets his gaze rest upon his son. A project of some sort is needed, something to bring them together. After all this time, there is still much they do not know about each other. Too much. And yes, he can hear the malcontent voice in the back of his mind demand, How much can any of us truly know another? To which he answers, That is beside the point. I must make the effort.

The boy is watching him again.—What now? he demands.—You keep staring at me that way you do sometimes.

—Think nothing of it, grimaces Cain, turning his attention once more to his supper.

The boy doesn't speak. Cain has to wonder what the child means by *the way you do sometimes*.

Now is not the moment to broach the subject of a project. Time for that later. They have never lived together in one place as a family, and his own experience in this regard is not encouraging. He must wait and decide how to proceed. He must think carefully. He must hit upon just the perfect plan.

But first they must all work together to make this wild place a home.

# 36 *the mistake*

When they wake the goats are gone.

It is Zoru who finds the tethers bundled at the boy's feet. The child, barely five years old, sleeps the sleep of the innocent, but his mother stares at the boy in a haze of uncertainty, as if knowing that she must act swiftly, or these may be the last innocent moments of his life.

Cain watches as she twists the rawhide in her fingers. Her breathing is quick and nervous and she gazes about her like a fluttery squirrel, but Cain has gone to piss behind a screen of hemlocks. As the urine streams out, fury floods in to take its place. Cain voids himself and watches his wife and can almost hear her think: What to do?

Before she can decide, he is there like a vision. Like a swarm, like rage.—Where are they? he hisses.

Zoru glances as if baffled.—Where are what?

The palm of his hand spins her to the ground. Long moments pass before her face rearranges itself into pain. Black spots drip into the brown earth, spreading like spilt wine. There is something satisfying in this. A tormenting voice in his mind keens, More! More!

Had his father heard such howling?

—Vex me not, growls Cain. His hands tremble. Part of him wants to vomit in rage and fear. He has not felt this way for a long time.

Zoru blinks away saltwater and raises her head to see her husband looming over her child. The look on her face suggests that Cain has ceased to be human. In his hand he hefts a gray stone. Zoru screams.

•

Cain stands with the stone in his hand. It is a good stone, smoothened by wind and rain till its warm soft curves fit his palm like the skull of a small animal. It feels like a friend. It feels like the stiffest erection in history and something perfectly suited for the job at hand: to pulp the head of a child lying helpless on the ground. It has no sharp edges or brittle corners, nothing to cut flesh, draw blood, make a mess. It will simply stave in the skull of the five-year-old and crush the brain beneath to a useless tangle of sponge. Cain knows perfectly well what the stone will do and how to use it for maximum effect. After all, he has done this before.

Zoru screams.

It is a scream to wake the dead: in this case it wakes Henoch, who responds not by screaming in answer or jumping up to flee or diving into his mother's arms. His response is to lie as still as a lizard on a rock and stare up at his father with almond-shaped eyes the size of hen's eggs. Moss green those eyes are, like his uncle's. His dead Uncle Abel whom he's never met.

Perhaps his reaction saves his life. Run from the hunter and the hunter will chase. But lie still—

Cain stares down at the child, his son. Not his brother: his son. The boy gazes up like some small furry creature. Cain feels the battle swirling within his arms and heart and mind. The battle between the desire for blood and the desire for calm. Calm would make him feel better later. Blood would make him feel better *now*. He can almost hear voices beside him whispering, screeching, debating in measured tones. The boy needs to be punished, says one.

It was a simple mistake, says another. Have you never made one?

This mistake stands to kill us all.

He's just a boy.

He'll not get much older if we all starve to death.

Don't be dramatic. There's plenty to hunt, and fruit besides.

Nonetheless he needs to learn.

Exactly! To learn, not to die.

Cain's arms tremble. Something is burrowing through his bicep, some worm or centipede, that causes it to twitch. He flexes his arm, raising the stone alongside his chin, and Zoru shrieks: Don't!

—Oh hush, woman.

—Father, whispers the boy.

—It's all right, Cain mutters.

—Father, the boy repeats.—You're not going to kill me, are you?

—Of course not.

Shame crashes across him then like surf, like a cataract or water-fall, but not cleansing. Just the opposite—dirtying, like a bath of sputum. He wonders, What is wrong with me? What do I lack? What normal family feeling, what sympathetic connection to others has been left out of my frame? First my brother. Is it someday to be my son as well?

From the past his father roars *You are an abomination . . .*

Memories of the wolf-faced boy flicker beside him as well:—So in a way it's as if you killed *him* too.

Cain shudders back to the present and forces a smile—never his best skill—that leaves his face looking sepulchral. Through exposed teeth he grits, I could never hurt you. How could you suggest such a thing?

—You have a rock.

He looks down. He does not even remember picking it up. The stone rests in his hand with undeniable ease, a slightly embarrassing friend: an acquaintance from younger, more impetuous days, one who has witnessed such things as would cause scandal if unearthed now.

—This? It's . . . nothing.

The stone thuds into the earth a few paces behind him. For a moment the tableau remains, the three of them watching each other. Cain feels rinsed out and empty, like the skin of an animal that has had all its entrails removed.

He wonders how the hell he has gotten to such a pass.

From far off echoes the inquisitive bleating of a goat.

•

They spend the morning fruitlessly tracking the animals. It's no use: they have gotten too much of a head start. At midday the family finishes the last of the flatbread and Cain says, No point wasting more time.

—You intend on journeying further? asks Zoru.

—I do.

—Where?

—East.

She sighs thinly.

The boy wanders off to the woods to relieve himself. Cain takes the opportunity to say quietly but urgently, Listen. I know I lost my temper this morning. Maybe I was wrong, but you need to understand—those goats may prove vital.

—Or they may not, she says.

He nods at the possibility.—The point is, I was upset and I may have scared the boy. Perhaps I even scared you. But there was never any danger of anything happening.

She listens without comment.

—Do you understand what I'm saying?

A long silence then as she mulls his words. There are often such pauses between them. Always Cain is reminded of the first such: a silence filled with the creaking of cicadas and frogs from the nighttime darkness.

At length she looks at him and shrugs.

He says thickly, I want to be sure you understand.

Instead of answering him she says, You say we're moving on. Why? We've seen neither habitations nor caravans for months. Haven't we traveled far enough?

—No, he answers.

He says nothing more, wondering if she'll pursue this, or if she'll address his earlier point. Sometimes she does; sometimes not. The boy returns from the woods and regards them both with the expression of a cat that has woken up suddenly.

Zoru asks, What exactly are we looking for?

It is a habit of hers, this saying *we* instead of *you*. Cain considers for a time before admitting, I don't understand your question.

—How will we know when we've gone far enough? That we can stop?

Now it is Cain's turn to gaze around him.—I will know when I get there.

—That's not much of an answer.

There is a challenge in her voice. Perhaps she thinks it is safe to provoke him while he is still shamed from this morning's violence. And perhaps she is right. Zoru is an observant woman, Cain knows. She rarely pushes him to display his anger: this morning, when he struck her, was a rare exception. At such moments he is his father's son all over again—his brother's brother—and none too proud of it.

—It's all the answer I've got, he mutters, and stands to load up the donkey once again.

# 35 *the proposal*

The woman is neither young nor old, neither tall nor short, pretty nor plain. She is, however, slim. And brown, from both the sun and God's design. Her unruly black curls, threaded with silver, fight to escape the kerchief that struggles to restrain them. Her hands are as shiny as wood and probably just as hard.

Cain sees her fetching water from a well some distance outside a small village. He does not know the name of the village or whether it has a name. Years of wandering have curbed his curiosity about human habitations; he cares only whether they can provide him with basic commodities like food and whether they will treat him with open hostility or with sullen, subdued fear.

There are no other responses. Except one, which he struggles to forget: a narrow boy's wolflike features, hunkered eagerly over the fire, eyes glittering into Cain's.—If it wasn't for you, he'd still be alive right now.

Cain pushes the memory away, hard. Forces himself to focus on the woman.

She is bent over the low stone wall ringing the well, showing her hindquarters off to good effect. Her hips are ample and circular and Cain likes this. Cain has never had much experience with women but when he sets eyes on her generous backside he is filled with unapologetic lust.

He approaches her and asks for water. She looks at him, sees the mark upon him and looks again. Then she gives him the urn.

He drinks while she watches him. He wipes his mouth and says, You know who I am.

—I know your reputation.

28

—Then you know I am a dangerous man.

—I know you were said to be such once.

The reply gives him pause, and to conceal this he drinks again although he is no longer thirsty. By the time he finishes he has decided what to say next.

—So you know I am shunned by man and God alike.

With a wry smile she takes the urn from his hands.—Be thankful then that I am neither.

He is quite speechless. As she makes her way along the footpath back to the village, he stands and stares after her. It is possible that his mouth actually hangs open. It has been many years since any woman has chosen to have a civil conversation with him. Perhaps it is this, more than the curling black hair (with a few silver threads) or the generous haunches (round like cushions) that smites him. Or perhaps it is all of these things together, like a circle of palms rising out of the desert heat, wavering on the horizon: a promise of what could be.

•

He follows the woman into the village. People see him and conversations limp away like cripples. Men stand in the fields, sticks and scythes in their hands, and follow him with their eyes. Children cease their games. Women clutch sucklings a little closer. Crows and vultures seem unconcerned, but then, crows and vultures always do.

The woman ducks into a hut at the far edge of the village. Even by local standards it is modest. Walls sag like old ideas, holes gape in the roofing. The bricks are no more than cast-offs, broken pieces that would be discarded by anyone with a choice.

Cain waylays a scared-looking youngster and demands, Who lives there?

Snot dribbles from the urchin's nose. He wipes it reflexively, recasting the dribble as a shiny smear.—Zoru and her father. He's blind.

—And the mother?

—Dead.

Cain considers. The boy looks ready to bolt but is perhaps too afraid. Cain asks, This Zoru is unmarried?

—She's a charity case, the boy answers promptly.—People give her food out of sympathy. No man would have her.

Cain spits at the boy's feet and growls, What exactly would you know about *having* women?

The boy, scared again, backs away.

—You can go, Cain tells him, and he runs off.

Outside the hut he clears his throat but nothing happens. He does so again. Behind him he hears a rustle. Cain has the impression that if he looked over his shoulder he'd spot a dozen pairs of eyes boring into him.

Instead he says, Hello?

A voice floats out to him. Her voice.—Who's there?

—The man you're not afraid of.

There are shuffling sounds, sounds of things being set aside, bodies realigned.—What do you want?

This brings Cain up short. What *does* he want? The answer to that is both simple and very complicated. To sit down somewhere without worrying that he will soon have to run off again. To talk to people who do not shun him. To smell the air exhaled by a woman. To eat the food she hands him and see the flutter of her hands as she talks. To go home.

These are difficult things to explain. Cain turns away.—I should not have disturbed you.

He has taken three slow steps when she appears before him, more disheveled than ever. Brick dust limns her hair like a holy image.— That's the second time today you've presumed to know my thoughts and been wrong about it.

He has no words.

She rests hands on hips and drills her eyes into his. Several teeth are gone and the rest are yellow; something small is groping through her hair. He finds her unspeakably lovely. She says, I wasn't afraid of you by the well and I'm not disturbed by you now.

He casts about.—I am glad to hear it.

—You seem to think you have great power over me, she teases.

At this he nearly weeps.—It's not a power that I want, but—some sort of influence causes men to react. Perhaps it is this mark I carry.

She frowns.—The mark doesn't help.

Then she smiles and reaches for his hair with a thin, veined hand.—Or maybe it's this. Where on earth did you get such a color?

From inside the hut, a ragged voice:—Zoru, who are you chattering on with?

—A stranger, Father. A man from far away.

—Well then, invite him to eat with us.

Cain can scarcely credit the words, but the woman is already gesturing to the hut.—Come.

—But this—Cain indicates the mark.

—He is blind, the woman laughs. Then suddenly, whispering in his ear.—He can't fear what he doesn't see.

•

The hovel is wretched, managing to be stifling and drafty at the same time. The hard ground batters his backside like a wrestler, and the food Zoru stirs over the cookfire smells distinctly burnt. Cain settles contentedly, savoring the sensation of belonging somewhere.

The old man lies huddled on a mat. Thin as a leaf, wiry white hair pooling greasily around his neck. He makes up for his blindness with a quick wit and a mocking smile, along with preternaturally sharp senses of hearing, smell, and touch. Fondling Cain's garment he declares, Linen from the west if I'm not mistaken.

—You are not.

Fingers probe Cain's timeworn sandals, rubbing grit between fingertips.—Come from across the desert, have you?

—Some months ago, yes.

—From your accent, you've traveled a great distance, further than either the desert or the linen. Or so I would guess.

—You guess correctly. I've wandered for many years, Cain acknowledges. Then he blurts: —So much so that I'm unsure where home even lies.

The old man nods, furrows creasing his brow like dry riverbeds. Leaning close he commands, Say something.

For no reason Cain can fathom he states, I have done terrible things.

The old man sniffs Cain's breath, then sits back.—It's been some time since you've eaten your fill.

Cain laughs aloud.—That's true for most anyone I can think of.

—As is your remark about terrible things.

He leans back against the bony brick wall.—Oh, I don't know about that.

The woman Zoru has been watching throughout, stirring a stew-like mash that bubbles over a smoky fire.—Shall we eat?

•

He stays. He tries to reclaim the stony patch of ground in back of the hut that has lain fallow since plague carried off Zoru's brothers, but he has not been much of a farmer for years now, and he knows that any attempt to plant crops is doomed beforetime. He has been told this after all. So he turns his attention to straightening the kinks in the hut's walls, filling the holes and constructing a new roof. He has a gift for this type of work—it reminds him of his previous exile, before this current one—and it comes easily to him. When he is done the hut feels twice as large as before, snug without being stuffy, airy without being cold.

Not that he spends much time there. Zoru is an unmarried woman, and the old man, blind or not, is her father. Cain takes his meals outside except in the most merciless of storms, and sleeps under a lean-to of gazelle hides. After years of wandering, even this feels like luxury.

The other men in the village get used to him. They still keep their distance, but they don't stare so much. They remark his work on the hut and nod thoughtfully. When he helps with the harvest he gets a portion, and when Oldag's barn collapses, it is Cain who directs the reconstruction. For this he is gifted a half dozen hens and a rooster. One evening lightning torches an absent neighbor's field and Zoru and Cain single-handedly contain the blaze, saving the man's crop. The next morning a pair of goats stand tethered by the hut's entry-way, bleating like damned souls.

After the harvest Zoru's father grows suddenly weak. Day by day he wastes away, thinning like a forest in autumn: where once grew leaves, now only branches show. The real wonder is that the old man is not dead long since.

One night he calls Cain inside the hut.

—I must speak to you both, he says.

Cain squats and hears Zoru shuffle closer. A low cover of haze has clotted out the sky, so they speak in darkness.

—Are you there?

—We're here, Zoru says.

—Attend me you two, the old man murmurs.—You both are suited to each other. The girl is past her youth and doesn't have much childbearing left. But you, boy. Are you there?

—Yes, says Cain.

—You have some great sadness about you. I don't know where it comes from or what form it takes but you must pass through it and leave it behind.

—Some things are simpler to say than to do.

—True. But do it you must, or you'll be eaten away like a corpse.

—It won't be easy.

—Do it anyway. For my daughter's sake. For your wife.

No one says anything. Outside, cicadas and frogs throw a chorus up at the sky, as if begging the moon to show her face.

—So then, murmurs the old man.—Will you accept her?

Cain clears his throat. He has often thought of this moment and is ready for it.—So I will, if she'll have me.

—And you, daughter?

Cicadas and frogs. Frogs and cicadas.

—Zoru? Daughter?

Her voice is calm, a filament in the darkness like a spider depending from the ceiling.—Yes, Father, so I will.

—So it's settled. Splendid. Now I can die peacefully.

—You're going nowhere, Father.

—You've never spoken truer. Son, bring your sleeping mat in alongside your wife's. Starting tomorrow you'll have this home to yourselves.

The old man was right. In the morning he lay deflated and still on the ground, as cold and gray and dead as a fish.

•

Cain will wonder about that hesitation for a long time. When the old man had asked And you, daughter? and there sang that prolonged chorus of cicadas and frogs in lieu of her quick, breathy agreement.

•

The village grows. Families trickle in from the west, light-skinned and dark, large-familied and small. They bring with them strange accents or headgear, new tools, unfamiliar crops, startling ideas. Some, it is rumored, come from across the sea or south of the desert. Cain cannot imagine what all these people are doing here. When he was a child, he and his brother and his parents had been *everybody in the world.*

One thing all the new arrivals share: an aversion to Cain. When they see the mark upon him they point, they stare, their jaws flap soundlessly, like mute senseless creatures. Season after season, it grates on him.

Worse than that, it makes him restless. He says to Zoru, I need to leave soon.

She nods. She's seen the signs.—Where will we go?

—East.

The expression on her face suggests that she is struggling to align this idea with the expectations she had been holding for her future, and is finding the fit less than perfect.—How far?

His hand flutters.—Far enough to get away from *them.* Till we come to a place where I am unknown and can live in peace.

She nods as if this is reasonable. Cain suspects she thinks otherwise. Zoru is no child, and her husband's fame has spread far past the horizon. They both know that searching for a place where Cain is unknown is likely to prove a fool's errand.

—Maybe we can delay our departure till spring, she says.

His eyes cloud over.—But it's only late summer now. Why delay? We'll go right after the harvest, while we still have plenty of supplies to take with us.

—The journey will be far more difficult for me in a few months' time, she says.

—And why is that?

She smiles coyly and pats her belly.—Guess.

# 34  *the strangers*

The desert waits for him. There is no gate saying *Abandon Hope, fool* but there might as well be.

He considers turning back but he knows what lies behind him and he wants no part of it. Just as it wants no part of him.

He considers trying to find his way across the hellish sand, and thinks, Why not?

He thinks, Other men have crossed it.

He thinks, And other men yet have died in the attempt.

He thinks, It might kill me too. I might collapse and provide a brief, noisy meal for a few vultures. Years from now, some camel may puzzle over my bones, half-buried in the dunes, while men wonder who I was and what brought me here to die. They might even pray for me. Imagine the irony of *that*. Then again they might not. Most likely, none of this will ever happen. I'll be covered by the sands and lost forever.

Then he thinks: There are worse fates than being forgotten.

He waits for dusk and makes his way out onto the hard desert plain.

•

There are caravan tracks, so he follows them. Where they lead is a mystery but he reckons his likeliest route across is where other men have already been. He travels at night, by the light of the moon or stars, always east. The trails lead in this direction, and in any case it is easy to make sure. The sun sets at his back each dusk, casting his shadow before him like a net, while every dawn glows like a beacon on the horizon. In the silvery moonlight the caravan tracks glimmer like hope, but morning reveals them to be dry, rutted things, pocked with stones and sinkholes. He treads carefully and tries to breathe through his nose, not his mouth, to save water.

As the sun climbs high he seeks shade. Most mornings he must create his own, draping his cloak over a dry shrub or a few sticks, then arranging himself in the miserly shadow. Once he comes across the bleached bones of some enormous creature with white ribs reaching toward the sky like beseeching fingers. He drapes his cloak across the top and sleeps inside, stretching his own tired bones alongside the vertebrae.

Days wheel past. He feels himself drying, shrinking. The sun leaches moisture from his body and leaves something leathery in its place. When he wakes in the evenings his tongue has paradoxically shriveled and expanded and he must ration his water, sipping the warm mouthfuls to make them last. The drops seem to soak into his tongue before even reaching his throat. Absently he wonders how long he will manage to continue living.

Still he wanders on.

He feels the sun toughening him, transforming his clay into brick. One thing he is grateful for: his mind is not so burdened as it had been with anger and self-pity and doubt and guilt and rage. The voices that whisper in his ear from time to time have fallen silent. He has only so much energy in his body and right now, all is concentrated on staying alive. So in a way, he finds some measure of peace. Or if not peace exactly, then—stillness.

•

Birds hover far overhead. Vultures, he suspects, or hawks. He wonders if they are even hotter than he is, being closer to the sun. Or if they are in fact cooler, being far away from this burning plain of sand.

He has brought a quantity of mutton and fish to sustain him. It has been salted down and the bite of this leaves his mouth, miraculously, salivating, while his cruel thirst grows even more relentless. But the dead flesh does succeed in rejuvenating his own, at least for a time.

Scorpions jitter by, milky yellow. Ugly things like God's mistakes. The sight of them chills his loins: he knows they would kill him without a thought.

●

One night a shadow looms up some distance away and he finds himself walking toward it. The shadow grows larger and blockier and suddenly resolves into a grove of trees, lurching outward at odd angles like a group of ruffians interrupted in the midst of some crime. Within the circle of trees lies a small dusty spring. Cain disrupts a pair of small desert foxes with ludicrously big ears, and collapses into the water. Owls comment from the palms above him. The pool is shallow but deep enough for him to dunk his head. He pulls up sputtering and hears himself laugh for the first time in a long while.

●

His waterskins are nearly empty. Once refilled, he drinks them dry, then fills them again. The sudden intake of brackish water causes him to vomit. Slowly, a few mouthfuls at a time, he drinks again. By morning he is fast asleep under his cloak's shadow.

He stays there four days.

He feels the water fattening his tired flesh. At the same time he knows he cannot stay forever. His supplies are half gone.

The next leg of the journey is even harder for the brief respite he has enjoyed. Heat bouncing up off the sand pummels him even at night, and he wonders if he has stumbled into Purgatory, or perhaps some outlying district of Hell. For ten days he sees nothing living, aside from scarabs and silvery-leafed twigs no taller than his ankle. Even the scorpions and raptors have vanished.

On the eleventh day his food runs out.

His water is reduced to a few gummy mouthfuls in one waterskin. Cain takes to chewing on the other skin to battle the ache in his stomach and throat. He wonders if he has the energy to catch a few scarabs, and if he does, whether he could bring himself to swallow them. He decides: probably not.

There is no shrub to drape his cloak over in this wasteland, nor any skeleton save his own. So each morning he burrows into the sand with the cloak spread over him to ward off the sun. An irreverent part of his mind notes that most people wait until they are dead to get buried. He assures himself that it is a common habit among the denizens of the desert, the beetles and snakes and mice.

He lies there all day and into the night. The night is when he should rouse himself, get moving, but it is so hard to stir.

So hard. Night glides by on black wings, and then it is morning again.

—Here, take a little of this.

Cain protests weakly, rolls over, seeks oblivion.

—What's that on your face? Some kind of. Oh.

A pause then. Heavenly silence. Cain groggily hopes it will last for—

—Oh. I see.

Heavy hands on him then.

—Doesn't leave me much choice, does it? I'd rather be abed, but you'd be dead by evening.

When Cain next flutters awake, the earth pitches beneath him. The sun is at his back, low and orange against the sky: it is sunset again, and he rides on a camel. He falls forward nearly prone on the animal's back, but his feet have been tied to stirrups so he cannot slide off. The smell of the thing is heavy in his nostrils, a surprisingly sweet blend of fur and grass and shit. A fly crawls on Cain's face, and after some time he notices it and rouses himself enough to shake his head and then straighten up. Another camel is in front of his, someone riding it, leading his own mount with a tether.

Cain tries to speak and hears a coarse grating. He coughs, clears his throat, and tries again:—Who are you?

The other rider turns to face him. He wags back and forth as his camel plods on.—So you're awake.

—Seem to be. I owe you my life if I'm not mistaken.

The man grunts as if this is no great debt. Black eyeballs glitter from beneath dense brows, above a mustache that grows long and droops like a cat's whiskers.

—What is your name? Cain asks again.

—Yarin, the man answers.

—I am in your debt. My name is—

—I know who you are, Yarin says quickly, as if afraid to hear Cain say more.—Rest now. You're weak and wrung out, and I don't have enough water for the both of us.

They ride in silence. The camels wear thick metal bracelets that clink, clink as they step across the hardpan, a homely sound against the vastness of the sky. To Cain there is a strange kind of poetry in this, and he feels peculiarly nostalgic for this sound he has never before heard.

—Why do your camels wear jewelry? he asks as the first stars glimmer in the turquoise.

The man regards him as if seeking hidden messages in this question.—So I can find them when they wander off.

And a part of Cain is a little disappointed at this utilitarian purpose.

At dusk they reach another spring. The man is so casual about it that Cain wonders if such things are marked in some way that he has overlooked. Beside the muddy puddle the camels hunker down, burping and farting, while Yarin lights a fire and grills a pair of fresh rabbits he produces from somewhere. In silence he skins and roasts them on a spit he swiftly constructs from a few fallen twigs.

—Thank you, says Cain when he is handed one of the still-smoking carcasses.

Yarin grunts.

Cain remarks his companion's stiff silence, his nervous glances flickering into the darkness around them. He asks a few questions about the man's travels and business and receives one-word answers. Cain's impatience swells. Finally he growls, You needn't look over your shoulder quite so much. It's not as if I've got the demons of Hell at my command.

Yarin squints at him.—That's a promise?

He does not seem to be jesting.

—If you're so afraid of me, Cain says, you could have left me where I lay.

Yarin meets his gaze with a black-irised one of his own. Behind that drooping mustache he looks distinctly unhappy.—Let me tell you something. If I could have, I would.

—Why didn't you then?

Now the man looks frightened, as if he has spoken too much. He attacks the rabbit flesh, masticating it as if the poor creature has given some offense.—You know why. I'm a man of God, and you carry the mark.

Involuntarily, Cain reaches for his face. Stops himself.—The mark is merely a warning, he says. He wills his voice to remain steady, as if talking about the alignment of the stars, or the differences between a cactus flower and a lily.—To prevent any man from murdering me. No more.

Yarin nods and chews his food. Chews some more. Swallows hard.—And if I'd found you lying there in the sun, and left you? What would you call that if not murder?

—It's not the same, Cain mutters.

—Is to me. A man who witnesses a death without trying to prevent it is as responsible as the man who causes it.

Cain ponders this. Under those circumstances, who would qualify as his murderer—the sun in the sky or the God who put it there?

There seems no point in asking this question, so he gives up on small talk and Yarin does the same. The man is reacting out of obligation and fear, and Cain is familiar enough with those two impulses to be uninterested in spending any more time in their company than absolutely necessary.

As the night thickens around them, the two men hang their cloaks on opposite sides of the spring and prepare to sleep. Yarin says, Listen. We'll stay here tonight and tomorrow so you can rest.

—Thank you.

—Tomorrow night we'll move on and by morning we'll reach the first villages. Keep your face out of sight and you'll save me a lot of trouble.

—All right.

—Past the river Tus you're on your own. When I wake up after that I'll be happy to see you gone.

Not bothering to look at the other man, knowing he watches closely, Cain nods. What is surprising is not Yarin's sentiment but how much it stings. This rejection, this cold unthinking hate. How much it pains him, like a slap against a burnt patch of skin, even after all these years. The unkindness of strangers.

There seems to be no end to the inventiveness of God's torments.

He rolls over and burrows into sleep.

•

After the desert there remains a part of Cain that is forever dried and hardened, like a shriveled nut lodged in his mind or heart or belly. When he thinks about it, which is rarely, he feels as if some of his guilt and fury have been scorched away by the sun, leaving only this hard kernel that will remain with him forever. He knows it is there but ignores it as best he can, which is usually well enough to get through the day without trembling, without weeping, without running outside to vomit.

•

Some weeks later Cain is caught in a lashing downpour. He staggers on under the howling sky until he happens upon a hut, open and abandoned.

Inside is musty and dim. The charred remains of a cookfire occupy the center of the floor. There is only one window, small and high up, and no furniture at all. In the roof beams is a nest of jays who squawk and rattle at his arrival. Cain stretches out on the dirt floor, taking care to avoid the cold cinders, and scowls at the birds, whom he half expects to empty their bowels on him until he leaves. He wonders whose hut this is and why it is remote and empty. The world is not so filled with accommodation that people can casually walk away from one house and expect to find another.

No answer is apparent. Cain sups from cold provisions he carries, almonds and dried fruit, hard cheese and olives. Then he rolls onto his stomach—thus has he slept since childhood—and falls into heavy slumber.

He dreams of fire and is awakened by its flicker against his eyelids.

Jerking upright, he takes some moments to realize that the hut itself is not engulfed. Rather, a campfire has been built in the middle of the floor, a small pyramid of logs that chats happily as it is consumed.

—Welcome friend, says a voice like a feather.

There is a figure crouched on the far side of the fire, someone thick draped in rough pelts.

Cain finds his voice.—I'm sorry to have intruded. I'll go now.

—'Sall right, says the voice. It is a soft voice, breathy, and strokes him like a caress. Somehow it doesn't suit this husky shadow.—No intrusion, and no need to leave either. I'm proud to call you my friend.

Friend.

It has been a long time since he has heard that word. A sudden feverish flush smites his face. Perhaps this man is mocking him.— Do you know who I am?

The man's eyes glitter.—Hard to guess wrong with that thing on you, he says, and Cain knows he means the mark.—I'd be a dog to tell you to go. And I ain't a dog.

Isn't this a puzzle. Cain sits up properly and squints across the firelight.—Come here so I can see you, he says softly.

The figure draws near, his face lit by garish flames. Little more than a boy, perhaps sixteen years old. His nose is enormous and hangs before him like a predator's muzzle, a wolf's perhaps, surmounted by a pair of glittering colorless eyes. His smile carries an air of supercilious contempt for the world and everything in it.

Cain is not sure that he wants to be considered friends to such a boy—man?—as this. Then another wave of fatigue assails him: perhaps he can beg off further conversation and go back to sleep. The irony does not escape him that the first person in years to have welcomed his company is, in fact, distasteful to him.

Ironic or not, it is true. He leans close to the fire.—Do you not understand this mark upon me?

Instead of withdrawing, the smile on the face broadens.—Sure I do! says the boy.—It's why I stayed here instead of going home.

Cain is confused.—Isn't this your home?

—Nope. This hut belongs to Ohar. Or it used to.

Cain asks, And where is he?

—Dead.

—I'm sorry.

—I ain't, grins the boy.

Cain says nothing. The child sits near with an air of expectation, as if waiting for him to speak. Cain's eyes drop to the fire, where a finger of flame has split a thick log and now burns hot and white out of the crease.

—Ain't you going to ask how he died?

—Not interested, Cain shrugs.

—I killed him, the boy says. When Cain looks up the boy adds, I used a rock.

—Why, says Cain, would you do something like that?

The boy appears surprised.—I thought you'd understand, you of all people. I wanted him to die so I did it. I figured maybe you'd want to know *how* I did it, not *why*.

—I don't care how you did it.

—I used a rock, giggles the boy.—Just like you did.

—I didn't—well, not exactly.

—I used a *rock*.

They remain silent for a time. Cain feels chilled by the boy's revelation but cannot say exactly why. It's nothing he hasn't done himself, after all.—He must have wronged you greatly to be so abused.

—I didn't even hardly know him, says the boy.—He just had some stuff I wanted.

—That's stupid, snarls Cain.—How could you kill somebody and not even know why you were doing it?

Distress splashes plain across the boy's face.—Don't call me stupid. You were the whole reason I did this. You were the, the, inspiration.

—Don't be ridiculous, snaps Cain.—You're either a murderer, or you are *not*. I have nothing to do with it.

A note of hysteria has edged into his voice.—A man has to be born capable of such a thing. No one can teach him how to do it if he is not ready in his own heart.

The boy looks about to start crying.—That's not true, he blurts.—I never thought of anything like this until I heard about you. Then I said if he could do it to his own brother, what's wrong with me? I said nothing'd stop me and nothing did. I used a *rock*.

Cain is silent. There is no point to speech. The fire crackles merrily: laughing even in death, Cain can't help thinking.

Still the boy gabbles on.—And you know what? It wasn't like I was alone when I did it. You were with me the whole time.

—Your imagination is making me tired, Cain says, which is nothing less than the truth.—I'm going to sleep. It's all the same to me whether you stay or go.

—So the thing is, it's not my fault, says the boy.—I never would of known how, if you hadn't shown me. If it wasn't for you, he'd still be alive right now.

—Sleep well, Cain mutters. He lies on his side with an elbow over his ear.—I'm not interested in hearing any more.

—Yeah, he'd probably be in this hut right now, talking to you, instead of me.

Cain is wide awake but pretends not to be.

—So in a way, the boy says, it's like you killed *him* too.

For a long time Cain stares at the orange firelight flickering against the walls of the hut. The shadows carry images of his brother. Cain watches them wearily, trying to call up the rage he once felt so reliably. And fails.

When he does finally manage to sleep, his dreams are profoundly unpleasant, and he wakes up more than once, sweating and disoriented.

•

In the morning the hunt is silent but for the patter of drops on the roof. Overhead the jays mutter. Was it all a dream? he wonders. He hopes it was. Just an illusion, a metaphor of some sort.

No, it wasn't.

Cain sits up. The boy is curled into a ball by the entryway, as if wrapped around a treasure he clutches to his midriff. Cain decides to forgo breakfast, choosing instead to step past the boy and make his way out into the drizzle. He does not know where he is going. All he knows is what he is trying to get away from, to leave behind. It is all he has known for quite a while now.

# 33 *the years previous*

Thereupon follow Cain's long years of exile.

In a way, the entire rest of his life is an exile, but these first years are the most difficult. Later he will meet Zoru and beget Henoch and plan the city that will bear his son's name. And although those years will not be without trial, they will not lack joy as well. Fleeting as a firefly's burst in the night, but real all the same.

These first years, though, there is no joy at all. Why should there be?

That might be the worst part of all: that he himself cannot argue with his fate. He is a murderer, a fratricide. The blood is still wet and warm on his flesh. He trembles when he thinks of the moment, the stone in his hand, his brother half turning to him, mouth open as if about to speak.

Cain carries that picture before him always. He sees his brother's face in stone outcroppings, in the dust of the trail, in a cloud. Always the living image, the bland joyous righteous infuriating face. Never the dead face, half-collapsed, unrecognizable, attracting ants and crows where it lies jumbled and broken at the bottom of a ravine.

Cain's own face burns with the mark. He avoids pools of standing water, troughs and rain barrels and still ponds. There is nothing he wants to behold less than the sign of God upon him.

•

He walks east, encountering few people at first. In this still-new world there are few enough people to encounter. The world is raw and freshly scrubbed, barely adolescent and very nearly empty. As he wanders, his meetings with strangers are rare and pass without incident. The odd solitary shepherd, a pair of young girls bathing in a stream. The occasional caravan or goatherd. On two occasions he spies people having sex. Everyone he meets is young. This is something he will remember, later, when he himself is aged and aching: in his youth, there were no old people. Nobody is older than his parents, themselves barely into middle age.

For some months he wanders through rolling grassland that gives way to low mountains, then more grassland. The weather cools. He is reduced to hunting small rodents and scavenging their burrows for hoarded nuts. He has never been fat, but now weight melts off him and he becomes lean and stringy. Despite his trials, his eyesight grows acute and his arm steady: one morning he fells a gazelle with his spear and feasts on roasted flesh for five days. He is thankful for the cold then for preventing the carrion from turning foul.

After this, Cain becomes more confident in his ability to survive. He raids beehives at night, while the furry mass of insects is sluggish, and enjoys comb and honey for his efforts. He surprises nightjars roosting on the ground and snaps their necks, gobbles their eggs raw. He collects locusts and fries them in fat. Their legs snap as he chews, pieces dribbling from his lips as if still trying to leap free.

Once he encounters a boy leading a string of goats along a river.—Hello, he says.

The boy sees the mark upon him and bolts. Reluctantly, Cain takes the string of animals and continues on. The goats treat him like their trusted uncle and keep him alive through the winter.

By spring he has reached the edge of an enormous inland sea. He tastes the water: salt. Turning southeast, he follows the shoreline. Surviving is easier now that he can dig mussels and clams along the beach, pull crabs from tidepools and net fish in the shallows.

The summer sun bleaches his hair into spun gold. Salt and wind abrade his flesh to a freckled pink-brown. Still he sees no one. The sun burns in the sky like a fever. He walks on.

After a time the sea falls behind.

One day he realizes with a jolt that he is following a trail, a thread of worn earth winding among grassy hills. Has he inadvertently returned home? But no, he quickly decides this cannot be. It is impossible to determine whether the trail is worn by human feet or by animals, but he turns his steps to follow it. Late in the day he tops a rise and looks down upon a village.

His shock is considerable: Who are all these people? Who begot them?

There are a dozen huts in a straggling line, hand-formed bricks piled into uneven walls. Stone fences and animals pens and a dusty lane running through the middle of it all. Cain squints at the silent, scared faces peering at him from doorways and shutterless windows. By all rights they should be his family—nephews and nieces, if not brothers and sisters—but he sees no kinship here. They are small people, pale with black eyes, and though there is recognition in their faces, it is not the recognition of fellowship and welcome. It is the pinch-lipped recognition that says: *Plague begone from our houses. Leave us be or we'll chase you out. Keep walking if you know what's good for you.*

Cain ignores these unspoken commands. He is curious about these people, and it has been a long time since his last conversation. How long exactly? A year, two? Five? He cannot remember.

He says, Hello.

They do not answer. Some of the men hold staffs or rocks, but Cain knows he is safe with the mark upon him.

—What do you call this place? he asks.

Safe, but not welcome. They do not speak, except with their pinched mouths and frowning eyes.

—I have wandered a long time. A cup of water would be appreciated.

No, not welcome at all.

A stone hits the back of his head. He whirls about and sees empty huts. Another strikes him from behind and he whirls again. The stones are not large enough to do damage, nor are they hurled with any great force; but they are unpleasant. They are intended to harry, not kill him.

Suddenly he is engulfed in a hailstorm of fist-size stones. The villagers no longer bother to conceal themselves: perhaps their numbers give them courage. Children and women join in the attack. Cain holds up his hands but it is useless: a sharp-edged missile slices his brow, another momentarily stuns him and the world turns black. When his vision clears he finds himself running, staggering in uneven steps across stony ground. He continues long after he has left the village and its cold welcome behind.

•

It happens again at the next village he approaches, some months later, and the next. After that he treads warily around human habitations, like a wild dog or a serpent. Flinching at every chance encounter, and holding himself ready to flee.

This goes on for years.

•

It is during this time that a singular thing occurs.

Cain is in the mountains, where he has fled to escape the hatred of people he does not know. He lives on cactus fruit and less water than he is used to, with the effect that his bowels are compacted and uncomfortable. One morning he is squatting between two rocks, trying to void himself as best he can, when behind him a voice says, Do not turn around, brother. It is I.

Cain's guts clench. He knows the voice but says anyway, Who?

—Your brother.

He begins to straighten up but the voice arrests him.—If you try to look I'll go.

Cain halts, his back to the voice.—I thought you died. I thought I—killed you.

—You did.

A pause then, silence filled only with the chatter of jackdaws and the wind's sibilant hiss. Cain forces himself to speak with a jauntiness he does not feel.—So then? You've come back to haunt me?

—I've come back to ask you a question.

—Then you must let me ask one of you.

—Maybe, murmurs Abel.

Cain snorts.—I suppose you'll ask why I did it?

—I don't care about that, Abel tells him in a dismissive tone.—Some things are bound to happen sooner or later, and I guess that was one of them. This is more important: What do you know about our brother Seth?

—I know of no brother Seth.

—He's just recently born.

—There you go then. I have not been home for years. There is little chance that I shall go in the future, so I'll continue to know nothing of this Seth or any other new fledglings in Father's brood.

—Too bad. I'd hoped . . . I've heard that Mother bore him . . .

—Yes?

Abel's hesitant voice is filled with wonder.—That she bore him to replace *me*.

Cain laughs aloud: it is the sweetest joke he has heard in some time.—Is that such a surprise? Lose a hut to fire, build another one. Lose a goat to the fox, breed another one. Lose a child to some horrible crime, conceive another one.

He wonders if Abel is thinking the same as he: *And if you lose a brother?*

But instead Abel admits, I hadn't thought I'd be so easily replaced.

A kind of grim satisfaction fills Cain at this.—I imagine it would be a shock. Precious little you can do about it now though.

Abel's voice grows breathy, as if the breeze is filling it up.—I suppose not.

—Unless you go and, and—haunt them. Like you're doing to me.

—I think I'll spare them that.

A thought occurs to Cain then.—What about that girl you were so keen on?

—Girl?

—The one you were planning to marry. Have you ever gone to see her? Aren't you curious?

—Ah . . . no. I'll leave her in peace, I think. It was just a misunderstanding between us. Farewell, brother.

—Wait! I get to ask a question of you!

—You just did . . .

Cain jolts around but there is nothing besides gravel and mountains and spindly scrub bushes. Nonetheless he cries out, Do you forgive me? Abel! Do you forgive me?

The echoes come back to him: *Forgive me? Give me? Give me!*

•

The vision or visitation or whatever it is preoccupies him for many days. He descends from the mountains where he has sought isolation, and for a time he pays no heed to the stones and curses hurled at him by the farmers and villagers on his path. But it is only a matter of time before his brother's presence fades from his memory, and the immediate reality of bearing all humanity's loathing becomes once more his daily preoccupation.

Despite this, he can't help wishing he'd called out a bit sooner: Do you forgive me? Any answer at all—yes no it doesn't matter—would have been better than silence. Would have helped Cain come to terms with where he finds himself. Which is, he is beginning to realize, nowhere at all. Regardless of where he wanders he is still, always, nowhere.

# 32 *the conversation*

—How would I know? snarls Cain.

An awkward silence ensues.

God, in the form of a gray-bellied cloud, drifts lazily across an afternoon sky of unimaginable blueness. Cain had been staggering along the river's edge in the miasmic shade of a cypress grove, listening to the blood scuttling through his arteries, when the Almighty had appeared, demanding, *Where is your brother?*

Now God asks again: *Have you not seen him today?*

—No, Cain snaps, I haven't. I'm not his keeper, nor his mother either. Go ask *her,* she's likely enough to have her arms around his precious head.

His head. His brother's head, broken and stove-in at the bottom of the ravine. Twisted at an angle that God never intended. His tongue, bit through by his own teeth, lying in the dust beside him.

God is there as a cypress now, tall but not so tall as some of the others. Together in the grove they look like columns holding up the sky's vault. It is past midday and sunlight angles through the treetops in golden-green fingers, lending the place an air of holiness that Cain could happily do without.—*Do you think you can deceive me?*

Exasperated, Cain turns at right angles away from God. The river confronts him now and he has no choice but to cross it, stepping along a series of half-submerged stones slick with algae. In fact he'd never planned on trying to deceive anyone, God least of all. But recent events had shifted faster than his ability to keep up. And so, having at last done what he'd long dreamed of, Cain is left wondering: Now what?

God waits for him on the far bank in the form of a large flat boulder. Lichen patterns it in particolored stains.—*Your crime will not go unpunished.*

Cain, knowing he is beaten, stops and says nothing. Stands ankle-deep in cold river water and waits.

—*Confess what you have done,* God commands quietly. The voice is reasonable, soothing even.—*Do not compound your sin by denying it.*

—I have done nothing! spits Cain.

Why is he lying? He cannot say. Some primeval impulse to cover up, to dissemble: the child's urge to escape the wrath of the parent. Cain knows it is useless but there's too much noise in his head to think clearly. Rage tumbles through his mind like a plague of frogs. He both tries not to think, and can't help thinking, about his brother's easy smile, his eyes green like this cypress grove at dawn, the creeping grin as he turned toward him.

They had stood at the edge of the ravine this very morning. Cain's blood sang in his veins. His rage was the melody. He had resolved to murder his brother and felt oddly detached from the proceedings. Insofar as motivation went, there wasn't much more to it than that. There was no single thing that had cemented his resolve—only a thousand tiny things built up over the years, accruing higher and higher into a great termites' nest of revulsion.

In the time it took to draw a breath, Cain recalled ten reasons to kill his brother:

1. The way he smiled vacuously at anything he didn't understand.
2. His certainty that all conflict could be resolved if people just tried a little harder.
3. Preferential treatment from Eve and Adam.
4. Preferential treatment from God.
5. *You should* and *You shouldn't.*
6. A breathtaking inability to see another's point of view.
7. The unbearable way he treated the younger children.
8. Smugness in all things.

9. His effortless ability to mouth platitudes that, unconvincing though they were, still left Cain feeling a misfit.
10. Obliviousness to all of the above.

None of these reasons was especially valid, Cain knew. Or perhaps they all were. Perhaps it came down to this: his brother annoyed him, so he would die. Annoyed him, enraged, infuriated, humiliated him. And made him feel he deserved it. These were good enough reasons, weren't they? They had seemed so that morning, when both men had stood atop the cliff overlooking the ravine. Abel leaning out, peering down at some imaginary curiosity that Cain had pointed to. Against the small of Cain's back pressed his hand and in it was the stone. The stone was large but knobbed, affording an easy grip as if formed especially for this purpose.

Formed by whom?

Cain had pointed to the bottom of the ravine, some sixty cubits below.—Look! What do you suppose that is?

His brother squinted down.—What?

—There. Do you not see it?

—I see nothing, brother.

And then Abel leaned further into the abyss, stretching his slight, brown-haired frame, before deciding his elder brother was having a joke on him. And as Cain hefted the stone, arcing his arm with all the power of his shoulder and back to hurl into the impact, Abel turned to face Cain with a little half-smile and some word left forever unformed on his lips.

Cain felt as if someone else were propelling him, guiding his hand, the trajectory of the rock, the bleak anger in his center. As if some other force were in control of things: destiny perhaps. For long disorienting moments Cain hovered outside his body, calmly looking down from above at two young men tussling at the edge of a cliff. Then one of them became a murderer and the other one died.

And then Cain was back inside his body, flushed and jittery, breathing hard, and wondering what his brother had been about to say.

•

Did the stone kill him, or was it the impact at the bottom of the ravine that snapped his neck? Cain doesn't know. He will never know.

His brother made no sound as he toppled through the emptiness. There were some birds in the distance, big white ones in a line, egrets perhaps. The sky was cloudless. Far off meandered the silver-white glitter of a river. Beyond that, the hills.

Cain watched as his brother fell and fell. It seemed to last for days. And then he stopped falling and lay lifeless in the dirt.

•

Now Cain sweats in the afternoon stillness. It is warm but not that warm. He is walking fast, trying perhaps to outpace God.

God will not be outpaced. In the form of the wind He rushes alongside Cain, tousling his hair and nipping at the hem of his tunic. God whispers in Cain's ear, *Your brother's blood cries to Me from the very earth.*

Cain squeezes his eyes shut but continues walking. He has left the river and the cypress behind and now climbs along a series of low rolling downs. With eyes closed it is just possible that he will misstep and topple into some unexpected chasm. He wonders if he is hoping for this.

*—Listen then, Cain, as you are unwilling to confess or repent of your crime.*

It occurs to him that there are two kinds of people in the world— those who long to hear God say their name, and those who dread it. Cain shivers to hear God say his name.

*—The earth has opened her mouth and drunk your brother's blood dry, and the cost of this shall be a curse upon your life forever.*

Cain stops and opens his eyes. The downs extend in all directions, and the day is inordinately clear and sunny. Small orange-and-purple wildflowers lie scattered in all directions.—So be it, he says.

*—Know this too,* continues the wind at his ear.—*The earth sickens of your crime.*

—She seems to have plenty of company.

—*A fugitive and vagabond you shall be until the end of your days,* declares God. In the sunshine a ladybird glimmers like a drop of blood on a knee-high stalk of grass.—*Should you till the earth to bring forth food, you shall reap nothing but nettles and poison plants.*

Cain snorts.—Thanks.

—*You bring this upon yourself,* God intones severely.

—You think I don't know that? bellows Cain.—I have killed my own brother. There! I said it. And what happens to me now? There's not a man on earth who won't murder me given half a chance. Even my father.

He pauses.—Perhaps *especially* my father.

A distant flock of swallows wings by, a shifting whorl of dots against the blue. Perhaps they are just birds, but perhaps they are really God. Cain is losing the ability to make such distinctions anymore.

In any case, the voice is still there.—*You needn't fear. No man shall lift a hand against you.*

—And how will you arrange that? snaps Cain.

Bad question. Without warning he is on his back, thrashing amid the wildflowers. Such pain as he has never known courses through him, as if his very fibers are being rearranged. The agony has as its epicenter his forehead, a burning spot of liquid fire above and between his eyes. He blacks out.

God is gone when he wakes. The flowers are still there, the wind, the odd ladybird and myna, but they are no more than raw physical clay.

Cain fingers his brow gingerly. Nothing obviously different apart from a residual tenderness: the burning is gone. But there is a mark of some sort, he is sure of it, and he wonders what its effect will be.

He finds out soon enough. A group of children are playing among the hills, and they stop and watch his approach. Cain frowns as he draws near and does not recognize them. This is a mystery. There are few enough people in the world, and he should know them all by name. But these urchins, five or six of them, are strangers; and he remembers his brother's conversation this very morning.

The children recognize him, though. As he waves a hand to hail them they back away, fear writ plain on their faces. The youngest burbles hysterically and the oldest girl scoops the child into her arms before turning to run. In moments they have all fled, leaving Cain quite alone in the shadowy lee of the hill, wildflowers his only companions.

He thinks on this.

He does not much like what he concludes. The mark on him, whatever it is, may prevent his murder but it will also prevent much else. His brow wrinkles as he wonders what to do. There is no one to discuss this with: his brother is dead, his father is a stranger, and even God—he senses this now—has left him forever. Night thickens about him and offers no comfort.

A little sob escapes him and he wonders: Where will I go?

The stars are well out when he begins walking again. Not that he has decided on a destination, but the air is chill and he must keep moving to keep the cold away. He does not return home.

Footsteps lead him east, away from his parents and the life they have carved for themselves out of the wilderness. Part of him is hardened in his resolve; his father banished him long ago, and there has been little enough affection between himself and his mother. But another part admits to a sadness at not saying something. Anything at all, even just: I am leaving now. You'll not see me again. Cain senses that he has a long fatiguing journey ahead of him, and he would have liked to mark this moment in his life, this transition from one form of existence to another. To say farewell, even if only to his parents—who made so many mistakes, who have so much to do with this situation in which he now finds himself. Now, ironically, as he turns his back on them forever, Cain feels himself almost ready to let them back into his life.

It is just possible, he supposes with a frown, that they did the best they could.

He does not allow himself to follow this thought very far, for if he did so, he might soon reach another conclusion—that to punish his parents, it was not necessary for him to kill his brother. That Abel too could have been forgiven, not murdered.

Don't touch that thought, whispers a voice at his ear. Leave it well alone.

Cain's footsteps hurry across the grasslands, every stride taking him further from home.

# 31 *the murder*

At last, he smites his brother with a rock and kills him.

**book two** *the brother*

# **30** *the murder*

Abel's bursting to tell but he can't, not yet. It's crucial to wait for the right moment. He wants to surprise his brother but at the same time, the surprise shouldn't be too startling: unfortunate results have come about in the past when Cain was faced with the unexpected. So Abel will wait for his moment to reveal his plans. But it's hard to keep the news in, so sure is he that Cain will be delighted.

*Delighted* is not a word often linked with Cain's name.

In the meantime there is the day to enjoy, even as the seductive whisper of his plan brushes against his mind. Abel follows Cain across the meadow, making for the river. Black and orange butterflies swarm across the sky, willows bend pale blue over the river's edge, yellow sun burns over it all like a benediction. Clouds? Maybe some other day. Dragonflies hover like weightless jewels while swarms of vermilion birds swoop to devour them. A breath of wind lingers soft against his flesh like a kiss, like a lover, only he's never known a lover. Maybe soon, though. Maybe one with almond eyes and hair to her waist and a clavicle that throws puddles of shadow across her chest.

Abel shivers and says, It's a great day to be alive.

There is no answer.

Abel's eye falls on his brother and his mood dims a bit. There are colors here too: eyes the hue of robins' eggs, hair like tangled sunshine, the chapped pink of gaunt cheekbones. But somehow the effect is not so joyous. Cain has been moody as long as Abel can remember, and now he's momentarily unsure of himself and his news. Maybe Cain won't like the idea; maybe he won't respond the way Abel expects. Even though it was Cain himself who first made the suggestion years ago.

Would he even remember?

Chewing his lip, Abel strides on after his brother. This might prove harder than he had expected.

•

They find the spot on the sandy bank where the river widens into a shallow pool. They've played here since childhood. Abel wades into the waist-deep water as Cain throws himself onto the ground and stares gloomily at the willows arched above them.

—You should join me, Abel calls.

His brother says nothing.

Shrugging, Abel dives into the deeper portion of the pool, wriggling underwater like an otter, delighting in the gold webwork of reflected sunshine that bounces across the pebbles at the bottom and the clouds of tiny orange darters that wait till he is nearly upon them before zooming away. Breaking the surface, Abel hauls himself to shore with easy strokes and plonks down next to where his brother broods. It must get old, Abel reflects but does not say aloud. This constant foul temper.

Instead he says, You'll be glad to hear we're all well.

He has decided to break the news in a roundabout way, approaching it from the side rather than head-on.

Cain says nothing. He has scrounged a stone from somewhere, misshapen and heavy-looking, the size of a fist. It drops from hand to hand as he juggles aimlessly.

—Mother is pregnant again, says Abel.

The juggling continues.—The old man certainly enjoys his hobby.

—Don't talk like that, Abel protests.—You should go see her.

Cain sighs thinly.—Don't you ever get tired of telling people what to do?

Abel ignores this petulance.—It'll be nice to have another little one about.

The downward arc of Cain's mouth suggests otherwise.—I can

hardly keep track of them as it is. How many does this make? Twelve, thirteen?

Abel tries ticking his siblings off on his fingers but loses track after ten. Numbers have never been his strength.—Anyway, they managed a good harvest.

—I'm so happy, Cain deadpans.

Maybe the harvest is a topic best avoided, Abel thinks, considering the history. Well, too late now. Is he his brother's keeper? The news is good so there's no reason not to share it.—Father says there'll be enough for the winter and some extra besides.

—Why keep extra? frowns Cain.—It will just go to waste.

Abel says, We'll trade it maybe.

Cain is peering at him queerly.—Trade with who? There *isn't* anyone, besides us.

—Actually, there are others now, Abel says after some hesitation.—Though to be honest I don't understand where they come from.

Cain stares.—Others?

—Strangers. You know, people like us, only not us. I mean not our kin. It's confusing, to tell the truth.

—Bizarre more like, murmurs Cain.—How many of these strangers are there?

Abel's fingers flutter, then fall still. Numbers have never been . . . —Quite a few. Several families have moved to the area. They seem—they're as we are, and have animals and children. Including daughters, Cain.

He mulls this over.—Intriguing.

Abel licks his lips. He has breathed not a whisper of this to anyone, not even his father.—There's one girl in particular, she's special. She's really something.

His brother watches closely.—All right.

—We are—we're to be married.

Cain is satisfyingly speechless. Abel rolls onto his back and pictures her floating above him.

—That's some news, Cain murmurs at length.

That's not the half of it, Abel thinks. But still doesn't say anything aloud just yet.

•

—Her name is Shana, Abel says after a time. He wonders whether to admit that the arrangements aren't quite final yet—but speaking like this seems to make things more certain somehow, and the last thing he wants to do is stop.—You'll like her, she's lovely. Quite like Kerod in fact.

—Married, Cain says finally.—The first of any of us. Think of it.

Abel permits himself a shy smile.—Believe me, I have.

Cain doesn't grin in response. Once he might have, Abel reflects. When did this change? A pause stretches taut between them, grows awkward, then lasts so long that it moves past awkwardness and becomes relaxed again. Abel wonders if Cain is bitter that he's not getting married himself, but before he can say anything Cain interrupts him.—Trade for what?

Abel stares blankly until Cain reminds him, You mentioned trade.

—Ah. They have linen, a kind of—he pinches his gazelle-hide tunic—a kind of thin skin, but made from plants.

—That's absurd.

—We thought so too. But it's lighter than wool and comfortable in summer. Plus they have something to eat called lentils, and another thing called wine.

—Which is?

—A drink made from grapes.

—Sweet then.

—It makes you laugh at first and then puts you to sleep. You should try it.

—Extraordinary, Cain says with venom.—And for this foolishness Father is willing to part with his hard-earned crops?

Abel says nothing but they both know the answer. After a time he asks, And you? Your harvest was fruitful?

—My storehouse quite overflows, Cain declares bitterly.

—Praise God.

Cain hocks.

—From Whom flow all blessings, adds Abel.

Cain lifts his hand as if to strike his younger brother.—That may be true for you. You always manage great rewards from minimum labor.

Abel thinks this unfair but he understands where it comes from, so he keeps silent.

—*My* blessings flow from the sweat of my back and the toil of my limbs, Cain glowers.—When it comes to God's gifts, I find Him extraordinarily tight-fisted.

Abel casts about to change the subject, to mend fences.—Maybe you should meet with some of these strangers. You can barter with some of your surplus, if you have any.

—They've nothing I need.

—They might have a wife for you. You should marry, it might— ease your mind.

Cain hocks again. A new habit?—You spend too much time with animals. Am I some goat that thinks of nothing besides what's be- tween my legs?

Abel blushes.—You used to think about it all the time.

—Maybe I've grown *up*.

—Well then . . . Abel reaches into his tunic and withdraws his most treasured possession. The knife is as long as his hand, the or- ange blade polished to a blinding shine. A handle of bone has been whittled to fit his grip. Even in the shady half-light of the willows, the thing reflects the sky and glimmers with an oily sheen as Abel ex- tends it, haft first, toward his brother.

Cain stares a long time before accepting it. He says nothing but Abel can see by the respectful way he handles it that he is impressed.—And what might this be?

—A knife.

—The knives I know are made of flint.

—This one's better. The metal is called copper and is found in mountain rocks. Heat the rocks in a fire and the metal runs out.

Cain is squinting at his brother.—You discovered this?

—The strangers tell us it's so, Abel concedes.—The edge is thinner and sharper than a flint. It's easy to skin an animal or gut it or—kill something. Abel's voice clots up. The last bit is hard to say because, shepherd or no, he hates killing anything. He should get used to it—he often tells himself so—but he can't.

For a time Cain hefts the knife as his look darts from the blade to his brother and back again. And again. And again. Then with unexpected viciousness, Cain's arm pivots and slams the knife down, burying it to its handle in the loose earth between Abel's legs.—Keep your knife, he rasps.—And I'll keep my harvest. You can direct those strangers to barter elsewhere.

—But what—

Cain is already on his feet. The misshapen rock passes from hand to hand and the vacant look on his face is chilling. Cain's voice is as emotionless as a cicada's buzz as he says:—You think you're so smart. Take it from me, you don't need a knife to kill a man.

Monkeys squabble in the trees overhead.

It is some time before Abel finds his voice.—I don't think anyone ever had the idea of using it on a *man.*

•

By midmorning they have climbed the steep trail that leads to the cliff top and meanders along the edge of the ravine. The cliff drops away in a sheer slice and the ravine winds through it, its walls nearly vertical until the sudden stop sixty cubits below. A scatter of broken boulders looks up at them from the bottom. As children they had been forbidden to play up here, but now it is one of Cain's favorite retreats.

Or so he tells Abel. Abel, for his part, is none too enamored of this place and its vertiginous prospect, but he senses that his brother needs his attention and he resolves to do whatever is necessary.

Sometimes Cain baffles him, presenting him with a facade as expressive as a stone wall or a heel of bread. Other times, Abel feels he can look past the transparent surface of his flesh and see all the activity bubbling away inside, like dinner simmering over the cookfire. Today is one of those days. Cain's jitteriness is palpable in the way he fusses with everything: his thin beard, the long grass by the river, that pointless rock he insists on hauling from one place to another.

Abel knows perfectly well where this anxiety comes from. This whole senseless episode of the past—how many years? Four, five?—has dragged on entirely too long and now Cain is at last ready to let it go. Well, not before time. Someone has to make the first move, and it won't be their father. Adam is a good man but treads carefully on new ground, emotional or otherwise. For that matter, God seems reluctant as well; and being God, He can't really be blamed. So that leaves Cain to make amends.

Not that Abel is without sympathy. He sympathizes *wholeheartedly*. Rejected by the God who had already rejected his father! Banished by the man who was banished by God! Harsh treatment by any measure. But Abel can't see the point in clinging to the sense of injustice and hurt, and is mightily glad that Cain has reached the same conclusion at last.

It seems.

Abel peers over the edge of the ravine and doesn't like what's down there. He swipes the hair from his eyes and says to Cain, So this thing you wanted to discuss.

Cain blinks. He is staring at him but does not really seem to see him. Again Abel gets the sense of bubbling froth, a kind of fizzing going on just beneath the surface.—Eh?

Abel says, The other day you said you wanted to discuss something. Remember?

Cain makes a noncommittal sound and sidles up alongside him. He stares past the edge of the cliff as if reading some secret glyphs spelled out on the rocks below.

—I know it's hard, Abel begins, but you're right to want to do it.

Cain continues staring over the edge.—Do what?

—Make peace with Father.

Cain stiffens. Very slowly he leans even further over the edge. He is standing awkwardly, with his hands behind his back, and Abel resists the urge to reach out and steady him.

—It's the right thing to do, difficult or not, Abel goes on after a moment.—I'm not saying to go live with them again. What you've built here, it's a real achievement.

He spreads his hands. Maybe now is the moment to tell his news. But no: Cain is still glowering. So Abel doesn't say, I've grown to respect all you've done. More than that: I almost *envy* you. Imagine! In fact, I was thinking . . .

Instead he says, Even if you stay here, at least go talk to Father again. It'd make him happy and that's our duty, after all.

Several long moments slither by. For some reason Abel becomes aware of his heart beating in his bosom. *Thub-ub, thub-ub* . . . At length Cain says, Is that what you think? It's our duty to make them happy?

—Of course it is.

Cain squints as if trying to focus on something.—What about their duty to us?

—I don't follow, Abel admits.

—Don't Father and Mother have some responsibility to treat us fairly? Doesn't God? Though I realize there's little precedent for that, he mutters.—Or does it all just move in one direction?

Abel has no answer to this. The sense he had moments ago, that he understood his elder brother perfectly, has swiftly evaporated. After all these years, Cain can spring a surprise on him. More than a surprise: a conundrum, a bafflement so profound that it leaves him feeling foolish for *not* being snotty and bitter and hurt.

Abel shrugs. He doesn't want to be bitter. He doesn't see the point.

Cain sees the shrug and flicks his eyes away.—You're just like them.

—Maybe I am, murmurs Abel. A sort of desperation wells up and he hears himself babbling, trying to reach out with words that he knows are pointless even as he speaks them.—Why shouldn't I be?

They're my parents and yours. You ought to be more like them, too. At least try. Get married, maybe have a few children. Forgive and forget. Who knows what might happen? You'd be happier at least.

All the emotion has drained from Cain's face.—You never will get tired, will you?

—Tired of what?

Cain doesn't answer. Wind licks Abel's face like a pup. It's a beautiful morning: below them the river winds away like a silver thread with trees bordering it; green meadows spill away like something dropped from a great height. The two brothers stand silently surveying the vista until Cain frowns and says, What's that?

—What?

He is leaning well out over the edge, pointing straight down.— There. Do you not see it?

Biting back his vertigo, Abel gingerly leans into the void, gazing down, following his brother's pointing finger. And there he sees boulders, scree, wildflowers, shadows. But nothing more: no secrets, no revelations, no glyphs. He listens to several more of his own heartbeats as he frowns down at the hard stony earth, before realizing that Cain is having a joke on him.

The words come to him then: Brother, I've decided to join you in your exile, so you'll no longer be alone.

He is about to say: Years back you invited me to leave home and live with you. Now I've decided to get married and take Shana and do as you've suggested.

If it's all right with you of course.

But Abel says none of these things.

He is ready to. He has inhaled the breath that will carry the words from his tongue to Cain's ears. And Abel feels an easy smile slide onto his face as he pulls back from the cliff, away from the danger, and turns to face his mysterious, unpredictable elder brother.

# 29 *the girl*

The girl is long and slender and appears to be his age or a little younger. She sports a prominent clavicle and hair to her waist. Oil keeps it shiny and free of tangles. Abel knows this is so because it is oil that she applies now, handfuls of it scooped onto her scalp and then massaged gently down the length of the strands. Then she combs it through and her hair glitters like black water in moonlight.

The girl is naked to the hips. Abel's breath is quick and shallow. He hides behind a stand of bushes and watches without moving.

Suddenly she looks up and Abel holds his breath. Has she seen him? She gazes toward him, not directly but close enough for him to see that her eyes are the shape and color of almonds but much larger. He lingers no more but ducks away and runs off, breathless before he even starts. From behind him floats a startled voice: Who's there? Hennara, is that you?

Her voice is music. Abel nearly falls.

•

After a time he rejoins his flocks and walks among them dazedly, the girl floating in his imagination like a spirit. Sometimes he modestly drapes a scarf across her shoulders. More often she is half-naked or altogether nude. Around his ankles the sheep butt and jostle but he pays no mind.

What is her name, he wonders, where does she come from, what makes her smile? Would she be willing to talk to him? In his experience, girls can be confusing. His sister Kerod is a solemn problem-solver, while Lya, only a year younger, starts chatting at daybreak and doesn't stop till night. There seems no consistent pattern.

Admittedly there is none with the men, either.

In the distance two of the younger children, Tovi and Shel, have taken one of the rams and dressed it in a girdle of leaves and a necklace of poppies. When they spot Abel, they dash away to hide behind a boulder. He ignores them. They peek out and watch as he passes, as if waiting for him to come and scold. He does not. He doesn't tell them to undress the animal and go help their mother. He doesn't remind them—again—that the sheep are not dolls. He barely registers them at all.

The children's faces reflect amazement and delight as he passes.

•

Abel decides the girl's name is Shana. This is based on nothing but the way the sounds feel on his tongue. It makes sense to him that the girl would have such a name.

He decides also that she prefers blue flowers to red, butterflies to birds, and moths to butterflies. She would rather walk along the river at twilight, he is sure, than feed twigs to a bonfire. Honey is her favorite flavor and fall her favorite season. Doubtless she is more impressed by a still winter morning than a raging summer thunderstorm. Truth be told, she'd rather live with him than with her family. Her favorite pastime would be to bathe with him in some shallow pool of their own discovering, far away from either of their families.

After their marriage, of course. When they have moved to . . . where?

The answer when it comes is obvious. Abel won't bring his new wife into his father's house. As her husband, it will be his responsibility to provide a home of their own. So they'll find empty land near his brother's, build a hut alongside Cain's, and tend sheep and crops side by side.

And if Adam doesn't approve? Well, he'll have to swallow his disapproval. Yes. About this, Abel is suddenly adamant. He'll make preparations, and move out to join his brother. And he will take the girl with him, if she will come.

Abel is confident that she will.

Thinking this way is disorienting, even to imagine himself opposing his father's wishes is something new. Abel feels as though a threshold has been crossed, and it's troubling and a little thrilling all at once. Well, so be it. Abel glances up as he walks and the jays and rollers seem more lively than before, the stream more vivacious. It's time, he decides, to take charge; time he made a few decisions for himself, and grew up.

Abel walks in a haze of preoccupation, his plans growing more elaborate as morning twirls slowly into afternoon.

# 28  *some weeks previous*

Abel finds the twins hunkered behind a clump of boulders at the far side of the wheat. He has ambled this way in search of a particularly stupid ewe, whom he refers to mentally as Rockhead. The last thing he expected to find at this remote spot was a pair of errant siblings ducking their chores.

—Well well, he chuckles.

The twins mutter and look away. The boy Epon clutches his newest drum, a wide bowl of carved cedar with a goatskin taut across the top. The girl Epna fingers the reed flute she has lately carved, larger than her last and with more holes.

—Shouldn't you be at work somewhere? asks Abel. Not harshly— it's important not to be too harsh with the little ones. But firmly, as befits his station as elder brother.

—We *are* at work, whines Epon. The boy rarely speaks, for which Abel is grateful, for as often as not his words are some variation of this protesting squeak.

—Are you now? And what are you working at so hard?

He is teasing them and they know it. It's something he shouldn't do, maybe, but better surely to tease than to bully and snarl the way Cain would. Or worse, Cain wouldn't even pause to bully them— he'd simply leave them to their own devices, letting them get into the Devil's own mischief. That wouldn't do at all.

So Abel's correction settles into a course of gentleness. He says, It looks an awful lot like you're playing.

—We are, answers Epna, meeting his eye with her own.—We're playing *music*.

Epna is the feisty one. Abel often forgets this but he remembers

75

now, as her ten-year-old's stare bores flatly into his. The child carries herself with confidence. Her hair is dark and feathery, but a pink flush straddles the bridge of her nose, above which rest eyes as black as her father's.

Abel clears his throat.—Playing songs is fine, but—

—We're *writing* songs, interrupts Epna. Her little voice is like a bird's: clear and insistent and surprisingly loud.—We're doing *work*.

Abel squats on his haunches.—I'm not sure Father would agree.

—Father told us to do this, Epon whines, tapping his drum.

Epna adds, He said to take all day if we wanted.

This unnerves Abel. His siblings are not known to lie, whatever their other faults—which are many enough, God forgive them. But he finds it hard to fathom that Adam doesn't need them in the fields or tending the goats or cleaning the well or digging a new latrine or helping Porad with the barn or Eve with the children or . . . something.

The twins see the hesitation staining his face.—We're writing a song for the new baby when it comes, explains Epna.

Her simplicity throws Abel.—Oh.

This has become something of a tradition. The twins have written songs to celebrate the harvest, the full moon, the arrival of spring, the first summer storms. There are songs praising Eve, Adam, God, each other, the river, the bee-eaters, the rain. And, starting with Tovi six years ago, the twins have fallen into the habit of writing a song to celebrate the birth of each new child.

—Father wants this?

—Yes.

Abel frowns.—But the baby won't come for—he tries to calculate the days, and fails—well, it's not here yet.

Epna shrugs.—He wanted us to have it ready.

Abel nods as though he understands, which he does not. Part of him can't help reflecting that Epon and Epna have never written a song for him.

A mild stutter: Epon's fingers dancing across the goatskin. The mouth of the drum murmurs and chuckles as if laughing at Abel. Epna raises her flute to her lips and exhales gently, and a lilting melody rises into the air like mist over the river. Between the two of them a tune escapes, writhing about itself, half-formed.

Abel stands.—I've work to do, so I'll leave you to this.

They have forgotten him already.

•

Several days later he is yet again disentangling Rockhead from a tangle of thorny bushes when a shadow falls across the twilit sky. It is his brother.

—There is something I wish to discuss with you, says Cain.

—Okay.

Abel gives a final wrench, and dead wood snaps free. Rockhead scampers down the hillside. That task complete, Abel is done for the evening. His duties extend no further than sitting on a hillside watching his flock. There are far too many for him to count, but each animal is distinct to him by its voice, and from where he sits he can track the location of each to within a few paces. He will spend the night sleeping out among them beneath the stars, and he is happy to loll and pass the time talking to his brother.

But Cain licks his lips.—Not now. Come visit me sometime. There is no hurry.

—All right. At your hut then?

Cain's eyes dance.—By the pool in the river. You know the place?

—Where we used to play as children.

—Yes. There.

Abel frowns at his waddling dams.—The ewes are getting ready to drop their lambs. I'll be busy awhile.

—It will keep.

Cain's face is pale and sweaty and his eyelids flutter. Abel wonders if he is falling into fever. Blue eyes are hooded in the evening shadows, but some trick of the twilight sets them to shining. Abel says, Are you feeling all right?

—Oh I'm great, he snarls.

—You should take better care of yourself.

Cain shuffles off, caught up in some sort of coughing fit. When he is gone, Abel sits and listens to the night cooling around him. The sheep have bedded down for the evening and murmur to one another. Abel muses on his mysterious brother but quickly grows bored. Sometimes he makes sense; sometimes not. After all these years, there isn't much to say that hasn't been said already.

•

That night under the stars is his fourth in a row, so the next morning he coaxes his flock back toward home. By the time he arrives the sun is well up and he is hungry.

The eating hut is empty: most of his family are working the fields, breaking the tough soil into arable rows. A commotion comes from the kitchen, where his mother hunches over the cookfire while Lya and Epna use timbers to pound wheat in a large stone pestle. Their smooth faces are blank as their bodies heave up and down, thrashing the grain into powder. Dust ascends in fine clouds, coating their brows and lashes.

—Hello Mother, says Abel.

She smiles distractedly and returns to the fire. She is so far along in her pregnancy that she has trouble squatting, and appears ready to topple over at any moment. She has taken to tying her hair back with a bit of rawhide, revealing both her sagging jowls and her startling gray eyes.—Help yourself to breakfast, she says.

Lya catches his eye.—Unless you want to help with this instead.

—We've been at it all morning, chimes in Epna.

What cheek! He chuckles at them to show he takes no offense, but they don't smile back. In the eating hut he sits with a chewy piece of salted mutton and a handful of dates. The pits collect in a little pyramid as he consumes the fruit.

After a time his mother joins him at the table. Abel tells her, I saw Cain last night.

—How was he?

—The same.

Eve shakes her head.—Some things never change. He has such anger in him.

—You shouldn't blame him.

She meets his eye with her own: flat and gray with minute flecks of gold, wide enough to look perpetually alert to some new alarm.—Why on earth not? Just as I can credit you for *not* being so.

Abel shifts his rear end on the hard bench. It is not a comfortable line of reasoning: If Cain can be forgiven his impulses, then why should righteousness be admired? But if he cannot be forgiven, then are all sinners born doomed? Abel sees no quick solution to this puzzle so he quickly puts it out of mind.—How is Father?

—No different from four days ago, his mother smiles.

He smiles back.—Some things really don't change.

—You're wrong there, says Eve. She snitches one of Abel's dates and pops it in her mouth whole, spitting away the pit a moment later.—Your father's changed a lot. Wouldn't believe to see him now, but years ago he was scared of everything. Even rabbits.

—Rabbits?

—They've got big teeth after all.

Abel muses on this. It's hard to picture. Maybe his mother is teasing him.

—Goats and sheep too, continues Eve.—And birds. The whole world really. You have to remember, when we first started out we knew nothing at all. *Nothing.*

Abel has no response to this so he remains silent, idly wondering what else went on in those years before the children. There is a whole span of his parents' lives that has only been discussed elliptically. So he doubts he'll ever know: Does Abel take after Adam as a young man? Or does Cain do so more?

He looks past the doorway to the figures of his brothers in the distance, hauling lumber, hacking logs. Among them the half-finished barn shoulders up like a groggy, awakening giant.—He's certainly throwing himself into his work.

—His energy is remarkable, agrees Eve, unconsciously patting her belly.

As if thus beckoned, the man himself stoops through the doorway a moment later, gaunt and bowlegged and coated in a fine sheen of sweat and wood shavings. Bits of debris cling to his beard and deep furrows bisect his brows. He grunts at Abel, asks his wife how she feels, and passes through to the kitchen. Returning with plate piled high with boiled eggs and roast lamb, he sits beside Abel and attacks his food.

—Good progress on the barn, nods Abel.

—Porad's a great help, and even little Shel does his part.

Abel nods again. The supreme wonder of his siblings is not their number, though that is in itself remarkable, but the variety of skills in which they are all so prodigiously gifted. Just as Cain is with husbandry and Abel with shepherding, so too is Kerod a wonder at weaving and Lya at spinning. And talking, if that's properly a gift . . . Porad displays extraordinary skills at carpentry and the twins at music. Even Shel, whose years number fewer than Abel's fingers, has shown himself precociously gifted at designing efficient structures.

Adam turns his black-eyed squint upon Abel.—What news?

—Nothing special. The flock is fine. No sign of that gout this year. Getting ready for lambing, and the shearing after that. Warm weather's come early, so the fruit trees are in bud already.

—Praise God.

—And what of those strangers, Father?

—Praise God for them too. They've odd ideas, I admit, but some have proven useful already. Their tools have certainly speeded our labor.

—Have they moved on, or . . .

Adam talks rapidly while devouring his breakfast.—They've taken the valley across the river. The man told me he liked the site for his family. As we've no plans for the land, I saw no reason to object.

—They're here to stay then?

—So they are. And their daughters too.

His throat suddenly tightens.—Is that so?

Adam leans close, brushing his shoulder against Abel's.—Indeed it is. Perhaps we'll celebrate the harvest together, in the fall. Give thanks for God's bounty, hem? He smiles at this, revealing big square teeth that glow against his complexion.

Adam seems to be talking about more than just the crops but Abel isn't sure. He blushes but is secretly pleased that his parents have, somehow, acknowledged something about him. That another man's daughters would interest him. That his childhood has passed. He is a shepherd after all: he knows the difference between rams and ewes.

He finds himself wondering what will change now. What kind of accommodations will be made, and by whom. His family has never lived close by strangers before. There have never *been* strangers before.

He wonders too what these daughters look like, and whether their voices are soft, like his mother's, or shrill, like his young sister Epna's.

His parents are smirking at each other and he knows it is because of him. Still flushed, he blurts out something to change the subject.—I saw my brother yesterday.

—Which one?

—The eldest.

The mischievous moment vanishes. Adam pauses in his chewing as if considering his reply. He swallows carefully before saying, That is no concern of mine.

—Father.

Adam resumes his rapid speech.—The barn should be large enough for our needs. The oxen will fit easily and if there is a very cold stretch like last winter's we ought to be able to squeeze the goats and sheep among them.

—Father . . .

—The roof will take some doing though. The walls will be twice as high as normal, so we can store hay and silage up above, on a kind of roof within the roof.

—Father, please. Talk to him.

Adam's face stiffens: every wrinkle round the eyes, every sunken ditch across his forehead looks etched in onyx. His beard is short and whitening and tangled, and Abel has plenty of time to study every fiber as his father swallows several times.—I have nothing to say.

—He looks unwell, says Abel.

Eve blinks.—You said he was the same.

—I didn't want you to fret.

Adam stands up, though food remains on his plate.

Eve says, Is he sick?

—Sick with bitterness.

—Oh, that.

Adam is still on his feet. Before storming back outside he barks, Don't waste my time further with this foolishness, do you hear me? Sons I have but he is one no longer.

Then he's gone. Abel tries to imagine his father scared of rabbits but somehow he just can't picture it.

Eve snitches another date. Abel says, Mother, you should talk to him.

—No point, she says, and spits the stone.—You know how he is.

—But his own son.

She shrugs.—My son too, don't forget. And it pains me to see them like this. But it's something they've both chosen. You can't save people who don't want to be saved.

Abel says nothing but stares at the scuffed earth between his feet. He thinks it is too easy, that dismissal. Too glib. Too much a way of saying: Let them stew.

—Besides, says Eve, placing a hand on her enormously swollen midriff.—I have enough to think about already.

# 27  *the old man*

Winter comes. Days shorten. Nights brood and glower and threaten to take over completely. Meanwhile Abel frowns over questions of age and death and regeneration.

It's a conundrum all right.

Abel has watched generations of lambs being birthed, suckled, and weaned before growing into maturity and bearing offspring of their own. Later in life most are slaughtered for the family's needs, but those allowed to grow old will eventually die of illness or injury.

This is not perplexing. This is the order of things, and there is even a comfort in it.

But when Abel considers himself and his family, his bemusement grows acute. Eve and Adam are much older than their children—themselves born lamblike and helpless to suckle their mother—and Adam's beard has turned silver these past years, his once-sturdy stride has grown noticeably slower. Eve grows thicker and more sluggish with each child.

The bit that baffles Abel is what happens *next*. For years now he has felt stirrings in his loins—strange things are happening down there, things he'd prefer not to countenance. Not to mention his dreams. But if he can see the similarity between himself and a randy ram, who then is to be his ewe? His sisters are all too young, and besides, any good shepherd understands the need to keep sibling bloodlines separate for at least a few generations.

So then, a conundrum. A problem with no solution.

•

His brother Porad is young but clever, adept with his hands, nimble in the design and construction of things. His skin is a shade of brown much lighter than Adam's, peppered with dusty freckles. Even his pale green eyes are speckled.

—Porad, listen. There's something I don't understand.

Perhaps Abel's tone of voice—quiet, conspiratorial—makes the boy look up. He is squatting in the dirt, sketching lines in the sand. Plans for some new project no doubt, some improvement. Porad's a great one for improvements.

Porad says, Just one thing?

Abel isn't sure but he thinks Porad is joking. He's a great one for jokes too, or so Abel assumes: every time the child opens his mouth, all the others titter.—Listen. How old is Father?

Porad squats while Abel stands above him, the sun at his back, so the boy must squint against the brightness.—I'm busy.

—Come on, says Abel.—I'm no good with numbers.

—Funny thing to say, with all the animals to watch.

Abel fumes. He wonders if Porad is being cheeky but he can't tell: the child is expressionless. Like Cain, Porad has mastered the art of remaining stone-faced; whereas Abel, like Adam, lets every shift in emotion flit across his face like a windswirl of leaves.—I keep track of my animals just fine. But Father's age baffles me.

Porad waits, as if to see whether Abel will get distracted and leave. When he doesn't, the child sighs.—Let's work backwards. People tell me I was born twelve summers past, two years after Lya and three after Kerod.

Abel tries to remember but can't: one year bleeds into the next.— I guess so.

—So, how old were you when I was born?

This is just the sort of thing he'd been hoping to avoid. There were the summers he'd shared with Cain alone, remembered as one long hazy time. Then the dead child, then Kerod, then Lya. Three children in three years like beads on a string. Then two years before Porad's birth. That made—wait. Abel counts on his fingers, then counts again and gets a different result. The third try produces the same number as the first.—I was eight I think. Or seven.

—All right. Let's call it eight. I'm twelve, that means you've been alive twenty years now, a nice round number. One for each of your fingers and toes.

Abel nods, appreciative of round numbers.

—Cain was born the year before you, that makes him twenty-one. Father and Mother were together some time before having children, and they probably didn't start before they were Cain's age. Call it twenty-five, plus Cain's twenty-one, that makes Father in his middle forties now. Mother is a little younger. Do you follow?

Abel tries to grasp the numbers but they are too huge: they swarm away like a mob of swallows, flitting between his fingertips before he can catch them. The numbers threaten to overwhelm him. To help remember, he collects pebbles and makes little piles. Four piles of ten, another of seven or eight.—No wonder Father looks so tired lately. He's turning into an old man.

Porad squints up at him.—He already is, isn't he?

Abel has no idea. There is no one to compare with. One thing he doesn't need to ask Porad about, though: the process has accelerated since Cain's banishment.

•

Weeks later Abel sits with his family around the remnants of a bonfire that had blazed huge in the empty space in the center of the compound. The younger children had built it for no other reason than to celebrate the release of winter's slow strangling grip, and the family took their dinner in its dancing light. Now Abel watches as weakening flames claw at the night sky like mournful things, throwing handfuls of sparks against the stars as the pile of slash timber collapses and is consumed. Within the pyramid of thicker logs at the base, coals glow orange and flames hum with diabolical ferocity.

His mother sits a few paces away, Kerod beside her. Once again Eve has grown heavily pregnant: Abel can hardly remember a time in the past ten years when this wasn't the case. Kerod is showing her the mechanism of the small hand loom she has invented. Big rolls of spun wool lie between them. Kerod, a somber girl who rarely laughs, instructs her mother with characteristic severity. Beside them sits Lya, staring into the fire while her hands quietly tug at a bundle of wool and spin it into thick yarn. As her hands flutter, her voice spins an endless tale that no one seems to listen to.

— . . . so the King of the Owls said to the mouse, That is my decision and from now on you shall scurry along the ground and live in holes beneath, and we will leave you alone during the day but at night we shall hunt you as we please, and the mouse said That's not fair! and the King of the Owls said Do not bother me about fairness, it is the way of things and the way it must be, and all the mice began wailing and grinding their teeth and moaning What will happen to our children? . . .

To Abel's left sit the twins. Epna toys experimentally with her reed flute: tentative melodies flutter through the night while Epon taps along on his drum. Depending on where his fingers strike the skin, the drum offers up a higher- or lower-pitched sound. This fact, mildly diverting to Abel, seems to preoccupy all of Epon's waking hours.

Beside them Adam rests elbows on knees and leans into the flames as if seeking revelation. The flickering orange highlights his loamy complexion and throws into relief every crag of his face and snarl of his beard. Abel is struck again by how tired he looks.

Perhaps sensing his son's eyes upon him, Adam turns to Abel.—I met your friend the other day.

—My friend?

—The skinny fellow with the hair.

For a time Abel had been unable to stop dwelling on his bizarre encounter with the strange man. But after his disappearance, as abrupt and complete as his arrival, he'd nearly put him out of mind.

—He is no friend of mine.

—Nor your enemy either, Adam reminds him sharply.—At least not yet, despite all your violent fantasizing.

Abel hangs his head.—That was just talk.

—You were quite adamant at the time.

—It's passed now. Forget it.

Adam wears a mysterious smile.—Anyway, with a family like he's got, I doubt he'll be starting any trouble.

Abel gapes.—Now there's a family too?

—A wife and three daughters.

—Daughters? he blurts before he can stop himself.

Adam chuckles. Abel blushes and says nothing, staring into the fire where the flames hold no answers.—Did you ask where they came from?

—West, he told me.

—That would mean the—the Garden, then?

Eve watches like an owl in the night.

Adam frowns.—It doesn't seem so. He mentioned something about a forest and steep mountains and rocky soil no good for husbandry. But when I asked about tame lions and stars of many colors, of honeycombs free from bees and flowers that never wilt, he just stared at me as if I were raving.

—Bizarre, mutters Abel.

—So it is, nods Adam.—Either he's hiding his true origins, not wishing to admit his own sin, or else he's genuinely from another place. Either way it's no crime to us. And if he truly has daughters, well then. Adam smiles gently at his son.—We may find ourselves all one family soon enough.

Images fill Abel's imagination, strange but familiar at the same time: girls his age or younger, but unknown in feature. Sharp-chinned young women with hooded eyes and noses like hawks. In his mind they go about their daily tasks: cooking and stitching and weaving, fashioning clay pots, threading flowers through their hair, bathing naked in the river—

Hurriedly he shakes the images away.—But if they're not from the Garden, then who is there now? Or did God abandon that place once you left?

The question hangs unanswered in the night air, like the swarms of sparks ascending in their short-lived, doomed arcs. Adam says nothing and Abel senses it was a mistake to broach the subject of his parents' origins. It's not something they like to talk about.

Everyone sits quietly as the bonfire burns down to ash.

Abel stays out after the others have all retired, his eyes reflecting the glow of the coals hissing like serpents against night's black-flung shawl. When his mother brings him one of Kerod's new wool blankets she tells him, If you plan to outwit God or even just understand His workings, be ready to stay out here a long time.

# 26 *the stranger*

The man says, You stare at everybody, or do I merit special l

Abel searches for his voice, finds it, drops it. Finds it a
don't know you.

—Expect not. I don't know *you*, either.

And then just stands there, waiting, as if this were the mo
ral thing in the world. As if it might happen every day.

Abel had seen the stranger approaching over the downs
light. First he'd thought it was his father. Then his brother. Th
mother, mysteriously transformed. And then the man had sto
fore him, a vision, a hallucination, saying: You look like somec
miliar with this bit of God's green.

Now Abel stammers, I know everybody there is. My parent
sisters and brothers. We're all the people in the world.

The man gives him a sideways squint.—Interesting point of
that.

He is older than Abel but younger than Adam: none of his k
has yet whitened, and there is a mischief in his eyes quite mis
from Abel's father. Milky complexion, hair straight and shiny. Lt
of a nose and small hazel eyes.—You don't much take after any
in my family, Abel admits.

The man grins.—Be surprised if I did.

—Though we all look different anyway . . .

The man's voice is funny too, rasping like a crow's and witl
drawn-out timbre to the vowels. His frame is slight and small b
moves quickly: eyes dart about and give the impression of taking
everything at once.—As I say, you seem familiar with the area. Ca
you give a stranger some idea of the lay of the land?

They stand on a low hill. Abel points out the river, the distant grasslands where his family lives, bluffs to the east where Cain has made his home. After a moment's hesitation he adds, My brother is not the friendliest of men.

—I'll avoid him then. I suppose he had some falling-out with your father.

—Yes, in fact.

The man nods with satisfaction.—Shame when bad blood rends a family.

He speaks as if from experience. Abel frowns.—Are you staying in this place?

—Thinking about it. Looking for some decent land and this might be it.

Abel nods as if this makes sense but really his mind froths. Nervously he turns his ear to his flock, almost hoping that one has turned up missing so he has an excuse to go.

After a time the man says pleasantly, You're not the talkative kind, are you?

—Ah . . . compared to my brother, I never shut up.

The stranger rolls his eyes.—Then I'll definitely stay out of his way.

And with that the odd little man saunters off, across the downs and away, until he disappears back to whatever mirage spawned him.

•

Adam is troubled by the news. He masks it well, no doubt to avoid frightening the younger children, but Abel knows his father's silences and can read them like the weather or the birds.

They sit in the eating room, packed on the hard benches bracketing the table. Both table and benches are new and uncomfortable but nobody is allowed to complain: they are designed by Shel and built by Porad. Constructing the furniture was the children's first major project, and even though the table is splintery and the benches tend to wobble, Eve and Adam don't want any of their children to be unduly discouraged. Not after what happened with Cain.

—A small kind of build, you say?

Abel nods.—Hardly taller than Mother. And thinner than me.

—Curious, Adam grunts.

Eve passes a terracotta dish.—You've barely touched your food.

He helps himself to a steaming slab of tongue, one of his favorite meals, and sets to chewing the tough meat thoughtfully. There was a time once when the family had needed to conserve their animals in order to maintain their flocks, but those days are long past now, thanks to Abel. And to God of course.

After a time he says, What shall we do about this stranger?

—There's nothing *to* do, Adam says softly.—It's not as though we've ownership of the land. If he stays, he stays. If not, so then.

—And if he makes trouble?

The idea just pops out. Abel wonders where it came from: there is no reason to expect trouble.

Adam seems caught off guard too.—Then of course, we'll . . . suggest that he make it someplace else.

Abel gets working on another chewy mouthful. For some reason, he can't shake off this line of thinking: it's like a snake with its fangs in his ankle, clinging on no matter how hard he kicks.—Suppose he did something terrible, like, I don't know. Like burning the house down.

—The house and huts are made of brick.

—The barn then. Or he steals the sheep and slaughters them for his own use.

His little sister Tovi stares at him with eyes as wide and gray as her mother's. Barely four winters old, she still can understand his words.—Who's stealing the sheep?

—No one, Eve assures her. Then to Abel:—Stop this. You're scaring your sister.

But Adam squints at him from under a ledgelike brow.—Go on.

—Well, what would you do? If he did something so foul that it couldn't be tolerated, but he refused reparation or banishment. You should think about this now, before it happens.

—I suppose I ought, concedes Adam.

—He's not your son but he would require correction. Would you whip him?

—Enough of this! cries Eve.—Why make problems when there are none?

Abel licks his lips. He feels reckless, and wonders for a moment whether the spirit of Cain has somehow possessed him. Quietly he asks, What if he killed one of us?

Eve jolts to her feet, ushering the younger children into the evening cool. The look she throws at Abel is somewhere between exasperated and furious.—Come along Tovi, let's sit outside. Epon, Epna, let's have a song. You too Shel.

The children all seem happy enough to join their mother, leaving Abel and Adam alone to face each other over the long eating table.—What if he killed *me*, Father? This strange man you know nothing about. Justice would demand his death in exchange, would it not?

His father's face looks troubled, but Adam is not a man to duck a moral dilemma.—I believe it would. But it is too monstrous to conceive, son. The very thought of stripping a man of that which God has given—no. He shakes his head as if bewildered.—It is too much to countenance.

—Yes, probably. But it *could* happen, couldn't it?

Adam frowns.—Why are you so taken by this stranger? I'll grant he's a mystery, but we face many such.

Abel cannot answer this question.—He seems . . . significant somehow. Like an omen or something.

—You've never been one for omens.

—I know. And maybe he's perfectly harmless. But . . . Abel gropes.—Where there's one, there may be others. This time next year we could be facing a flood of them. And isn't it possible that some of these newcomers won't be so innocent? Some might wish us harm, for whatever reasons, greed or envy or just ill will. One of them might decide to do something about it.

He leans across the table, his fingers clenched against the splintery edge of the wood. It's difficult to sit still, as if some strange energy is buzzing along his limbs.—One of them might think about doing something unthinkable. We should be prepared.

—Perhaps, Adam concedes without pulling back from his son's

stare.—But I believe it unlikely. The idea that one man may end another's life, for whatever reason, is destined to remain an unrealized nightmare, praise God, for all time. Of that I am confident.

Abel is not so sure.

# 25  *the conversations*

—How long is this going to last? demands Abel.

Cain straightens up and wipes away sweat.—Riddles never interested me much.

Abel rolls his eyes.—This living alone foolishness. It's been years already. How long do you plan to keep at it?

—Ask Father.

—Be reasonable.

But his brother returns to his labor, clearing the brushwood from a patch of land he will till next spring. The field he's been using for the past two seasons is not as successful as he would like. This bit near the river is thick with lush undergrowth and promises to be more fruitful.

Despite himself, Abel admires Cain's industry. The way he has carved a home for himself out of this wilderness, all alone—under different circumstances, he would be tempted to join him.

But no. That would divide the family even further.

—Oh Cain, Abel sighs. Two years this fiasco has dragged on, and he can easily imagine it lasting many more. Until the mountains tumble into the sea, for example. His family are like that sometimes.—*Cain.*

Cain blinks at him mockingly.—You have more to say?

—Kerod asks after you, he says helplessly.—She'd come herself but Mother keeps her busy.

—Tell her I'm fine, Cain nods.

This summer Abel is seventeen years old, more or less, and carries with him the certainty that reason can overcome irrationality. As time goes on he will grow to question this belief, but at the moment it is strong inside him.—Cain, you ought to go to him.

—And do what, exactly?

Abel licks his lips.—Tell him you've thought things over a bit. Tell him you've reconsidered and you're willing to admit you overreacted.

Cain spits: a wet glistening gob smears the earth. It is just possible, Abel reflects, that he needed to do so at this particular moment. But probably not.

Abel says, You must admit that what happened is partly your own fault.

Cain's eyes widen and for a moment he looks plain mad. His fingers clench the hand ax.—I'll try to forget you said that.

—I didn't say it was all your fault. He's to blame too.

Cain says, But you want *me* to apologize.

—Would it kill you to do so?

—Would it kill *him*?

Abel's eyes skip sideways.—It might.

Cain barks a laugh and swings the flint-and-timber ax into the ground.—For once we agree.

—If you apologize I'm sure he will too.

Cain barks again.—And as ever, our agreement is fleeting.

—As ever, sighs Abel.

—If you're so intent on playing peacemaker, go talk to *him*. He's the one who needs it. I'm not at fault here, whatever you think. I didn't banish myself: he did it. You want that taken back, you need to talk to the man responsible.

—So I will, Abel resolves.—Just watch me.

•

He finds Adam digging clay out of the riverbank: sloppy work, but bricks are needed for a new hut. Adam slogs through knee-deep muck, and Abel waits for his father to throw himself onto the bank for a moment's rest before saying respectfully, Father, about Cain.

Adam's lips are pressed tight.—What about him?

—How long is this going to go on?

Adam picks away specks of clay from his beard.—You refer to what?

—This living apart business. This banishment.

—Ask him. He chose it.

—He told me to ask you. As it was your decision, he said.

Adam laughs then, a dry deep rasp devoid of mirth.—His memory must be deficient. Or perhaps far superior to mine, if he can remember whole conversations that have escaped my retention.

Sitting on the gravelly earth, Abel digs up a handful of small pebbles and tosses them one by one into the river. The ripples are carried downstream, simultaneously expanding and receding.—Maybe you should speak to him. That's all it would take.

Adam's face is a carved mask.—And what would you have me say?

At seventeen or thereabouts, Abel feels he should be taken seriously. If not exactly an *equal* to his father, he is at least enough of an *associate* to be worthy of a hearing. Thus he speaks more directly than he is wont.—You should tell him you have thought things over a bit, even reconsidered your position. You should—if you felt comfortable, I mean—you could tell him that perhaps everyone overreacted.

Adam's abrupt grin is broad and unexpected.—Look at you, growing up all of a sudden and giving me advice.

Abel smiles back, then looks down, unsure whether his father is mocking him.

—What you really want me to say, Adam continues as his grin slips off, is not that *we* overreacted but that I did. Is that not so?

—It would help, Abel says quietly.

—You want me to apologize.

Abel shifts his backside on the stony ground.—Someone has to start . . .

Adam holds up his hands.—Nothing would be easier, believe me. Nothing could be simpler than walking up to your brother at this very moment and saying Cain my son, I was wrong. Or as you would have it: Cain my son, I overreacted. I'm so sorry. Try to forgive me, and if you cannot do that yet, then at least find it in your heart to return home and live again as part of the family.

Abel says nothing. The way Adam declaims the words, they sound both perfectly reasonable and breathtakingly stupid.

Adam has been speaking toward the river but now his head pivots toward Abel. His black eyes have grown squinty and his brows ripple like thunderheads. Brown hands tremble against brown earth.— Nothing would be easier for me.

Abel remains silent though inside he seethes: Why not say it then?

—But pride is a terrible thing, muses Adam, as if he has heard Abel's thoughts.—Your brother suffers from a surfeit of it. Teaching him that he was correct to do what he did, that it is right to nurse his grudge and has been right all along, will only make that pride worse. It will swell and grow like a child in his belly, and when it is finally born, O what a monstrous issue it will be.

—I'm sure, Abel murmurs, that if you made overtures, he would respond in kind.

Adam exhales sharply.—He said as much, did he?

—Not exactly, no.

This time Adam's smile is thin and bitter.—Your faith in your brother's better nature is touching, but you place your eggs in a basket with no bottom. If you want your brother's exile to end, you need to have this conversation with him.

—Maybe I'll do that, sighs Abel. His voice is thin and uncertain, like sunshine in winter.

•

He finds Eve in back of the outhouse, collecting sweet purple berries off the low-growing shrubs that cluster there like lambs. Her fingers are dotted with welts where the thorns have snagged her. Lya and the twins help. Lya is telling some endless story about a caterpillar and a butterfly. Eve stands slouched, as if her barely visible pregnancy is already pulling her down.

—Mother, how long is this going to go on?

She stares at him in bafflement.—Until the child is born, of course.

—I mean Cain. You know, my brother. How long is he going to live alone?

—Oh that.

A note of peevishness creeps into Abel's voice.—Yes *that.*

— . . . so the butterfly said, You will never be like me, you are doomed forever to crawl on the dirty muddy ground, which made the caterpillar so sad it curled up in a ball and wrapped itself in its fuzzy blanket and cried itself to sleep. . . .

Eve tucks a strand of copper-colored hair behind her ear. Sometimes when she fails to wash it, as recently, it takes on a distinctly grubby cast.—I can't say. I was under the impression it was a more or less permanent arrangement.

Lya natters on but the other children have fallen silent and listen now to their mother, as purple fingers pluck, pluck-pluck the berries from their stems.

—Mother, be reasonable. We can't just pretend he's gone off and *died.*

Eve winces and Abel remembers the stillborn child and regrets his choice of words. It is one of those things left unmentioned. . . . But when Eve resumes her berry picking, apparently uninterested in discussing the matter further, he feels his annoyance creeping back.— You should talk to them. It might help.

She looks startled at the thought, but then, she always does.— Talk to who?

—The both of them.

—What should I say?

—Tell them they've both overreacted.

—Well, that's nothing but the truth.

— . . . and when the nightmares finally ended the caterpillar woke up and came out of its blanket and lo, it wasn't a dirty little grub anymore but a beautiful butterfly whose wings were orange and scarlet and purple and aquamarine and yellow and black and a kind of dusty pink that you see sometimes during sunsets after there's been a storm . . .

Abel seizes the chance.—Then make them see the folly of what they're doing to each other. *And* the family.

Eve's voice is noncommittal.—You know how they are. Wringing an apology out of them will be like pulling meat from a tree.

Epon giggles at that and dumps a handful of berries in Eve's dish.—Meat from a tree! he squeals at his sisters, and they laugh and echo him. Lya even breaks off her story.

—Meat from a *tree*! And berries from a *goat*!

—Mother, can we get meat from a tree? Can we get it and eat it tonight?

—And, and, and—

—Berries from a *goat*!

Abel grimaces. Suddenly he's so tired he can hardly speak. Why is this so hard? Why does this problem even exist? There's no reason for it.—Would it be so impossible for either of them to admit he's wrong?

She halts her berry picking then and gazes at him.—Exactly which family have you been living in all these years?

—I know, I know. But I'm sure if one of them made the first move, the other would feel obliged to follow suit.

—That might be true, she says vaguely.—But getting that first move is the hard part. Isn't it.

—Seems to be, Abel sulks.—I thought you'd want to help.

—Certainly I want to, she answers, but it's not in my hands. The difference between us, Abel, is that I recognize when things are beyond me. This argument is between your father and his son. If you want to resolve things, you'll need to talk to them, not me.

Abel is not prone to sarcasm but he feels himself sliding into it.—Now why didn't I think of that?

—I don't know, she answers, oblivious.—You're a good boy but a trifle naive.

Abel turns to go.—Thanks for your help, Mother.

She doesn't answer, distracted by her berries.

— . . . so the butterfly says, Where have you come from I don't recognize you, and the other butterfly says Oh but I never forget anything, and I definitely recognize *you*. . . .

Abel wends his way back to his waiting flock. Crows swoop and flutter in the sky above him as he goes, laughing and taunting in a thick murder overhead.

# 24 *the previous two years*

No ordinary flock is this: that much is clear from the start. The ewes are plump and fecund, the rams docile and satisfied. Both carry great shaggy swaths of wool that are softer than an infant's hair. They never wander beyond Abel's hearing and they grow fat on whatever greenery is at hand. Any wildness that may have once flickered within them is quite extinguished. When the time comes to slaughter (and he hasn't slaughtered many) the animals all but hurl themselves against the knife. Their meat is tender and sweet, their fleece don't grow foul or muddy, and their wool is easily spun. Abel's clever sister Kerod has recently invented an ingenious mechanism for weaving together strands of yarn, and now the family enjoys soft but warm wool blankets to guard against the winter.

The sheep are numberless beyond comprehension. Abel knows his joy should be equally incomprehensible. And yet.

As the days darken and diminish toward midwinter, Abel's mind can't stray far from his brother. The sheep give him no less pleasure than before, but it grows increasingly tempered with concern: there has been no sign of Cain around the family compound ever since the great falling-out. No one speaks his name except the youngest children, and when their questions are quelled with tight-lipped silence, they soon stop asking. Adam has immersed himself in threshing and storing the grain in a makeshift hut and talks often of the need for some larger, more permanent structure. Eve spends her afternoons tanning the leather that she'll cut into new garments for them all during the long winter evenings. The children collect firewood or play in the stubbled fields or tend the animals. With the harvest in and the days short and cold, they have an unaccustomed amount of free time. In the evenings they sing songs: Epon has taken to pounding out rhythms on a block of wood, while his twin sister Epna shows an impressive skill for whistling simple tunes. The rest of the family gather about them in the gloaming and invent songs and throw their offerings skyward amid much laughter.

Abel is both a part of this world and outside of it. He is the eldest now, with Cain gone, and he feels the burden on him. He is fifteen summers old, or so his mother tells him; Kerod is eleven, so she says herself. The gulf between them seems immense. His sister Lya is younger still, and the others are but children with children's concerns. Abel misses his brother. His thoughts turn often to Cain out there in the winter night, unaccompanied by music or laughter: only a wrap of skins shielding him from the wind.

Cain has gone to live atop the bluffs that look out past the river. Not far from the very spot Adam took them on the Night of Revelation. For one reason or another, Abel has contrived to avoid visiting him for all these months of exile.

Has it really been months? Well then, so it has.

No longer. He makes up his mind to go the very next morning.

•

It is the shortest day of the year. The sun limps above the horizon like a misfit, glaring weakly down on the dormant earth. Trees are bare or cling to weak girdles of brown, shamefully masking their nakedness. Willows hang above the river like spectres and the river itself is rimmed with thin ice along its banks.

Abel's breath precedes him in misty gusts as he strides across the hills toward the bluffs where his brother lives. He steps carefully: the area is littered with gray stones, sharp-edged blocks the size of his head whose corners reach out to snag his ankles and toes. In the dim morning light they are easy to stumble over. Abel wears his leather tunic and a bulky shawl Kerod gifted him, and he is still cold. He has half a mind to leave the shawl with Cain, who doubtless needs it more than he.

Cain's residence appears on the horizon like a pimple. Abel draws near, frowning. He'd expected some improvised lean-to, hastily assembled of branches and skins, but this is solid and square. Then he is looking upon a squat structure built of the very stones he has been striving to avoid. Cain has gone to some trouble to find complementary blocks, so the flat surfaces and sharp corners of one lie more or less flush against the next; smaller chips are meticulously set into the crevices. The walls have been clay-daubed from inside, leaving the interior murky as a cavern no doubt, but snug as well.

Roofing timbers support an array of flat stones, cleverly angled to channel off rainwater. The entryway is so low that Cain must crawl through on his knees. It faces south, away from the coldest winds. The whole affair is barely long enough for a man to lie outstretched, but Abel is nevertheless struck by his brother's industry.

He clears his throat.—Are you in there?

Cain's head pops from the doorway as if he's been awaiting Abel's arrival.—Hello.

—Hello yourself. You've been busy, I see.

—Like it? Cain grins. For a moment he looks like what he is: a teenager overly pleased with himself.—Took me a week to build it. On the seventh day I rested.

—Oh stop.

The grin slips off: Cain looks as jagged as if he'd been slapped.—Worked morning till dusk and damn near froze in the meantime.

Abel suspects his answer—*You should have just come home*—wouldn't go down well, so he keeps silent.

—Anyway it's done now, says Cain. He wriggles from the tiny hut like a snake.—What brings you all this way? I see no sheep. Don't tell me you've misplaced that glorious bounty from Heaven.

Abel ignores the sneer in his brother's voice.—I came to see how you were.

Cain appears simultaneously embarrassed and cynical.—Well then. Here I am. And he holds his arms wide as if to say, Behold!

—Yes, says Abel.—Here you are.

The question dangling unvoiced on his tongue is, For how long?

Cain lights a cookfire and shows Abel the holes he has dug in the rocky soil to store his harvest.—Later we'll check my traps, he says.—I've dammed up a narrow bit of the river and strung some nets. The fish are remarkably stupid so I needn't fear starvation.

—You plan to stay here all winter then?

Cain squints at him across the smoldering fire.—At least. Come spring I'll have to find some decent land for my crops, and a more sheltered spot for the hut. There were plenty of stones to hand here so I didn't look further, but it's too exposed and the wind out of the north is brutal.

They squat by the fire. Cain stirs unground wheat into steaming water, lets it simmer for a time before mixing in honey and a splash of milk.—Bet you're wondering where I get milk from when I've no goats of my own, Cain winks.

In fact Abel hadn't noticed.—Now that you mention it . . .

—It'll stay my secret.

Their mother makes a point of having some dried apricots or dates on hand, and Abel craves them now. But Cain has none such. So he accepts a steaming bowl from his brother and tries not to wrinkle his nose.—You won't consider coming home then?

Cain blows across his own breakfast, and steam flows flatly away: he looks as if he is breathing smoke.—You heard the old man. I've nothing to come home to.

—Ah now, that's not true.

They eat quickly and in silence. Better this, they seem to agree, than fighting. When they finish Cain says, Let me show you my pantry.

In the river, fish as long and heavy as Abel's forearm clog the nets, which have been strung across a narrow cataract. A dozen full-size specimens and twice as many youngsters flail against the weave, pinned by the current.—Give me a hand here.

They let the juveniles go and toss the rest onshore to flop and die. Cain swiftly guts them, stacking the slabs of bloody flesh into bricks and wrapping them in goatskin.—I'll dry some of this and salt it, he says.—It'll keep me healthy another two weeks.

He catches Abel's eye and there is a challenge in his voice as he says, You be sure to tell Father that I can take care of myself. And Mother.

—Okay, he says.

—Tell them I'm fine.

—I will.

—Tell them that whatever they hoped would happen to me, isn't happening.

—They didn't hope anything, Cain.

—I'll clear my own fields this spring and do my own planting and hunting. I can live out here as long as necessary. If that turns out to be years, well. He shrugs.

Back at the hut Cain throws a little tinder on the coals and the cookfire chuckles back to life. He fries some of the fillets and he and Abel consume them like wolves.—Good, concedes Abel.

—There's a plant that grows on the riverbank. Like thick grass with little purple flowers.

—I know the one.

—You take a handful and throw it in with a little salt and the fish, and it's like you're eating some other animal. More?

—I wouldn't mind, grins Abel.

They devour four of the fish before they're satisfied. Cain smokes the rest over the coals, which he feeds with thick handfuls of still-green grass from the bluffs. Abel watches. Cain's yellow hair has grown knotted and lank, and dangles down his back like an obscene tail. But his pale eyes flash defiance. It's almost as if they are boys again, playing hidden games all alone in the world and Cain telling him impossible stories they both half believe. But at the same time Abel feels a heaviness in his gut. They aren't children anymore, not really, and he's aware suddenly of the heavy weight of something that's gone missing. Something he can't name, but important nonetheless.

Abel clears his throat and says, You're sure then, about staying here?

Cain flips the drying meat, barely visible now in the sheath of gray smoke.—Yes.

—Even if it means living alone for months? Or longer? It'll be a cold winter.

—So it will, Cain nods, and for that moment he reminds Abel so much of their father that the resemblance is dizzying.—Company would make it easier though.

It takes time for Abel to understand.—Company?

—You could think about it.

This is so preposterous that Abel half thinks his brother is joking. Camp out here, in voluntary exile with Cain?—I don't think so. There's the flock, and of course Mother—He stops. The idea is outlandish.—You shouldn't even mention such things.

Cain's mouth twists.—Figures you'd say that.

The sad thing, Abel muses, is that a part of him is quite impressed by Cain's tenacious refusal to quit. Living independently as he does, making his own decisions, has an undeniable appeal. But Abel pushes that appeal to one side. He has come to heal wounds, not to incise fresh ones.

Disoriented, he struggles to restore some kind of warmth to their parting. He shrugs out of the heavy wool shawl Kerod has woven him.—If you won't come home, then at least take this.

Cain rubs the cloth between his fingers, testing its heaviness.—Nice work.

—Kerod made it. She's very clever, always coming up with something.

—Yeah she is. You're sure you don't need it?

—I'm sure you need it more, out here alone at night. You can return it when you come back, even if it's months from now.

—Longer than that, most likely, Cain tells him.—Years I'd guess. Brother, I fully expect to be out here for *years*.

Frowning, Abel nods as if he understands everything perfectly, these passions that seem to control his father and brother. But he doesn't. In fact he doesn't understand them in the least.

In some inarticulate way, he feels obscurely grateful for this.

# 23 *the judgment*

Smoke hangs heavy in the windless air, like the echo of something obscene. Cain rages at God while the others watch.

—At least explain Yourself, You coward! At least show me that much courtesy! Or is that too petty a concern for one such as You?

His arms whirl: he actually *punches the sky,* and Abel winces at the futility of the gesture. The acid in Cain's voice is painful to hear. Or maybe it's just the smoke of the recent fires, hanging low in a motionless pall, that has roughened his throat.

—The Hell with You then!

Cain storms across the fields, past the bushels of peas and wheat, the pyramids of onions, the heaps of melon. Half-charred now, reduced to cinders: smoky haze hovering close over the earth like a supplicant unwilling to leave. Abel watches his brother go off ranting but knows he'll be back. O yes he'll be back, and Abel braces himself.

It's a good harvest. A bountiful harvest, the best anyone can remember. Dates dangle fat in the orchard, apricots and grapes swell like testicles. Piles of grain and peas and wild onions—blackened now, scorned—lie in once-orderly rows like a promise for tomorrow. Cain is responsible for it, or most of it anyway. Responsible for the hard work: he'd taken upon himself the task of bringing in the harvest and displaying it as an offering to God. Adam approved. Eve arched an eyebrow. Abel stayed alone with his flock while the younger children helped, but everyone knew it was Cain's devotion fueling it all.

And then God turned His back on it.

This is a hard blow to his brother, Abel knows, and yet difficult to attend to properly. For God has accepted Abel's own offering as warmly as He disdained Cain's, and now Abel's flock stretches before him, miraculously increased fortyfold, serene and docile and munching the long prairie grass that grows in tufts along the edges of the plowed fields. If the phlegm-inducing smoke troubles them at all, they fail to show it.

Sheep had been Abel's offering, and now sheep he has beyond number or near enough. Beyond any number he can manage, anyway. Abel stands caught between wonder at this demonstration of God's bounty, and anxiety at Cain's overwhelming resentment. The flock is scattered before him, a blessing made flesh, three-dimensional figures of Grace. Their fleece is unsullied and they glow like angels come to earth. Unnervingly stupid angels, it's true, but angels nonetheless.

Movement nearby: his father, silent throughout the proceedings and Cain's subsequent tirade. Abel says, He's taking this badly, not that I blame him.

—He'll get over it, Adam declares. He wipes red eyes with a sleeve, smearing the ashes that coat his face.

—What about you?

—This smoke, Adam grunts, is undeniably a trial.

While Cain wanders off to vomit on God, the others scurry to store the harvest as best they can. Though much has been lost, there is yet an abundance. The twins set to stashing the fruit in the newly expanded cold cellar. Grain and legumes are stacked in baskets in the sleeping huts and eating room.—We'll lose much to insects and mice, Adam observes sourly.—Some sort of proper storage is needed, a barn of sorts.

Abel barely hears.—Why did God spurn Cain's harvest, Father? It was a good one and did Him much honor.

—Don't question the Lord, Adam commands quietly.—He does as He sees fit.

It crosses Abel's mind that the same could be said of Cain and this would be seen as no admirable thing, but he holds his peace.

●

At lunchtime Cain returns to the compound, his pink face flushed nearly purple, his blue eyes brimming with hate. Blond hair cascades down his neck like fire. The rest of the family avoids him as they would a wild dog.

Except for Abel. He has been standing outside, staring silently at his flock since morning. Now he asks Cain, Where have you been?

—Talking to God, he spits.—Or trying to. You never actually have a conversation, do you notice? It's a bit more one-sided than that.

A nearby ewe says, Baa, as if in agreement. Cain scowls, looking ready to stone the beast.—As if there weren't enough of these before. We'll be tripping over them now.

Abel scuffs the ground between his feet. They stand outside the eating hut with the family inside, no doubt listening.—What did He tell you?

—Oh, the usual. Everything and nothing.

Abel nods. The fact that he's not heard God speaking to Cain doesn't undermine his belief in his brother's words. God speaks to whom He wants when He wants, in the manner in which He wants.—We put the harvest away, Abel says just to say something. Cain looks ready to scowl at the clouds till nightfall. Or maybe sunrise.

—You know what He says to me? He says, *Why are you angry?* Astonishing question I'd say, considering the source. All-knowing and all-seeing and all-everything.

Abel clears his throat as if to speak, but finds himself without words.

Cain spits into the dirt and grinds the wet gob with his toe.—It's something isn't it? You break your back cutting and reaping and collecting and stacking, and then you say a little prayer and say Well God, here it is. And what does He do?

Cain stares off, lips pinched tight. Abel doesn't answer: they both know what God did. He finds himself wishing they could be children again, playing games in the woods, exploring the world. During the time before Cain's realization that the world had done him wrong, before he carried his sourness around with him like a talisman.

Had there ever been such a time?

—He says, *Your offering is not pleasing to Me.* Cain's voice contains equal measures of wonder and scorn.—Then He asks why I'm angry about it. While you—and your damn goats—

He chokes off. Abel says nothing. Cain's eyes are wide: they do not roll back in their sockets, but it wouldn't surprise Abel if they did. Years back their young brother Shel fell into a fit, flopping about on the ground like a fish. Adam declared him possessed and stayed up all night praying. Abel, eyeing his elder brother, wonders now if another such episode is imminent.—You shouldn't dwell upon this, he says, felling as he does so the inadequacy of such advice.—His judgment lies outside our ken.

Cain's eyes flash bloodshot and wild. A little fleck of spittle dots his cheek.—The advice of the blessed. Easy to say when *your* offering has found favor. You and your useless idiot animals.

His fists are clenched at his sides. Fear scampers up Abel's backbone: his brother looks capable of anything at this moment, even something unthinkable. Violence against the innocent sheep, for instance. Cain's hands flex as if grasping an imaginary club with which to pound them all to pulpy smears.

—I'm sorry, says Abel sincerely.—I'd reverse the judgment if I could, have God accept your labors and reject my own. It's what He should have done, it'd be fairer given all your work and how little I've had to do.

Cain squints at him a moment before snorting sharply and relaxing his fists.—I think you actually mean that.

—I do, Abel says earnestly. It is no lie. Why not sacrifice a little to make his own brother happy?

Cain shakes his head.—A pity *you're* not God, you'd make a better job of it. Not that that would be so difficult.

—You watch your tongue, interrupts a voice as rough as splitting timber. Adam has emerged from the eating room and now stands scowling at them. His face remains sheened with cinders and soot, and Abel knows he must look much the same. Like a very creature from beneath the earth.—Your disappointment is understandable and much can be forgiven because of it, but do not push forgiveness too far.

Cain looks ready to spit again.—What do I need with forgiveness?

—Loose words against God are not easily erased.

—God is nothing to me. God is a coward and a capricious child.

Adam's eyes grow round.—Say not such things.

—God rejects me, so, snarls Cain, I reject Him. Go to Hell, You bastard!

This is at the sky but Adam rushes forward as if it is he who has been insulted.—I'll not hear this!

Cain puffs out his chest.—Then leave, for I'm not done speaking.

Abel sidles between them but they stare through him as if he is wind.—Take back what you said, Adam rasps. He is dark as a plum.—Take it back and I'll pray for your soul and perhaps, one day, you can return to God's favor.

—There's nothing to take back, replies Cain.—Every word is true. He throws his head back and yelps at the sky, Are You listening, You useless bastard? I hope You're enjoying Your sick games, You crippled son of a bitch!

—Get out of my sight, gasps Adam.

Cain's grin is wicked.—Throwing me out of the Garden, Father?

—Get out *now*.

—Must run in the family . . .

Adam charges and very nearly succeeds in knocking him down, but Abel manages to take most of the impact while Cain dances away. (Why not sacrifice a little to make his own brother happy?) Adam all but froths, Don't come back until you're ready to beg forgiveness on your knees. To me and God both.

—I won't be back at all, don't fear, until you come begging to me on His behalf.

Sputtering, Adam spins away.

Snorting, Cain stalks off.

Bewildered, Abel stays put.

In the doorway stands Eve, taking it all in with wide gray eyes. Briefly Abel wonders if she'll call out to Cain, beg him to wait, not be so stubborn, cool off a moment. *Think.* Or perhaps she'll implore her husband to show a little mercy, consider what the boy's been through this day, grant him another chance. *Wait.* Abel wonders what his mother will say, and to whom.

He gets his answer when Eve turns away to disappear into the eating room.

When Abel glances over his shoulder, he sees his father knee-deep in the stubble field. The blanket of smoke, thinner than wool but denser than stone, is already obscuring him. In the other direction, Cain is a thin silhouette against the green prairie, making for the hills. Walking fast from the look of it, as if he has a destination in mind. As if he knows where he is going.

Abel wishes *he* did.

# 22 *the offering*

For weeks they labor ferociously. The harvest signifies something more than the simple gathering of food; beyond all else, it is a recognition of the gratitude they hold toward God, so their task takes a new urgency. Even the youngsters seem to feel it, and abandon their games to solemnly lay dates and apricots in neat rows to dry, and collect the sheaves of wheat that Cain has hacked down, carrying them by the armful to the roasting fire that Eve tends in back of the compound.

—It looks to be a singular harvest, frets Adam.—We should have built a larger shed.

Eve smiles at him.—You say that every year.

There isn't time to build any new sheds, so Adam decides to expand the storage pits. They are little more than shallow holes in the ground at present, but they keep food cold through the winter, and Adam decides they must be enlarged and lined with clay or stone to keep the water out.

—Don't overdo it, Eve warns, but he just shrugs.

—No point working for all this bounty if it just goes to waste.

Meanwhile Cain outdoes them all. He is the first up and the last to come in for supper. Abel suspects he'd work by torchlight if his exhausted body would allow it. He observes Cain with confusion and surprise mixed with not a little joy. In the field Cain's body rises and falls like a hoopoe. He has fashioned a long slender blade of flint, wrapped at one end in hides: a scythe, he calls it. With this he hacks rough bites out of the wheat, chopping the stalks at their ankles. He works down one edge of a field, dropping the scythe at row's end to gather the stalks and tie them into bundles. Working his way up the row he has just hacked down, he leaves a trail of sheaves that Kerod and Lya and Porad collect. By the time they have threshed the grain and brought one row's harvest to Eve's roasting pit, Cain is finished with the next. The rhythm lasts for many days: Adam's family has grown much and the farm has expanded many times over.

Besides the wheat, there are chickpeas and green peas, and after that the fruit. By midautumn Cain is growing gaunt.—You should rest a little, Abel tells him.

—I'll rest when I'm done.

Or when you're dead, Abel thinks but fears to say, lest it come true.

For his part, Abel tends the flock. Not much labor is involved, but Adam tells him, You have a knack with the animals, and they must be watched and watered.

—One of the youngsters can do it. I should be helping with the heavy work.

Adam waves him off.—We're fine, he says, then stumbles away. Watching him go, Abel is struck by his father's ginger manner of stepping. Is that the hint of a limp in his left leg?

Cain spends another two weeks on his knees. He is permanently filthy with a kind of grayish tint that never fully washes out. Even his hair is, for once, the color of Abel's. The work is obviously backbreaking but Cain has little to say about it before dropping into sleep each night.

—He'll collapse before long at this rate, Abel murmurs one evening, on the floor of the eating hut. Adam has been promising a table and benches for years now but thus far nothing has materialized.

—He's a strong back, Eve says.—He'll be fine.

—But how long can he keep going?

—He won't need to keep at it much longer, grunts Adam.—Work is nearly done.

Eve smiles and pushes a plate of cheese in olive oil toward him. It's his favorite food and she knows it.—Then we can all have a nice long rest.

Abel thinks: Cain needs the rest more than any of us. Devouring the cheese and oil, he resolves to tell his brother to slow down a little. Let things follow their course. Those onions in the ground aren't going anywhere.

So the next day he asks, Why are you pushing yourself like this?

Cain looks up. A half-filled basket rests beside him.—I thought you'd be pleased.

—So I am, but you seem almost, I don't know . . . possessed.

He squints.—That can't be good.

Abel looks away.—I get up in the morning and you've already left. When I sleep out I hear you walking to the fields. You're up before the sheep are. Sometimes you're up before the *sparrows*, and I wonder how you can even see, much less work. You barely stop for lunch, you go home after dinner and fall asleep like a dead thing.

He pauses. Cain sits for a time before saying, I'm missing your point.

—My point is: Why?

Cain scowls.—Some people are just never satisfied.

—Listen, Abel continues relentlessly.—We manage the harvest every year. So this time is bigger than usual, it'll take longer. That's fine, the bad weather is still weeks off. The way you're acting, it's like you're trying to do it all yourself. Like you think it'll all disappear one night if you don't.

—That's not what I think, says Cain quietly.

—Well what then? Is it because of—that time? When Father found you, you know—and chased you through the woods? You told me what happened, what he called you. . . . Abel doesn't know if he should continue along this vein. Cain's jaw is visibly clenched, his breathing labored. Still, Abel pushes on.—Because I don't think he sees the connection. You've never really talked to him about it, have you?

Abel remembers the incident well. It was the last time he'd seen his brother cry. To make him feel better, he'd said that Adam wasn't actually being unfair: it was Cain who was at fault. This was no less than the truth, and anyway wasn't it better to admit a mistake than to think your father a monster? And it worked: Cain wiped his face dry and stared back dull-eyed, never mentioning the incident again.

Now Cain seems to be searching for words first in the soil, then off on the horizon somewhere.—This has nothing to do with that.

—Are you sure? Because it'd be normal to want to make amen—

—Shut *up*, Cain hisses.—Don't *ever* speak of it again, understand?

His voice is like two rocks scraping together. Surprised, Abel says, All right.

Long moments pass. Cain says, I'm just, I'm trying to do it his way. That's all.

—Whose way? Father's?

—Who else?

Abel squats. Every so often, but more and more rarely as they grow older, his brother surprises him. When they were children growing up it happened almost constantly. He realizes now that this is one of the things he most loves about him.—You think Father wants this?

—I don't know if it's what he wants, Cain says. Impatience darkens his voice.—But it's how he would do it. Throw himself into the task, not rest until it's done. You've heard it all. Idle hands are you know what.

Abel sits and listens. Cain's voice is like a stream bubbling over rocks, but he isn't really talking to him.

—So, all right. He comes to us and says, Let's take in the harvest and present it to God. My first thought is, Why bother? But my second thought is, Well why not? Maybe the old man's right. Maybe God's deserving of thanks and praises, and whatever happened between Him and our parents needn't concern us. So this time I'll do just what he says exactly how he says it. Let's see what happens.

Abel says nothing. His brother has always possessed an intensity of spirit quite alien to his own, but it has never revealed itself like this before.

Cain shrugs.—Maybe God will appreciate it.

—I'm sure He will, mumbles Abel. He is amazed at his brother's sudden turnabout and feels it can only be God's doing.

Cain adds, He might even let it show for once.

Abel wonders if Cain speaks of God, or of Adam, but hesitates to ask.

—Anyway, says Cain, I'm not holding any great hopes. I'm keeping up my end of the bargain, but from what I can tell, that's not always enough.

He indicates the sky with a dirt-stained hand, and this time it's obvious Who he means.—He likes a surprise now and then.

•

The morning after the harvest is in, rain lashes out of a rat-colored sky, rinsing the melons clean, dusting off the sheaves, scrubbing the acres of dried fruit. The storm lasts only brief moments and when fingers of sunlight probe down in golden shafts, the bouquet of wet earth and fruit and grain rushes into Abel and leaves him dizzy with its perfume. He closes his eyes and tries to count the different scents that assail him.

The family gathers, Mother and Father and Cain and Kerod and Lya and Porad and the twins and youngsters. Everybody, thinks Abel: everybody in the world is gathered in this one spot. Behind them is the family compound, and before them the harvest brought together to one place. Baskets and urns overflowing with grain sit shoulder to shoulder with heaps of onions and chickpeas and great pyramids of melon taller than the youngest children. The harvest far outweighs any containers adequate to hold it, instead lies flung like a number of great blankets heaped upon the ground. The presence of so much food in one place is both giddying and sobering at once. The food quite fills the empty area behind the family compound and even spills over the edges of the nearest fields.

Beyond the harvest, Abel's own offering, his lackadaisical sheep, lounge and slouch and chew their cud like bored guests, like jaded cynics unimpressed by anything. Their muddy, wet-wool presence compared to the grandeur of the harvest—Cain's harvest—fills Abel with momentary envy and then, immediately after this, shame at his own selfishness. God is just, he reminds himself, and will know his offering is made in good faith. And envy is a deadly sin, to be avoided at all costs.

The clouds slide away like dreams. Hot yellow sun washes over the scene, droplets sparkle on the fruit like jewels. Kingfishers holler in the trees; woodpeckers make a racket. Beetles trundle across the family's feet. There is only one cloud left in the sky but it's not a cloud, everybody knows it's really God. Abel feels his tongue swell and his bowels gurgle.

There comes a voice.

—*Adam,* says God, *have you brought together this your family to make an offering to Me?*

—Yes, says Adam.—From all of us, but especially from my two eldest sons.

—*That is good,* says God.

The voice does not come from the cloud, exactly. It is not loud like thunder, exactly, and does not echo in rolling peals across the world. Not exactly. But it has substance in the air, and it sounds to Abel like a quiet voice spoken at his ear, low-pitched and clear.

Cain is standing with his mouth drooping open and his hands limp at his sides. He looks, Abel thinks, about five years old.

—*The flock is the gift of the son Abel,* declares God. It is not quite a question but seems nonetheless to require some sort of acknowledgment.

—Yes, says Adam.

—*And the bounty of your husbandry. That comes from the son Cain.*

—So it does, Lord.

Abel watches his father closely. In the presence of God, Adam conducts himself as he does at any other time: a little preoccupied, a bit uncertain, but ultimately confident of his convictions. In Abel's estimation, his father deserves respect for maintaining such equanimity in the face of the unknowable.

—*Very well,* says God.—*Abel, I accept your offering and return it to you fortyfold.*

A dazzling light sweeps over them then, and Adam's family throws up their arms to shield their eyes. A stiff wind kicks up among them, tousling their hair, blinding them with dust.

Just as suddenly, dust and glare both subside. And there stretches a flock too huge to comprehend, jostling as it seems from one horizon to the other: forty animals where there had before been one, four hundred where there had been ten.

Abel's lungs feel strangely swollen in his breast: it is hard to breathe, much less swallow or talk. He faces Adam, who stares with awe and then, slowly, joy.

Eve's look of wonder mirrors his own. Even Cain is smiling.

Abel drops to his knees but no words come. He stares at the earth, each individual grain of soil distinct in his sight. No *thoughts* come.

Adam tries to speak but must clear his throat first.—Thank you, Lord. You are most generous as always.

—*That leaves Cain,* says God.

Abel looks up again at the cloud.

—*Know then: I reject your offering with scorn.*

As one the family stops breathing, but the cloud gives little away.—*Behold! I consume the better part in holocaust, and leave the lesser remnant for you.*

That glaring brightness again, the dusty wind, but when it subsides it is not to reveal the harvest multiplied fortyfold, but rather its consumption by hungry flames licking and sucking and teasing blackened welts of ash and cinders from the pyramids of their effort. Like a single fear-maddened creature, the family throws itself onto the harvest: stamping out flames, smothering fire with precious animal skins, emptying water troughs to create firebreaks. Quickly their efforts center on a few specific piles of food; others are too far gone to be saved. The effort is frantic, panicked, and ultimately successful. By midday the whole family is blackened. Ash and soot clog their noses, cinders stain hair and clothes; but the harvest lies saved. Some of it anyway. Abel surveys the damage and guesses they've lost half at least. Well, God promised as much. And doesn't God always keep His promises?

It's then that he notices Cain is missing. Come to think of it, his brother was absent during the chaotic dousing session too.

Adam is saying something but the words are faint. Abel is aware of pressure in his ears. He squeezes his nose, exhales, and his hearing pops.—Excuse me, Father?

Adam says, Have you seen your brother?

It is then that Abel becomes aware of a distant ranting.—No.

The ranting continues, rising and falling like dueling wildcats.

—But I think I hear him.

# 21 *the proposal*

Abel feels pleased when Adam proposes the offering. He's been restless lately and this gives him something to look forward to.

Even Cain, who looks at first as though he'll say, Why bother? ends up shrugging as if to say, Why not? And Abel thinks to himself, No argument! Imagine that. Maybe he's gotten tired of his old self, and has decided to try something new.

Maybe, thinks Abel, it's never too late to learn something new.

**book three** *the family*

# **20** *the proposal*

Adam worries. Nothing surprising in this: Adam has worried about one thing or another for most of his life, ever since he left that place where worry was never an issue. He tries not to think about it—but those were sweet days indeed. Since then, there has always been some need: to catch a meal, build a house, plant a crop, appease a god (appease *the* God), sire a child, nurse a child, appease a child, catch a fox, slaughter a sheep, appease a wife. Appease *the* wife. Is it any wonder he worries? No it is not. To worry is to plan ahead, to plan is to survive. He has tried to teach his children this: with some success. Say what one will about Cain (undeniably the boy has problems, and Adam shudders to remember one in particular), he's got a knack for the long view. A man can't plant a crop and expect any return if he doesn't pay attention, year after year, to the habits of the weather, birds, soil, pests. A certain eye for detail; a certain way of organizing information. And a certain way of acting on it, one that some people might characterize as *worrying*. Other people, Adam included, would characterize it as *paying attention to what is important*.

Then there's Abel. The second son, the ideal child and, Adam suspects, Eve's favorite (though she is careful to mask this). Outwardly at least, it is Cain who is problematic, who merits special concern, whose moody squalls and gusts of sullenness have spoiled many a family gathering. But Adam finds Abel's busybody vapidity hardly less annoying.

Or maybe that's too unkind. Abel genuinely tries to be helpful, it's just that his manner lacks finesse. His two favorite words are *you should*, followed by *you shouldn't*. Often the advice is perfectly reasonable, which, of course, makes it no easier to bear.

Anyway, sheep are ideal for him: he can order them about all day and they never answer back or grow truculent. But Adam frets as the boy grows into manhood and appears uninterested in anything else. He has only to touch a plant for it to wither. Any wall he essays will collapse. Sharp flints left in his vicinity somehow invert themselves to slice the user's flesh.

—I fear, Adam once said to Eve, our second son's only skill is with the most brainless of God's creatures.

—What of it? Eve demanded, always ready to defend her offspring.—The meat is fortifying and the wool is warm. I'd think that any man would be pleased with such knowledge.

She lifts her eyebrow as she speaks, impishly. It is a mannerism that dilutes her venom into flirtation; he is helpless to argue against it.

Nonetheless he tries.—I am pleased too. But a man does not live solely by meat.

—Nor on grains alone either, but I don't hear you harping on Cain.

The ugly way she says it (*Cay*-in) pains him. Adam lets the subject drop: she does not hear him harping on Cain, it is true. Nor will she. There are some things his wife need not know. That would make her look upon her firstborn in a most negative way—which would be of no use to anyone.

•

On this day it's not just his sons that Adam worries about. He also fears that his wife may be with child again. Fears too she may not. If she is, will the physical strain be too much to bear? They are both growing older; even as Cain's beard feathers out and Abel's mustache asserts itself, Eve's hair is paling from red to copper, silver strands coursing through it like ore. Her belly sags like a fruit gone soft, her haunches flap as she walks, her breasts splay sideways after years of hard use. She has birthed fourteen children in sixteen years, and suckled twelve of them past infancy. Yes, Adam did the hard work of tilling the soil and planting the seed, but reaping the harvest is the more demanding labor . . .

So Adam worries that his wife might be with child. After the previous one she said, Let this be the last, another may kill me. Since then he has kept his distance. Recently though, he approached her again. In the night her sagging haunches feel smooth and he thrills to them like a young man. Surely it would be an unnatural act to deny himself his own wife's flesh? Or to deny her his? For she enjoys it too. She makes no secret of this, reminding him only: —The difference is not in the pleasure it gives, but that I'm left to carry the consequences.

And if she is not pregnant? Even this is a cause for concern, for the Lord has made it clear that it is Adam's duty to multiply. The details of how long this should continue were left unmentioned. It seems impractical to keep going until they drop dead. Why have children if the parents expire before they can raise them? On the other hand there is God to consider. God said: *Do this.* God did not say: *Do this until you get tired and then stop.* God certainly did not say: *Do this until such time as you decide that My instructions are no longer relevant and then do whatever you want.* No indeed. In Adam's experience, which is admittedly limited but compelling in the extreme, God's instructions when issued are meant to be followed. Exactly. Until otherwise amended.

He finds himself faced with two possibilities and neither pleases. Adam would never use such a cavalier expression as Damned if you do, damned if you don't, but it would be fair to apply it here. (Where has he heard that expression, anyway? Cain most likely. The boy speaks little but can turn a pithy phrase when he chooses.)

•

This year spring comes early and mild weather lasts for months. There is just enough rain and at the right time, sweeping across the fields like messengers bearing glad tidings. The crops thrive, including the new patches of melon Cain has put in. They grow untidily like weeds, but Cain claims the fruit will be abundant and uncommonly sweet.

He manages to convey all this with a minimum of words. He

does not ask, precisely, to be allowed to experiment with the planting: his tone suggests that, whether Adam agrees or not, Cain's plans are already laid. That distance, the *strangerliness* that Adam has noticed—stretching back even to the night of the Garden revelations—is strong in Cain these days. As if his mind is off marking its own trails, seeking its own resting place apart from the family. Or perhaps trying to find its way back to them.

Maybe he is growing up.

Sometimes Adam gets the feeling that the farm is barely his own anymore. His eldest son has appropriated it somehow and instituted numerous modifications. Sometimes, but only sometimes, these take the form of suggestions.

—This new grain is good to eat, Father. I planted a larger patch than you wanted.

—The fields that grew peas last year should grow wheat this year, and the other way around.

Altogether Cain seems more comfortable with the company of plants than animals, especially the two-legged variety. Adam wonders if he should worry about this, then decides, So be it. If his eldest's talent in the field supercedes his own, well, such is God's plan.

For indisputably, God has one.

Besides the melons, Cain transfers wild grapevines to the orchard, where they hang from trestles between the date palms. Grapes are a great favorite with the younger children, but the bulk have always been lost to crows and orioles.—One of the children must have the job of running about and scaring off the birds, Cain suggests, or rather, instructs.—And when the vines grow thick they'll give a nice shade and the fruit will hang down for us to pluck.

And so it is done.

By midsummer Adam can no longer contain himself. He demands of Eve whether she is with child and, startled, she answers:—No.

—Praise God, he bursts out before he can stop it.

Surprised again, she laughs aloud.—I agree but thought you'd feel different. I've known for weeks but haven't said, for fear of troubling you.

•

Late that summer it occurs to Adam that it has been some time since his family has made an offering. Overdue really, and the approaching harvest looks like a good one. He proposes the idea to the boys: Abel of course is always up for a holy act but Cain seems only slightly less interested.

—All right, he shrugs. (How Adam detests that shrug, that studied indifference.) His eyes rest steady on Adam who again feels, while watching Cain, that shift from the familiar to the unknown and back again.—Why not? We've an abundance, I guess it would be the right thing to acknowledge it.

Adam is pleased, notwithstanding the shrug. He hadn't expected the proposal to be met so warmly, but there it is: unexpected things happen all the time. Maybe Cain is growing up. Perhaps he has grown tired of his constant gloom. Perhaps he is finally taking into consideration his immortal soul, and with characteristic foresight, is planning ahead.

# 19 *the previous winter*

The mistake was in hitting the boy. That much is certain, however much his wife protests that the blow was warranted. The more she says so, in fact, the more certain Adam grows that it was the wrong thing to do.

Nor has this been his only blunder. Adam is sure he has made thousands. If he etched the list on tablets, no doubt the stack of them would reach halfway to the sky. Not that he can particularly remember more than a handful—and not that he didn't have help.

The weather is vindictive too. Winter has settled in and with it come long cold afternoons, joyless nights, and bitter mornings. Rain slashes down every second day, even the occasional snow squall. Just the sight of this makes Adam tired: the distant mountains carry a perpetual mantle of white as if they too have grown as old as he feels.

There are chores enough to do while the earth lies comatose. Tools to make or mend, garments to repair, fires to tend. The whole family sleeps in the eating hut, the only warm room in the compound on account of the driving winds and pervasive damp. The fire is left to smolder as they sleep, and in the mornings Adam wakes to a stiffness unknown to his previous years. As if the very membranes of his joints are drying up, pulling his bones out of alignment.

Knees and neck are the worst. He squats painfully next to the ashes each morning and pokes them till he finds an ember, then blows on it, feeding little tufts of dry grass. He enjoys being the first to rise. Let the others rest. Before long flames are cackling, twigs and branches have begun spitting sparks while the rest of the family slowly come to life. But even while Eve fries the breakfast meat and the children giggle sleepily or argue grumpily, the tightness in

Adam's joints remains. Sometimes it's not gone till midday. He wonders if the development is permanent, if he has it to look forward to
for the rest of his days. He wonders if, one morning, he will find that
he cannot move at all, and if on that day he will be dead.

•

Cain avoids him throughout. Sleeps at the far end of the room by
the open entryway and doesn't linger at meals. Spends his days outside doing Adam knows not what. Abel is gone too but that is logical: the animals are outdoors.

One morning Adam steps outside. Abel lounges against the wall
of the eating hut, a couple of miserable ewes crowding his knees.
Across the fields the younger children approach the compound, arms
piled high with firewood. Even the four-year-olds, Epon and Epna,
do their part, dragging a Y-shaped stick between them that is nearly
as long as they. Adam smiles fondly upon them.

The children drop the wood in a heap at the end of the clearing
and have turned away for more when Abel calls out, Don't leave it
like that.

They hesitate. Epon and Epna look to Porad, who looks to Kerod,
who looks to Adam. Abel goes on, Stack it neatly or rats will nest in
it. And you two, Epna and Epon, try to bring more than one piece at
a time or you'll be at it all week!

Epon looks ready to cry, although his sister's face is a stone. Adam
steps forward and says quietly, You're doing a fine job. You two especially. Now go on and get a bit more. The sky looks threatening.

When they're gone, Adam turns to Abel, who protests, You'll
spoil them, Father.

—Hem.

—Just look at that messy pile. Vermin will be nesting there by
morning.

—Straighten it then.

Adam strides off quickly toward the woods, striving to outpace
his annoyance. Maybe he'll collect a bit of firewood himself this day.
He is tired of the huts and wants some activity to distract him.

(Sometimes when he forces himself to some labor, the stiffness in his joints subsides. Other days it grows worse. There is no discernible pattern.) This morning there is a thin rind of snow crunching underfoot, and the willows and hemlocks wear shaggy garments of white. Adam passes swiftly among them, seeking downed limbs or overturned trunks, but the children have been through this area many times and all the easy pickings are gone. He moves along, slower now.

A shadow to the right, and Cain is making his way toward him. The boy walks with purpose, and Adam wonders if he followed him out here. He stops and Cain stops too. They face each other across a clearing the size of a large room.

Neither speaks for a time.

Adam's inclination is to say, Yes? but he senses that to speak first would be to somehow give up an advantage. Perhaps the boy feels the same way. Around them the snow sighs gently as it settles into the crannies and crevices of the forest.

They stand and watch each other like rams.

This is getting ridiculous, Adam thinks as the silence stretches. He takes the moment to study his son. Cain is fifteen summers old now, and yellow feathers smear his upper lip like a kiss, though his cheeks remain pink and smooth. Adam feels a tug inside him: approaching manhood, the son is fully as tall as the father. Still with a boy's lankiness though, and a boy's uncertain movements, his sudden rabbit-quick stops and starts.

The picture comes unbidden into his mind, the memory of the child sprawled on the ground, legs open. In some ways he is altogether a man already.

Adam can bear this childish silence game no more. Whether he's giving up the advantage is irrelevant.—So then?

—There's something I want to ask, Cain announces.

Adam waits.

—God banished you and Mother from the Garden for disobeying Him, right? For sinning.

Adam sighs. The boy is simply obsessed, there is no other word for it. This has gone far beyond a healthy interest in his origins. Was it a mistake to tell him? Perhaps. But what's done is done. Adam answers, So He did.

—And Mother sinned first, you said.

—Correct.

—And then you. So my question is, if Mother had disobeyed but you hadn't, what would have happened? Would God have banished her but not you?

An intriguing question, Adam is forced to admit, and one that he has held at arm's length for many years. To explore it fully is to court regret, despair, and possibly madness. To ignore it (to ignore so many things) is to allow himself a good chance of getting up each morning and facing the day's demands without falling to earth in foaming, incoherent rage.

He admits none of this to his son, telling him only:—It is a foolish question.

—It's interesting to me, shrugs Cain.

That shrug again. Adam's jaw clenches.

—Because if she had sinned but you said no to her, then God would have been pleased with you, isn't that true? And He wouldn't have sent you away. Maybe He would have sent her away but you'd still be in Paradise.

—And you, snaps Adam, wouldn't be here at all. Your mother and I had no children until we left the Garden. He does not add what he is thinking: We did not know how. We were innocent—unlike you.

Cain considers this.—But God would have given you a new wife, don't you think? Unless you were running out of ribs, he grins.

Adam does not allow himself to be baited.—There is no point speculating.

—I'm just trying to understand you, shrugs Cain.—God rejects you but you cling to Him tighter than ever. God sends a poor harvest and you thank Him for it. God tells you, Don't do this one thing, but you let Mother convince you to do it without a second thought. It's confusing. . . . If Mother hadn't tempted you, you'd still be there. You spend your life taking care of her even though she made

such a mess of things. If she'd done it to me, I don't know. I'd be
tempted to slap her, or leave her rotting in a cave somewhere.

Adam clenches his molars and counsels calm. Obviously the bit
about slapping her is designed to sting him, but he reminds himself
that losing his temper only makes things worse in the long run.—
Speak of your mother with respect.

—Sure, the boy shrugs. (How Adam hates that shrug.)—I'm just
saying, don't you ever, well—blame her for what happened?

Adam's throat is constricted. Part of him is tempted to blurt: You
speak truer than you realize. In my bleaker moments I have felt just
as you describe. But another part of Adam wants to club the whelp
into silence. Doubtless this would be the wrong course, but he feels
no less tempted for that. And what is he, he wonders bleakly, but a
man who gives in to temptation?—As I said, there is no point speculating. What's done is done. God's will is done, always. Accept it and
be free, or fight it and remain a prisoner of your own limited understanding for the rest of your life.

This thought has just come to him. Adam is rather proud of the
neat way he has put it. Sometimes he has a way with words.

Cain squints at him from across the clearing.—Why are you so
afraid to *talk* about anything?

The question startles him. He gropes for an answer, blind like a
newt.—We talk a great deal.

—Not about things like this. The weather, the crops, the animals.
Mother makes up songs and you tell us how to pray. Lya's blasted
stories about the birds go on and on and never end. But we never, we
don't *discuss* things. Like, who will Abel and I marry? Who will we
have children with? Each other? Our sisters?

—That's enough! snaps Adam.

—It's a fair question isn't it?

He forces his throat clear.—All will be revealed.

—All right, but when? How?

Cain gesticulates while he speaks—an unusual mannerism for
him, as if angels are using him as a puppet. (Or demons are.)—It's
as if you're afraid to discuss things you might not know about. As if

you don't want to admit your ignorance of anything. But you're not fooling us—there's so *much* you're ignorant of. We all are. What are we supposed to do when you and mother die? Divide up the farm among ourselves? Keep living there as we do now? Fight over it? What's on the other side of those mountains? How come God made all those different animals but we're the only ones that can talk? And I'm serious about the marriage thing, Father. I know how children are produced—here he pauses, but Adam retains his dignified silence—I've seen the livestock busy with it often enough. Not to mention what Abel is thinking.

Adam winces.—Does Abel talk of such things too?

—Not yet, but he will, and then what? It's easy to say that all will be revealed, but does that mean we avoid discussing things altogether? Isn't there some use to having a conversation? You say we talk but we don't. What happens is that every once in a while you tell us to do something. Then when you're finished you ask if we understand, and we say we do, and then we get on with whatever it is.

He stops abruptly. This rant leaves Cain deflated and breathless. Never has Adam heard such a long speech from him, and he wonders how to respond. Clearly the boy's main point can be dismissed out of hand. Never talk? What then was fueling all these questions, if not the conversation Adam had had with his sons two summers back? No. This is clearly a case of Cain's feeling sorry for himself. Sad to say, it is a habit to which he is prone.

—You're not going to answer me, are you?

Adam coughs quietly.—There are no answers to the questions you ask.

—There are many possible answers, Cain counters.—If we discuss enough of them we might hit upon the correct one.

—I could make up stories if you prefer, as Lya does. Childish drivel about what the insects are saying to one another as they buzz and chirp. I could invent superstitious nonsense and imaginary stories to give the illusion that we understand our purpose and destiny. I can pretend, as you would have me pretend, that I can comprehend God.

Cain is silent.

—Or, I can keep my own counsel until such time as we are meant to understand. This is what I choose.

The boy waits a moment more, then turns his back, shuffling deeper into the woods as if in search of more kindling. Adam suspects this is not his real purpose. He watches his son depart with an expression that leaves vertical marks between his eyes as deep and unyielding as scars.

Self-pity is not Cain's only distraction. There is a new quality to his temper that Adam has marked lately and is more apparent than ever today. A kind of low-lying belligerence, a smoldering challenge. Yes the boy has always been demanding, but this is new. It reminds Adam of certain wild dogs that live on the periphery of the farm. When challenged, some dogs flee, but others rush the challenger, fangs bared. It is important to recognize which are which. Adam feels, since his mistake at the bonfire (his open palm, Cain's spraying nose), that Cain is starting to bare his fangs.

God help me, Adam prays. Help me comprehend this stranger, that he might comprehend me.

There is no immediate answer.

# 18 *the mistake*

There comes a year when the harvest is scanty and winter looms long and bleak. Adam thinks hard on what must be done before declaring, We must make a sacrifice this evening. A burnt offering seems especially appropriate.

Abel claps his hands.—Yes! A bonfire!

Cain says little but watches his brother as a falcon might observe a mouse.

The other children grow lively and rush to collect kindling and logs from the woods. Eve sits and suckles the youngest inside the eating hut, leaving Cain alone with Adam in the clearing among the compound's buildings. Autumn sun washes down on them but the breeze carries the hint of the cold weather approaching. Overhead a V of geese hurtles somewhere unknown.

—You seem unexcited, observes Adam.

Cain shrugs.—The children will enjoy the fire, he says, emphasizing the word *children*.

—That is hardly a proper attitude.

—It is the only attitude I have, shrugs Cain. Shrugging seems his favorite activity of late: at times Adam fights the urge to ask what is wrong with his neck. Other times he wonders if all his children will be like this at age fifteen. There is no way to know.

Now the boy says, But I will help if it is expected.

—It is indeed expected.

—I'll gather some wood then.

—Wait, says Adam.

Cain waits while Adam chooses his words carefully.—This offering will be more significant if it consists of more than a few dead

David Maine

branches and old animals. The harvest is slender this year and it seems right that, if we are asking for better times ahead, we should sacrifice some of what we have.

—Sacrifice some of the harvest?

—Yes.

—You mean burn it?

—I do.

—That makes no sense.

Adam bites back his impatience. He's only a child, he tells himself, despite everything. It's not his fault if he thinks he understands all the workings of the universe. (Is it?)—It makes a world of sense. We are asking God for a larger bounty, and what shows our commitment more than a bit of the bounty we already have?

Cain is almost smiling, but not quite, as if he thinks Adam might be having a joke at his expense.—You're saying that the best way to show how urgently we need more food is to set what we have on fire.

—Not all of it, Adam says. He is suddenly exhausted. From the direction of the forest the children are returning, bearing tangles of kindling. Inside the house Eve coos a song to her sleepy twins, to the drowsing Shel.—Just a part.

—How much? demands Cain.—A tenth? A hundredth? Half?

Adam tries a different tack.—Use your judgment. The harvest has been less than plentiful this year.

—Exactly! And you'd lessen it even more.

—The point, says Adam doggedly, is that God expects more *from* us before He'll give more *to* us. Adam is pleased with the phrasing of this: it is neat, and true, and will stick easily to the memory.

In the clearing the children are heaping the kindling before running off for more. Abel shows up with a pair of tottering sheep barely able to stand. They survey the confusion through leaking eyes while gumming their cud to liquid.—Shall we add these, Father?

—Fine, fine.

When Abel has staked the animals and gone off for wood, Adam turns to Cain and says, You see? Your brother is willing to sacrifice his animals and no complaining.

Cain rolls his eyes.—They can hardly stand.

—It's still plenty of meat we won't be eating. You think we won't miss it?

Cain shrugs.

In the end Cain delivers a few sheaves of wheat, a bushel of stale dates, a dish of moldy peas.—That's all we can spare, he tells Adam, who commands:—Then go get more. A sacrifice taken from a surplus is no sacrifice at all.

The boy shoots him an incredulous look but does as he is told. Adam watches him stalk off with no small satisfaction. There are some things, after all, that the sire understands better than the whelp.

•

The fire roars white against the night sky, quickly fading to yellow, then orange. The orange lasts a long time, flecked through with green and blue from the underbellies of logs; this is followed by hot glowing red, the coals and flaring embers and near-invisible flames that hiss and snap like beasts. The family sit in a ring around the flames and stare as if entranced. The smell of burnt sheep and roasted grain is sweet and pleasing.

With satisfaction Adam notes that Cain is no less hypnotized than anyone else by the display. Rather more than some in fact. A ragged fondness surges through him. His eldest son is a challenge, but so what? All the more reason to appreciate his strengths, which are many. If everyone were like Abel, then yes life would be more predictable. But a fair bit duller too.

Suddenly he feels ashamed of his harshness to the boy last spring. *You are an abomination in my sight.* Words spoken in anger could not be taken back, but the child should know that—transgression or no—Adam harbors no ill feeling.

Impulsively he stands and approaches Cain from behind, squatting behind him to rest his arms across the boy's shoulders. Cain starts so violently that Adam is nearly thrown backward.

—Excuse me—

—Sorry . . .

—I didn't wish to startle you.

—Of course. It's my fault.

They both stand, awkward now. Adam is quite out of sorts. Does he really embrace his son so little that his touch is so alien to the boy? Or perhaps he had just been lost in his thoughts. Yes. That was more likely.

Cain watches him, his adolescent face as smooth and expressionless as an egg.—You wanted something of me?

—Ah, yes. I wanted you to know how glad I was with your, hem, contributions. Adam gestures to the still-hot coals.—I am sure they were appreciated.

Cain shrugs. Again.

Something about that gesture needles Adam's skin like a rash, enough to urge him to continue speaking when, really, restraint is no doubt the better course. Nothing to be proud of but there it is. Adam needs to assert his correctness over the boy and has no better words to use than those he'd spoken before in his thoughts.—There are some things that the sire understands better than the whelp.

Cain blinks.—What?

—I think my meaning is clear. Youth has industry, but age—here Adam levels a meaningful glance—has experience.

—And a lot of good *that's* done you.

Adam frowns but Cain goes on, You think you understand how to keep God happy? A bit late for that I'd say, once He's already thrown you out. And how are you so sure that you've got it right this time?

—You quiet yourself, Adam growls.

—And if I don't?

—You will come to regret it.

Cain's laugh is doglike.—Listen to him!

The whole family is watching. Adam and Cain are on their feet but the others sit cross-legged or lie back on the ground, hanging on to every word. Some of the younger children have forgotten to close their mouths.

This situation is intolerable. Rounding on Cain he hisses, What I discussed with you and Abel was a private matter. The others are un-aware.

—Are they now.

—Indeed they are, and you will keep silent until I choose other-wise.

Cain shrugs.—But you must admit it's strange.

The boy just will not let up. Adam forces a deep steadying breath into his lungs, where he holds it, willing himself to calm.—What is so strange?

—This whole sacrifice business. Sure I can understand an offering to someone who makes the rain fall and the sun shine. But consider-ing your history and Mother's, I just don't know.

—You go too far.

—Well, what do you expect from an *abomination* like me—?

This in front of his mother, who stares in perplexity.

—This God of yours bullies you out of the only perfect place you'll ever know—

It happens with remarkable slowness but it happens. Adam feels himself outside his body, looking down as he pivots, weight on the left foot, leaning slightly forward as if for leverage, picking up mo-mentum as his body torques. Almost as if he is hurling a rock at a crow, except his hand is empty: there is no rock nor crow either, just fingers stubby and creased and getting more creased by the season, the nails bit short and crusted underneath with loamy soil, and his palm, wide and spatulate and calloused from years of hard work. The hand arcs through the night air as if independent of his arm but it's not of course nor is the arm independent of the shoulder, the back, the hips that twist into the blow, the mind that directs it all and is madly hollering I told you to stop and you'll stop!

These words are not said. There is no time to say them. His hand flashes in an eyeblink, catches his son's face (smooth, unlined, egg-like. Innocent? No, not that) across the front of his jaw, catches chin, clips nose, but does not—Adam can feel this—dislodge any teeth. Cain pirouettes away as if clowning, as if mock-dancing, loses his footing as if playing the fool for the delight of his younger siblings.

So one might think, watching him, except that this is Cain and Cain does not clown, does not mock-dance, and never ever plays the fool.

He spins heavily into the dirt and is still.

But only for a moment. Then he jumps to his feet, breathing hard, eyes wild. Blood streaks from his nose and is left unwiped.—You didn't, he gasps, gulping air, trying not to cry. He is the eldest after all, and has his pride.—Have to, do that.

Adam lets his silence speak: words would only dilute the lesson.

Cain's eyes flicker to Eve, who has sat motionless and wide-eyed throughout.—Don't you have anything to say about this?

—Listen to your father.

He snorts, then spits away the blood that is leaking from his nose onto his lips.—There's something wrong with all of you, he snarls before bounding into the night.

Adam watches him go. He is not proud to have hit the boy. It is not an indulgence he has allowed himself before. On the other hand he is pleased to have gotten some sort of reaction. Any response is better than a shrug, that non-response, that anti-response. Eve's support is welcome too, he'll thank her for it later. But still. He can't shake off the feeling that he has erred somehow. That one way or another, for better or for worse, everything has changed.

If he is honest with himself, he'll admit it already had.

# 17  *the abomination*

Adam clamps his jaw and tries not to howl. Blood thrums in his ears like a song while sweat whispers down his forehead. The boy lies in a sprawl on the ground, an expression of bewilderment and shame writ across his face like sacred text.

Cain's mouth flops like a dying lamb's. Adam raises one foot as if to stamp down on that mouth.—Have you nothing to say then?

Around them the simple noises of the woods start up again: squirrels rustle through dead leaves, redstarts twitter. As Adam watches, Cain's eyes shrink. From widened terror they transmogrify, shrivel to something small and hard like pebbles. The boy almost sneers— almost. Perhaps the wild glitter in Adam's eyes causes him to hesitate. A moment later he says, I didn't mean to.

—You didn't mean to, Adam repeats. The words make no sense.—Didn't *mean* to?

Adam had come upon his wife that afternoon in a clearing by the river, and something about the way her hair dangled in a loose strand past her ear and coiled on her bare shoulder had startled him into stillness. The gazelle skin wrapping her torso had slipped, revealing a knobby line of vertebrae extending downward from her neck, and the urge to run his fingers across those swells had stirred him with startling ferocity.—Where are the children? he'd croaked.

—Home, she answered. When she caught his eye, she smiled and arched her eyebrow.—The boys are in the fields, I suppose.

—Well then.

—Well then. Eve's eyebrow arched yet again. She might as well have thrown a rope around him, and pulled.

Adam seized her quickly from behind. The vertebrae beneath his fingers hummed against his fingertips as he thrust. Eve lay her head on a pillow of moss and closed her eyes, half smiling as if she were listening to a private song.

—Mmm, she hummed.

Adam closed his own eyes and forced himself to move slower than was his wont. Inside him a great swirling seemed to burn through his fibers, coalescing and solidifying into a mass that swung through him like lava. His thighs trembled. His loins opened. He looked up from his wife's hips to see, from across the clearing, his son's blue eyes staring into his own.

Adam shuddered. His mouth fell open a little further as his brain struggled to make sense of this apparition, and failed.

—Mmm, murmured Eve.

Cain's mouth hung open a little too. Adam's gaze lowered to Cain's hand clutched around his own purple erection. Adam tried to pull up, to arrest his plunging, but could not. Father and son climaxed at the same time.

Adam didn't linger.—I must go now.

He left the confused figure of his wife and dived through the brush. Cain fled before him, gangly as a fawn, but Adam was fueled by cold righteous fury. Branches snatched at him as he dodged trees and leapfrogged rockfalls. When Cain skittered down a rocky slope and tumbled amid a pile of dead leaves and broken ferns, Adam came to a halt beside him. For long moments there was no sound but that of settling dust and the squawk of startled birds winging off.

Cain's eyes were huge in Adam's sight. A pulse in his neck flickered like a feather but he kept quiet.

—Have you nothing to say then? Adam growled at length.

•

Now the boy makes an incoherent sound. Adam's foot still hovers above his face like a cloud.—And do you make this a habit, to follow your parents around and spy upon them?

—I wasn't following you, the boy protests.—I was—I was—

Adam waits.

—I was just by the river when Mother came. And then you—you—

This is the decision point, Adam knows: he can turn away or he can press forward. He could cough or harrumph disparagingly, tell the boy for God's sake to *grow up* (though to all appearances, he has done exactly this). And that would be that. Or he could do otherwise.

Adam reaches down and yanks away Cain's gazelle hide. The boy flinches. Semen has dried in a whirlpool on his thigh. There it is, plain as sunshine. No turning back now. Adam's mind recoils from the presence of the boy's—the man's?—seed, drying to a sticky gum, and he cannot help but wonder what had run through the child's mind at the moment of climax: his own mother, spread beneath him? Anger chokes his breathing; Adam suspects his face is turning red.—You are an abomination in my sight.

The boy's eyes, already shrunken, narrow even further. They gleam like small hard things, like blue jewels.—What are you then?

—What's that supposed to mean?

—We did the same thing. Didn't we?

Adam closes his eyes. Why me? he wonders. Aloud he says, She is my wife. She is your *mother*. What I did was allowed.

—But it's not for me.

—No.

—Because she's not my wife.

—That's right.

—But when I have a wife I'll be able to do this with her.

Adam finds himself grinding his molars again. How did this child grow up so quickly? It can't be normal. Just weeks ago, it seems, he was catching tadpoles with Abel, and finding pictures in the stars.

—Father?

He shakes his head.—Hem.

—When will I have a wife?

—When I see fit, he snaps.

—Will it be Kerod?

Adam shudders. Kerod is nine summers old. Adam tries to whisper, You monster, but the words don't come out because of the constriction in his throat. He shakes his head convulsively and Cain takes this as a negative.

—Who then? says the boy.—If not Kerod, then who?

Adam takes his time in answering. Partly this is because he does not know the answer, but partly this is because he knows the answer, whatever one he gives, is important.—We have to wait and see, he says at length, what the Lord decides to provide. In the meantime, you shall avoid self-pollution. Understand?

The boy hesitates only slightly.—All right.

Neither of them is convinced by the other, but Adam leaves the boy as quickly as he can: lying on his back in a pile of dead leaves, with a sticky patch of semen half-dried on his leg.

# 16  *the conversation*

The time comes for the boys to know the truth, so Adam leads them to a remote place one evening and sits them down and says, Your mother and I are not from here. We came long ago, years before either of you were born.

The boys look to Adam like a pair of baby birds. Abel open-faced and expectant; Cain frowning and sullen, a nestling buzzard perhaps. Both carry with them the expectation that this conversation will reveal momentous tidings. As well they might, Adam reminds himself. As well they might.

Cain turns his head and his yellow head flares in the flat twilight sun.—Came from where?

—There, Adam points.—West.

They sit along the bluffs, at the edge of a sheer cliff split by a narrow, twisting ravine. Their home lies three miles distant but they walked the entire way in silence, Adam thinking on the words he would say and the boys polishing their expectation to a shiny brightness. Now they look to follow Adam's pointing finger to where it stabs the setting sun as if lancing a fat red boil. They see trees and low distant mountains and the river unspooling from them, like a thread. Or slithering toward them, like a threat. But their blank faces reveal that they see nothing more.

—From the mountains? hazards Abel.

—Further, much further. We walked for years after we left.

—Left where? demands Cain.

He hesitates. The boys are thirteen, fourteen. It is time they understand everything, as much as is possible to understand. But this conviction makes it no easier to form the words in his mouth.—The place where your mother and I were created.

—You mean born, frowns Cain.

—I mean created.

The boys are watching carefully now.

•

He pinches some dirt between his fingers and mixes it with a little saliva in the palm of his hand. As the children watch, he fumbles with thick fingers and fashions a crude little figurine, roughly star-shaped.—Imagine you did this, he says.—Imagine you made the earth and sky and water and stars and the great emptiness all around.

Cain scowls. Abel smiles faintly as if he truly is imagining it and enjoying himself doing so.

—Then imagine you held this figure before you, Adam continues, and you breathed upon it, and it took your breath and made it its own and sprung to life in the palm of your hand. What would this make you?

—God, answers Abel promptly.

—Just so. And the man you made?

This answer is not so prompt, but after a moment the happy son answers, He would be the first man.

—Exactly.

—So God breathed on mud and dust and water and gave it life?

Cain interrupts contemptuously.—It's not the literal truth he's saying. It's a metaphor.

Abel is unfamiliar with the word.—Met a what?

—A way of explaining things, Cain answers impatiently.—Like saying time is a river. Time isn't really a river but it passes in the same way. And God didn't *really* breathe on a handful of spit and dust to make the first people. It's just a way of saying it, to show that God gives life to everything.

Abel looks at Adam.—Is that what you mean?

Cain looks at Adam.—Of course it is.

—No it's not, Adam says.

Abel looks more confused than ever while Cain just frowns harder. Adam says, God fashioned the first man of dust and saliva and breathed on him and gave him life.

—How do you know this? demands Cain.

—Because I am that man.

•

Time passes. The sun slips behind the low distant mountains and the sky turns aquamarine and purple.

—So dust and spit is all you are? says Cain eventually.

—Dust and spit is all any of us are, or ever will be, replies Adam.—Plus a little divinity.

•

Some time later Adam goes on, God placed me in a garden to live my life.

—What was it like? asks Abel.

—Impossible to describe, he says sadly.

—Try, demands Cain.

So Adam tries.

•

The boys consider for a time.—Then what? asks Cain.—Didn't you get bored?

Adam can't tell if he is being deliberately provocative, or merely curious. After all, Cain in the Garden might well have found *something* to complain about.

Adam says, Not exactly bored. But I will admit to a degree of loneliness after a time. Which brings us to your mother.

—Ah, smiles Abel.—I was wondering about her.

Cain's gloom deepens, if such a thing is possible.

Adam says, One night I fell into an unusually deep slumber. I woke to an awful cramp in my side and your mother standing at my feet. She was lovely. She glowed like the moon.

—More dust I suppose, barks Cain.—Dust and spit and God's hot breath.

The boy's eyes mount a challenge that Adam cannot meet. He wonders sadly at this anger blooming through his son like a black flower, and wonders what he could have done (what he can still do) to root it out. In a flash of intuition he realizes that whatever else this conversation may accomplish, it will do little to sweeten the bile that courses through Cain's arteries.

—And something else, too. Adam touches his scar.—From here. You've asked me about it many times. Now you know.

•

—So, says Cain, you live in a magic garden with Mother, where every need is met and you never have to work. Why leave then?

—It became necessary, Adam says flatly.—It's gone now. It has been taken away.

—By God?

—Yes.

Bats swirl over them in the deepening dusk, veering in wild leaps as if searching for the vanished Garden. At length Cain says, And why did God, in His *infinite wisdom and mercy,* do that?

Adam winces as if struck, then explains.

•

But there are some things he does not explain:

Eve's face gazing up at him from the ground, that first time. Red hair spilling crazily across green moss. A brightness in her eyes not entirely due to the sun overhead. Cheeks flushed. Her body like another garden under him—pressure bruises in little arcs on her ankles where he'd clenched. The mix of exhilaration and fear sweeping through his consciousness, the awareness of her raw animal form wet and prone beneath him.

And the sudden ache in his stomach, the looseness in his bowels, when he realized they weren't alone.

The brightness in Eve's eyes not due entirely to the sun overhead. Indeed.

Shadows falling across them at unruly angles, the fear a sudden jab to his gut. God with them of course. And knowing everything. Of course.

—My Lord—

God commanding *Be silent*, and Adam doing as he was told.

Eve sitting up now, hair bedraggled, eyes wide and startled. But lovely. Still unspeakably lovely. Her fingers seeking his, twining through, phantom-pale against his own tilled-earth-brown. Like a piece of artwork, although no one has ever thought to make artwork yet.

God growling, *You have until nightfall.*

—To do what? cringed Adam.

—*To leave.*

Feeling then that the earth had opened up, mawlike, to swallow them. Long moments of actually not sensing solidity beneath him— free-falling and tensing for the impact. Stomach lurching, guts bubbling. Feeling as if something had poked a reptilian finger into his intestines and was twirling it about. Hard to say which was more terrifying, God's cold anger or the prospect of leaving the Garden and going—where?

—Where will we go? he whimpered.

—*That is not my concern,* God replied thinly.

Eve speaking up:—How will we survive? Will there be food?

A pause then, as of God weighing His response.—*You shall learn.*

Somehow this answer was more frightening than any Almighty rant would have been. Adam managed to choke out, Learn how? but there was no reply. He repeated it:—Learn how?

—He's left, came Eve's voice.

Adam realized his eyes were screwed so tightly shut they hurt. He forced them open. Colors were strange, everything bluish. Eve watching him carefully. Still naked and lovely but he wasn't thinking about that now. Wasn't really *thinking* in any meaningful sense of the word.—What do we do now? he gagged.

—Don't have much choice, do we?

Eve scared too but covering it with coldness, with glibness. Adam looked around at the suddenly chill afternoon and felt anxiety clutch his lungs again. Hard to breathe. He rooted about for his girdle of leaves, stood up and pulled it on. Eve did the same, and for a moment he felt marginally better.

—Well then, he said.

—So, she agreed.

But his heart still pounding wildly as if he were being chased. He wondered if it would ever slow again.

Adam asked, Do you think He will return?

—Be surprised if He doesn't, she said softly.

Adam standing there, bereft, with afternoon cooling around them and clouds gathering on the horizon. Then suddenly blurting:—I wish we'd never done it! God! God, take us back, we're sorry! We won't do it again!

Eve looking away and saying nothing.

Adam fighting for control, not wanting to believe that their actions were final, irrevocable, but unable to believe otherwise. Eve wisely saying nothing, letting the feeling wash over him and pass, slowly dripping off like a puddle to collect at his feet.

The afternoon sun sliding behind a cloud, fat and gray. More clouds lining up to the west, a thick rank of them like soldiers. Adam had never seen clouds before—or soldiers—and he wondered what they portended.

Eve interrupting his thoughts.—Maybe we should make preparations.

He looked upon her as if at a stranger.—Such as?

—I don't know, she admitted.

After a moment's thought he said, Nor I.

—Everything is strange now, she whispered.

He didn't bother to answer. Standing there thinking, wondering, watching a mosquito hover into view and land on his shoulder.

Watching as it took a moment to select just the right spot. And then bite him.

•

Cain says, Let me understand this. There was only one thing you were forbidden to do?

—Yes.

—I would have done it then.

Adam murmurs, I do believe you might have.

Abel asks, But why did *you*?

—Both your mother and I were at fault, but she was led astray first. She was told that by eating the fruit of the tree, she would become like God.

—Are you sure this wasn't a metaphor? demands Cain.

—Oh yes, I'm sure.

—I *definitely* would have done it then.

Abel asks, Why would God tell her to do something He didn't want her to do?

—It wasn't God. It was the serpent, she told me later. An agent of the Devil, or perhaps the Devil himself.

The boys gasp. Cain cries, What was the Devil doing in this Paradise?

Adam has no answer.

Abel says, You're both lucky that banishment is all you suffered. It could have been much worse.

From the darkness comes an inarticulate gurgling: Cain searching for words.—This whole story makes *no sense!* Why would God create a perfect place and then allow the Devil in it, just to trick you? Why tell you not to do something when He could have just removed the tree, and so avoided the problem completely?

—I don't know, admits Adam.

—Craziness.

•

It is fully dark now.—After your mother ate the fruit she brought it to me, whether from fear of her act or a desire for me to share in it I don't know. Anyway when I saw what she had done I felt a certain recklessness. Even a little . . . pride. She had gone and *done* something on her own, and yes it was a foolish thing but at least it showed a little initiative on her part. So I took a bite too. And the first thing I noticed—

He stops, clears his throat. The boys sit attentively. Adam forces himself on. His offspring will soon be men, after all.

—The first thing I noticed was that your mother was naked. The second thing was that I was too. Your mother was a lovely woman.

—Yes, says Cain. His voice is cold.—We understand.

—I don't, admits Abel.

Cain mutters, What do your sheep like to do to make little baby sheep?

—Oh . . .

Adam goes on, Later we didn't feel it appropriate to go about unclothed as we had before, so we fashioned some kind of coverings for ourselves. Quite crude they were too, just skirts of leaves. That was our mistake. When God next returned to the Garden he saw them on the ground beside us and drew the obvious conclusion.

—He would have known anyway, says Abel.

—Quite likely.

—And that's when he banished you?

—So it was. He told your mother that she'd be under my dominion for the rest of her days, bringing forth my children, and He told me that I would toil and sweat and labor for my bread until the day I died.

They are silent for a time.—Oh, and when we die, we shall revert to the dust from whence we came.

Night has settled thick as fleece around them, lit only by a few brave stars glimmering overhead. At length Cain says, Two things I must be sure of. One, you had only one rule to follow. And you broke it?

A sigh escapes Adam's nose, whistling into the night.—So we did.

—And the second thing is, you still worship this God?

Adam's breath breaks off short at that.—Meaning what? God is God.

—Sure He is. And He gave you life, so all right, thank you. But then He sets a trap and when you fall into it, He takes away everything He ever gave, which is *every*thing, and lets you go rot. But you're still always going on about praying to Him and making sacrifices and all the rest, even though He's treated you more unfairly than anything I can imagine.

—God isn't *anything*. God is God. God made me, and you.

—I understand that. But you made me too, Father. And if you ever, I don't know, if I ever did something and you banished me from the house, I'd react differently.

—I would never send you away.

—All right. I mean, *good*. But if you did, I wouldn't spend the rest of my life telling my children how fair you were, and how benevolent and merciful, and how you gave me every blessing in this life. I would tell my children: Yes, my father has some good qualities, but he's also thoughtless and selfish and unforgiving and hateful and mean. That's how God's treated *you*.

Adam shifts on the stony ground. To be honest, some of these same thoughts had echoed in his mind over the years, at especially trying moments. But nothing useful will come from admitting as much to his sullen firstborn.—Let's hope it never comes to that, then. Let's hope I never take such drastic action, and you never give me reason to.

He pauses, expecting Cain to offer some concomitant reassurance. He is disappointed. The silence stretches on with only the crickets chanting among themselves.

—Amen to that, his son says finally. But it is his son Abel whose voice cuts the night, not his son Cain.

# 15 *two summers previous*

Early one morning Adam leans over the water trough, hands cupped to scoop his ritual waking-up splash, when something causes him to stop. And look. And see himself.

That is me, he thinks. My face, indisputably. But it is also a stranger.

He lowers himself to his knees and leans further over the trough. The water is flat and still; the sunshine low across the scene. He is reflected in every detail, and some of these details are not especially welcome. Baggy semicircles hang beneath his eyes as if he has been beaten. Tufts of hair mat his nose. (His nose? He raises a tentative finger to check: Yes, there they are.) A pair of vertical lines runs between his eyes and divides his forehead neatly in two. Seeing them he frowns, and the lines grow deeper and darker. Does he really frown so much, that physical marks should be left on his body like scars? He notices also the ropes of matted white whiskers twining through his beard. Still plenty of black on his cheeks and upper lip, but underneath (he cranes further over the water, the better to assess the damage) white hair is fighting for ascendancy. And winning by the look of it. Adam wonders that his wife has made no mention of this. And then, remembering Eve's own gray hairs, scattered in a fine wash across her head, he is not so surprised. Eve's gray has lightened her hair only a shade or two; against his own black kinks it is far more noticeable. In any case there is no point mentioning it: there is nothing to be done.

Adam wonders if this is a normal thing, this bleaching, this leaching of color. Or a sign of illness? He doesn't know. It's hard to imagine it as a sign of strength and health. But no one alive is older than he, so there is no one he can ask. If it is a sickness, though, both he and his wife have it.

His wife.

She has, undeniably, changed as well. He had thought it was the effect of childbirth many times over, the endless demands on her body made by other, smaller bodies. He had thought he would be spared. In fact he'd been rather complacent in this conviction: but what if he were wrong? What if the simple fact of existence left its mark on a person, the daily routines of labor, rest, food, sleep, sex, all leaving behind their stains on the vessel used to get through the seasons? The thought is unsettling. More than that: it is terrifying. Adam considers his children, squalling infants at birth, little walking bodies sometime thereafter; then playing, talking, working. A few years slip past and these infants are nearly people. A few more and they'll be grown. And he, Adam? If Cain is a man five years from now, what will he be? If Abel is his own age in thirty years—what will become of Adam?

His hands spank the surface of the water, shattering his image. *You will return to dust,* God had said. Adam had paid little heed at the time: there was too much else going on. Now the words reverberate through his sinews and turn his muscles to water.

Pressure in his bladder: the need to relieve himself is dire. He does so beyond the orchard but his unease does not abate. If anything it grows worse. Adam strides through the orchard, between date palms taller than he is and low, silvery-green apricot bushes. Without warning he enters a clearing and beholds his wife, squatting, gathering fruit. She must have risen while he was occupied and now collects apricots for the children's breakfast.

He is on her like a panther.—Hurry, he croaks.—I have a need.

Under his tunic he is straining for her. She sees his excitement and laughs.—You never tire, do you? But she stops laughing when she sees the anguish on his face.—What's the matter?

—Please, he says.

It is unlike him to beg. She lies back and lifts her own tunic. Blue veins lace her thighs and her rump spreads like yogurt. Her hair is the same red tangle it has always been.

Adam knows her quickly. Fear propels him, perhaps, or anger or the desire to deny what he suspects: that he is getting old. That he is dying day by day. That one morning he might be unable to do what he is doing at this moment. And what would *that* be but a foretaste of death? Dust indeed. His movements against his wife are sudden and lacking in tenderness, but she seems not to mind. She lies with eyes closed, smiling slightly, hair spilling like blood. While Adam knows her he forgets himself, his own white hairs, the lines on his face and spots appearing on his knuckles. His body soars as it did in his youth. There is only himself and his wife and the eternal dance that binds them. He feels, not to put too fine a point on it, young. The tempo of his thrusts increases. Absently Adam wonders how many times they have done this together.

Then with a gasp he is done. They straighten up quickly, adjusting their tunics and glancing about, but none of their children is visible. Eve raises one eyebrow and smiles.—It's nice to know I can still command your attention.

—You always have my attention, he says. He means it.

She kisses him lightly on the cheek.—Care to explain what that was all about, husband? Or am I to assume that my drooping backside is still enough to stir you?

—True enough, he mutters, suddenly sheepish. What is there to say? I fear to return to the dust whence I came, so I wished to lie with you one more time? Growing old (something I never really understood before this day) fills me with hot terror, so I tried to hold back its realization? No. He will not, cannot give voice to such things. They are foolish ideas if not downright sinful ones, the ungrateful preoccupations of a spoiled child.

So he says, There was no special reason. We are both here, and it is after all our duty.

—Ah, duty, she says with a smile. Her eyebrow lifts again (that mannerism that makes her irresistibly girlish).—And that is all?

He clears his throat roughly.—And you are still, I think you know this, pleasing to look upon.

—Why thank you, she laughs. But her smile lingers, and it is a smile that says: I don't believe you, but worry not. I understand everything, and if you're too proud to admit it, well, there are worse sins.

Adam leaves her then, feeling more confused than ever.

# 14 *the years*

After Abel's birth there follows a long fallow period. Adam throws himself into his husbandry, expanding the area given over to grain and planting a field of peas. Rather than relying on the wild patches along the river, he decides to cultivate them in a more organized fashion. This done, he wanders far and finds a grove of apricot trees and another of date palms, and plants two dozen of each in orderly rows beyond the wheat.—They shall take time to mature, he tells Eve.—But time we have.

For her part, Eve reaps wild berries from the thorny shrubs along the river, and mixes them with honey for Abel's breakfast. She cuts goatskins and gazelle hides into garments for the boys. Eve's needle is a sliver of bone; her thread is sheep gut. The clothes do a fair job of keeping the rain off, but they smell foul and are abominably hot in summer.

—Still, we can't just let them go naked, she says.

Adam agrees heartily.—Let's find some way to keep them from turning rotten. Perhaps if we soak them in something?

And this becomes another project for him.

The years slink past like cats. A year with no child and another year with no child and then nine months of Eve's quickening gut and swelling calves and lank hair and expectation on all sides. Nine months of Cain asking why Eve is getting so fat and Adam telling him to hush and help with the chores. Cain's chores, at age three, consist of collecting brush for the cookfire.

Abel at two doesn't have any chores.

Nine months of wondering, A boy again or a girl? Or maybe one

160

of both? And then the night, the labor, the quickening tempo of the contractions like waves pounding at Eve from inside, her sweat-soaked body on the mat, her mutters of Something isn't right, this isn't like the others. And finally after nine months the infant slipping silent into Adam's hands as lifeless as a graven image.

The boys are outside, wondering. Adam squats inside, wondering. The child lies cold and shiny in his hands.

Eve says, It's dead isn't it.

He nods.—If it was alive to begin with.

—Oh, it was alive all right.

He buries it far from the house. Far from the grave of the other child, the one they never mention. But before he pushes the dirt into the hole, he looks. The child is a girl. Was a girl. Would have been a girl, if.

When he is done and the child is out of sight forever, Adam can contain himself no more. He indulges in the luxury of hurling the vilest oaths he can imagine at God. This is perhaps unwise, but Adam is unconcerned with wisdom. He wonders aloud why God hates him. He wonders aloud if God thinks the hatred cannot be reciprocated. If such is God's thinking, He is wrong. He is wrong. Adam puts God on notice.

He taunts Him. He suggests that God is impotent and cruel and stupid and hateful. He suggests that Lucifer is correct in thinking God is afraid of competition. He considers the serpent his best friend, his only real friend, and thanks him loudly for passing the fruit to his wife. He thanks his wife, loudly, for eating it.

Adam keeps on insulting God until he can think of no more insults or combinations of insults that he has not already repeated several times. Then he stops, breathing heavily.

There is no reply.

After a time he gets to his feet, brushes his trembling hands, and makes his way unsteadily through the fields to the hut, where he left his children to comfort their silently weeping mother.

•

Another year gone. God never answers Adam's accusations, and as Adam's anger recedes, he finds himself wondering if he went too far. Knowing God, He would have informed him if he had.

Only once that winter does Eve squint at him over her stitching and say, We heard you howling out there but couldn't make out the words. What were you going on about?

—Nothing important, he says.—I was upset, is all.

Eve says nothing, but hugs Abel to her bosom and tickles him gently. The boy chuckles and she coos into his ear. Bubbles of drool cascade down his chin; she wipes them clean with her hair. Across the hut, Cain watches, till Adam pulls him into his own lap. Cain does not chuckle or drool, but squalls and writhes free.

Eve sighs.—He's got a temper, that one.

—Like his mother, suggests Adam.

She pulls a face.—Like his father, I'd have said.

The boys get older. Each time Adam sets eyes upon them, they have stretched, lengthened, grown more angular and lean. He just gets used to their crawling underfoot, when they begin toddling around. He accustoms himself to their weaving into everything— knees, doorways, the cookfire—when they start running outside. Cain is always a step ahead, as expected; but Abel hurries to keep up.

They invent games for themselves: tag and catch and run-the-circle and kick-the-stone. They watch caterpillars weave luxurious silken tents and emerge weeks later as butterflies drunk on the sun or moths obsessed with the moon. They collect small blue eggs with white spots and small white eggs with pink spots and big pink eggs with blue spots. They catch tadpoles in their hands and throw them back in the river and watch them transform into frogs. They put the frogs in the birds' nests to see if they will stay there. (They don't.) They put the eggs into the river to see if they will hatch there. (They won't.) They open the cocoons after two days to see if the caterpillars are done turning into moths yet. (They aren't.) They leave a smear of honey on a rock to see if it will attract ants. (It does.) They sleep out under clear skies and count the stars and fall asleep before they finish, or sleep out under cloudy skies and sometimes make it through the night and sometimes must run, giggling and snorting, back into the house when the heavens convulse and flood down on them. Their playground is the world. Their companions are each other. They are best friends: they are the only friends that exist.

Adam watches it all.

Cain tells Abel, When a sheep gets old it turns into a goat, and Abel, wide-eyed, nods in wonder. This is not precisely a lie on Cain's part, because he is not exactly sure himself whether it is true or not. He thinks it might be. But seeing Abel believe him so unquestioningly gives him a certain authority to think of other things that might also be true, and say them.

Once Abel asks, Can diarrhea hurt you? and Cain says, Of course, if it doesn't stop then maybe one time everything will come out. Your heart and stomach and everything. Again, Cain is not completely sure about this. But later that night Abel appears bawling at Eve's side, hiccupping his anxiety; and she throws Cain exasperated looks while comforting the younger child.

Adam watches all this, hears all this, and is filled with such love for both his sons that breathing is difficult: he is already so full that it is hard to inhale. He remembers his outburst against God and feels ashamed and wonders if he has been forgiven. In his experience, God's forgiveness is a variable thing. He giveth much but He taketh much away, and nobody knows this better than Adam.

But anyway. No point harping on it: what is past, is past. And if Eve is still a little reserved with her firstborn, well, is she not a little reserved with them all lately? Yes indeed, for she is pregnant again.

This time the months slide past with unnerving swiftness, almost as if God doesn't want the family to anticipate too much, and at the end of them bursts out Kerod, round-eyed and big-handed. Kerod greets the world with a full-throated scream as Eve slumps exhausted to her mat and the boys watch, rapt. Adam steps outside and prays thanks as feverishly as he had vomited curses the previous year.

Kerod howls lustily at first. She's a noisy baby who will grow (though nobody knows this) into a reticent child. As an infant, she's a storm. When she wails, which is much of the time, Cain smiles as if enchanted, while Abel stands next to her and says earnestly, You should stop now. You ought to be quiet. There's no reason to act like this.

After that there's no stopping the tide. Lya follows a year later, then Porad, then the twins, then Shel, Tovi, the other twins. Adam finds himself perpetually needful of expanding his crop in order to feed his multiplying family, and as the older children get big enough to help there is yet more to do as the younger children keep appearing. It is rather like climbing up a landslide, and feeling the stones give way beneath his feet.

Each time he says to his bedraggled wife, One more then. (Or two, as the case might require.)

And each time she arches an eyebrow and says enigmatically:— Looks that way.

He notices a pattern, starting with Lya and holding through the other children: when they annoy Cain (which is frequently), he leaves them. Abel, by contrast, proffers advice.

Not always the best of advice.

—Stop tormenting that beetle, Porad. You should either let it be, or else put it in the soup . . .

Adam watches his growing flock with love and pride mixed with apprehension and more than a little uncertainty. He adores his children ardently, beyond measure, but can't help wondering, How long will this continue? Exactly how many children is he expected to sire? And what should he tell them about himself and their mother? Already Cain is ten years old (how did that happen? A moment ago he was lurching across the hut on wobbly legs) and starting to ask awkward questions. Somehow he has grown guarded and watchful around his parents, and this saddens Adam. He wonders if, in attending the younger children, he has somehow neglected the eldest. But no: he has taught the boy the rudiments of husbandry, has in fact spent more time with him than with the others. Instead of drawing them closer, it has had the opposite effect. Cain stands in the fields now for half a day at a time, observing, calculating. Taking everything in.

In the evening there are always questions.—If you're *our* father, Father, then where's *yours*?

—There are lots of birds and goats and lizards. How come there are no other people?

—Where did you and Mother live before you had us?

Abel, forever parroting the other, chimes in too.—How come you have that scar on your side?

For a time Adam parries their questions by giving half-answers or non-answers or joking answers. But the boys won't be put off for long and Adam's jokes aren't very funny anyway. He knows he'll have to do something soon. Tell the truth, most likely. Confess.

Abel by himself wouldn't be much of a problem, but Cain is alert and sharp and sees the world through those thin blue eyes that slice past all dissembling. Abel is cheerful and inclined to give the benefit of the doubt. Cain is not inclined to give much of anything, least of all the benefit of the doubt.

Perturbed, Adam wonders what to do. If he were entirely honest with himself, he might admit that he wonders: If his firstborn is already such a commanding presence at age ten, how will he turn out as an adult? But Adam shies away from such bluntness, preferring to conciliate and compromise and make the best of things.

So he postpones what he knows is coming, and then again for a little longer, and then a bit more. There is always something more pressing, a pox among the goats, a new hut to be built, a marauding wolf. And of course the infants keep coming. A few more years bring a few more children; they're everywhere now. Playing in every hut, working the fields, tending the animals. Doing chores and getting underfoot and crying and laughing and sulking and singing: it all goes on, all the time, in different proportions from moment to moment. Toddlers fall over in the yard and sucklings dangle like pine cones from Eve's teats. And if Eve herself appears exhausted from her constant reproduction, the ongoing refashioning of new human beings from her own dwindling essence, Adam does not allow himself to worry much. What can he do about it anyway? He didn't make the arrangements here, he's just following instructions.

It seems to him that this has been the founding truth of his whole life.

# 13  *the second son*

Eve likes the second child better.—I shall name him Abel, she declares, tickling his chin. The child coos in response.

This pregnancy was much easier than Eve's first, and her reaction to the new child is closer to what Adam had expected. Now he scoops Cain from the floor, where he is chewing on a dead leaf.—I must see to the sheep, he says. Eve is busy tickling Abel's bottom and does not answer.

In the past year, Adam has taken Eve's idea of keeping a few sheep always near the hut and expanded on it, hoping that by so doing, the animals might be more easily caught and eaten. He was unsure whether this would work but discovered that, in fact, sheep are refreshingly dull-witted and easy to manipulate. He had little trouble ensuring that a few stayed always nearby, and in the spring, when the lambs were born, the newborns were even more docile. Once the lambs were weaned Adam struck upon the simple but ruthless expedient of slaughtering all the sires and ewes, hoping that this would leave the youngsters even more dependent upon him as some kind of two-legged surrogate father. This has succeeded beyond expectations, and now his little flock of six or seven adolescent sheep barely strays from sight.

Eve was well pleased with all that meat: they feasted for weeks, and lay at night on soft layers of fleece. The winter was harsh, the nights cold, the fleece warm and soft. Adam grins to himself in recollection. It was no surprise that his wife had got with child again so soon.

•

Eve's fondness for the second son grows more obvious with each passing week. She calls him her little man, her little green-eyed bear, her tiny hunter boy, and all manner of endearments that leave Adam vaguely queasy. The elder son she refers to as Cay-in. For reasons he cannot exactly codify, her pronunciation never fails to bring a wince from Adam.

He fears to broach the subject directly, dreading any reference to the elder son's troubled birth: he is sure that he does not want Cain to grow up hearing *that* story every day. Or Abel for that matter. Better to say nothing, perhaps, though Eve's intemperate favoritism makes this increasingly difficult.

Eve is not a dull woman. More than once she says to him, You think I'm uneven in my affections.

—Somewhat.

—And I suppose you think this unfair.

He spreads his hands.

—And you probably reckon that my feelings all stem directly from the older one's birth.

He clears his throat.—It is logical to see it that way.

She lifts a sardonic eyebrow: a mannerism he has always cherished.—But then you didn't *see* anything at all, did you? Being delirious as you were, and then just plain catatonic.

He says nothing in the face of the truth.

Eve goes on, I try to be fair, but it's not always easy. Look at them, sitting there in the yard. The one all pink and yellow-haired and chubby, while Abel's so dark and slender and quiet.

Eve's voice turns soft.—He reminds me of shady spots in the Garden, like the earth underneath the willows that overhung the pond where we swam. Before we knew each other as wife and husband, do you remember? We'd swim naked in the water before we ever knew what being naked *meant*.

—It is not the child's fault that we have left all that.

—Of course not, she snaps.—I didn't say it was. But neither is it Abel's fault that he helps me remember it.

Adam says nothing.

—He's as thin as the eels we used to catch for our breakfast, and his voice is as sweet and soft as the doves who nested on the earth where we slept. It was my home, Adam—it's where I'm *from*. And when I look at him I remember it, and can pretend I haven't been gone so long. And even, if I wanted, that I could go back.

Adam remains silent. She has never spoken so. They mention the Garden only rarely now, and never with such naked longing.

On the dirt outside Cain kneels next to Abel and gurgles a question. Abel, on his back, laughs an answer and slaps the ground.

—With Cain it's not like that, Eve shrugs.

Adam by now regrets this whole conversation but it's too late to stop.—Let him be, he sighs, knowing the request is futile.

—He's loud and bright and harsh like this place we've been sent to. His hair is the yellow of the sun burning too hot to bear. His skin is the burnt pink of something left too long in the open. Where did he get such coloring, anyway? Not from either of *us*.

—His eyes are blue, suggests Adam.—Unexpected I admit, but pleasant in its way.

—Not the deep blue of that stone we found in the mountain rocks, what do you call it? Lapis. His eyes aren't blue like that, no. Nor the dark blue of the summer sky, or of morning glories hanging on their vines like bells. Such flowers we had in the Garden . . .

—So we did, whispers Adam.

—His eyes are the blue of fading bruises and dead fish, the blue of mold growing along the edge of meat. They're a shade that never existed in the Garden and every time I look at them they taunt me—tell me that I'm banished and can't go home again.

Adam shrugs.—If such is how you feel.

—You may think me heartless, Eve presses, but I'm not. Despite all, I suckle him and bathe him and tend his needs and wipe the shit from between his thighs.

—Undeniably.

—So credit me that, at least. That I fulfill my duties and will never speak a word of this to him.

—I know you won't.

She peers at him.—Something yet troubles you.

He wonders how to begin.—You thought at his birthing that he was some manner of evil.

—I thought it possible, considering.

—And now?

—I withhold judgment, as you urged. But I remain doubtful. A falcon fledgling doesn't mature into a mouse.

—Yes . . . but still I fear that we may encourage the evil we fear to bring about. By treating him as something other than our son—something to be held at length—we will in fact *make* him into something other than our son.

Eve's gray eyes spark.—This conversation is pointless. You want me to feel more fondness for our firstborn? I can't. I feel what I feel and no more. You want me to feel less love for the second? I *won't*. I feel what I feel and no less.

—I only ask that you do your duty.

—And so I do, every day. First by carrying the child in my womb, which is a trial you know nothing about. Then by bearing them and nursing them and tending them the whole day.

Adam holds his tongue in the face of Eve's annoyance. She goes on, Your criticism of my motherhood is hurtful and unjustified.

—I apologize, he says sincerely.

She turns from him then and Adam rises to go. Stepping from the hut, he scoops his eldest son in his arms and feels something stirring inside him. Flesh of his flesh. Cain waves his hands and chortles and Adam says to him, Come along, son. Let me show you something.

Together they stride off to the near field, where the grain is beginning to sprout thin green shoots into the air, groping mutely for the sun far overhead.

# 12 *the previous murder*

Adam eyes the rabbit warily, keeping his distance. The rabbit, gnashing the long grass with vigor, eyes him right back.

Adam tries to remember if the thing poses a threat. He doesn't think so but it's so hard to be sure. So difficult to remember everything, all the little details. Which clouds mean rain and which mean only shade. What manner of wild pig can be frighted off with a loud clap and which will turn threatening. Which mushrooms can be eaten and which will leave him up all night, writhing and clutching his midriff. Experience is a reliable teacher but a ruthless one.

He feels a flash of hopeless yearning: in the Garden, none of the mushrooms had carried poison and none of the pigs ever threatened. All the plants were good to eat.

Except one.

And all the animals could be trusted.

Except one.

Or maybe two.

•

The rabbit bursts into sudden activity, scuttling forward until it is sequestered in the shade of some thick-leafed shrub. It gnaws busily at the foliage and seems to forget Adam altogether.

Indecision wracks the man. His wife lies untended in their hut, swollen near to bursting with their first child. She requires nourishment. They have never been through this before and Adam is quite alarmed at his wife's condition: she reports that the unborn infant kicks and jabs and worries her endlessly. It drains the strength from her like a parasite. She says it feels as if a very demon is within her, all lizard scales and dripping venom, seeking to claw its way out. These unpleasant images are discussed in much eager detail, until Adam begins to feel nauseous. Eve has been much prone to unpleasant images lately.

Again the rabbit erupts, this time into a flurry of violence: it tears off whole leaves, entire stems of leaves, until there is a carnage of broken greenery all around it which it then sets upon, masticating furiously. Adam watches with trepidation. He cannot help noticing the incisors on the beast, larger than his own on a creature a fraction of his size. All Adam carries is a net, painstakingly woven from tough ivy stems. Will it be enough to contain such an extravagantly equipped creature? Adam does not know.

He bites his lip. He finds himself wondering, not for the first time, how he got himself into this ludicrous position. Not for the first time a part of his mind offers the answer: It was all her fault, wasn't it?

Adam decides to leave the animal be. No telling what harm it could do, and certainly his wife needs a healthy and uninjured husband as much as a mouthful of bloody flesh. At least as much. Perhaps, when the animal moves off, Adam will gather a few handfuls of the leaves it is so happily consuming. If the rabbit is content to feast upon them, then perhaps they will suit his wife as well.

•

They do not suit his wife as well.

If he even has a wife anymore: sometimes Adam doubts this, never more so than now, as this grotesque harpy hurls the greens back at him amid howls, curses, and taunts of his manhood. Her hair hangs slack and greasy along sunken cheeks, the dull red-orange plumage of some unnatural fowl. A fine thread of sores outlines her jawbone. Gray eyes darken to slate as she hisses:—Get me proper food! I need nourishment, I need meat! Not leaves!

Adam backs away. Eve can barely sit up but he half expects her to levitate off the bed and float toward him, fingers flexed.

—Are you listening? Meat! Not fruit, not flowers, insects, nor honeycomb. Flesh. Cooked, fatty flesh! Get it for me now, or dismiss any notion of keeping wife or child in this world.

He stands in the doorway, the half-lit length of the hut between them. Outside the afternoon burns like a conflagration, and inside feels stuffy and thick. Mustering the shreds of his dignity he says, I'll do what I can. I have to hunt, you know. I have no power to beckon animals to me. We left that behind, he adds a trifle petulantly, in the Garden.

Eve makes an inarticulate sound and collapses onto her back. In the darkness he can hear her panting.—Wait.

He waits.

For some moments she is silent and he wonders what new discontent she will air. So he is confused when she says, Hear that?

—Hear what?

This is the wrong answer, Eve's long-suffering sigh informs him. When the sigh is past (it takes a long time, like watching a flock of birds pass overhead) there is a moment of absolute stillness, then the complaint of a lapwing, then another moment of stillness. Then the bleat of a sheep.

—That, says Eve.

—The animal?

—It is a sheep, says Eve. She talks as if instructing a child: her voice is slow and measured, perhaps due to fatigue. Perhaps something else.—I told you to catch one and tie it up and make it fat. Told you that weeks ago.

—I tried, he murmurs.—They are not so easy to catch.

—But you have done so, on occasion.

—Ah—yes.

—They're good to eat, there's a lot of meat on them.

—Yes yes, I know.

—Then you know why I want one now.

He taps his foot nervously.—It will not be easy. They tend to run away.

—Run after it then, my hunter husband, Eve snaps. There is ice in her voice, and irony.—Use the net or chase it up the hill and over the cliff. If you're lucky it will break its leg.

If I'm unlucky, thinks Adam, I will break mine.

—Use the flint to hack off some meat, Eve continues.—You know the part I like, the thick muscle around the haunch, and the liver. The brain is good too. Build a fire and roast the meat and bring it here.

Eve settles wearily onto her matting.—I feel my time coming very soon. If you do this for me tonight, we may be a family of three by morning.

•

He does as she commands. The sheep is young (as all the animals are) and stupid (as some of them are not). When it sees Adam racing toward it, arms akimbo, net fluttering overhead, whooping like a thing demented, the sheep turns tail and bolts to the cliff's edge and doesn't stop galloping until it has fallen halfway.

Adam collects the still-warm corpse and carries it home over his shoulder. The thing smells of mud and shit and damp bloody fur but even so he admits to a feeling of satisfaction, even pride, in his work. Never the neatest of butchers, he shreds the meat rather than cutting it, and spills most of the organs into the dirt. Nonetheless he presents Eve with just the meal she wanted, a thick haunch of mutton well roasted, and is rewarded by her saying, without a trace of irony:—Thank you, husband.

While she eats he fusses with the rest of the carcass. He cuts thick strips to slow-dry over the coals. He places other thick cuts into clay bowls layered with salt. He half fills the stone basin with hot stones and makes a stew by dropping in anything that looks edible.

Before he is done she's yelling for the liver.

Grinning, he serves her.—What do you think of your hunter husband now?

In the late-day sun she smiles back.—He's learning.

She is coated with sweat and the pulse in her neck flickers visibly.

Adam wipes strands of coppery hair away from her eyes, shamed now that he'd ever thought his wife a harpy.—How do you feel?

—Like an egg about to hatch, she whispers.—Like a boil about to burst.

He realizes how afraid she is. She hasn't said as much in so many words, but it is obvious how much she needs him. She can't do this without him. Well, so be it: she won't have to.

He resolves to get over this foolish anxiety about animals. Childish really. And isn't he an adult? It is time to put away childish things. God has placed him (and her, but really *him*) above all other creatures, sole regents over the dominion of the world. He, Adam, is the authority here. He would do well to remember this.

Early-evening sun burns low on the horizon, bouncing flat orange light through the entryway, across the hut. Adam asks, Anything you need?

—Some water.

He rises to get it. Halfway across the room he sees a jittery angular shadow smeared across the floor: a scorpion. Adam freezes. Is this a danger? Then he remembers his recent resolve. What is this little thing to him? Ugly, yes, but most likely as harmless as the sheep he just slaughtered, or this afternoon's rabbit. Still, no point sharing their hut with the thing.

Striding across the sandy floor, he glances at his wife with a smile.—Behold, your hunter husband is a changed man.

She looks at him quizzically as he swings his bare foot over the scorpion and brings it down hard, crushing the vermin under his heel.

The world implodes around him.

•

The blackness lasts and lasts. There are moments of shadowy half-light, winged figures looking down on him; then more blackness.

It lasts and lasts.

•

When Adam wakes he discovers himself a father. His wife squats in the doorway, using a twig to one-handedly stir the contents of the stone basin. In the other arm she holds a bald pink creature reminiscent in shape and hue to a piglet. This apparition slurps avidly on Eve's purple-veined teat.

The sight lurches Adam into awareness: he sits up suddenly, then cringes as nausea and pain kick the back of his skull. Eyes closed, he swivels his head and vomits. Nothing much comes up.

His wife is beside him now, tipping water from a shallow clay bowl.—Sip.

He does so and his head clears slowly, though the pain remains. His leg throbs as if afire. He hiccups but manages to swallow the water again, acid this time.—The child?

—Lives, she says simply.

Something is wrong.—What's the matter? Is he not well?

—Oh it's well enough. Has a grip like an eagle's claw and an appetite that never quits.

—Praise God.

Eve says nothing. She has set the child on the ground by the doorway, where it lies slapping against the dirt with intensity and focus. Adam cranes his neck to observe the boy.—He is quite bald.

—The hair is so fine as to be nearly invisible, Eve tells him, and downy as a chipmunk's belly. If you hold it in the sunlight you see a halo round its head. Quite unnerving actually. It's not something I like to see but I can't seem to make myself stop looking.

—Remarkable.

Adam sits up gingerly. Now his headache is subsiding and he is starting to feel famished, though his leg still tortures him.—And what happened to me? The last I remember . . . He rattles his memory but comes up empty.—There was a rabbit. No, a sheep. I killed a sheep.

—There was a scorpion, Eve says heavily.—Just as my labor started.

This last with a gesture toward the infant.

Adam isn't sure why she refers to the boy as *my labor*. But there are many confusing things vying for his attention at the moment.—A scorpion? Where is it now?

—You killed it. And it very nearly killed you in return.

This news baffles him. He strives to remember but cannot: some effect of the poison, no doubt.—How long was I smitten?

—Four days.

He gasps.

—You raved for two, then fell so silent I thought myself abandoned. Last night you returned to normal sleep.

More bewildering than ever! Sudden sheepishness (no, shame) floods him and he grasps his wife's hand.—And I left you to do the birthing alone. I'm sorry.

Her face is brick.—I managed.

—So you did. And it all worked out. But still.

There is a reserve in her manner that is unusual. He would have expected her to be jolly now her ordeal is over, thrilled that she has produced the boy, even teasing of his own incapacity at the time. The arched eyebrow, the sly smile. Why then this sourness, this dull holding back? Is she injured in some way? Were there complications, pain perhaps or blood? Adam has often observed the animals giving birth, the stoic ewes, the nickering donkeys. Had it been more difficult for his wife?

He studies her but sees no clues. Her hair is freshly washed, her cheeks and shoulders healthily pink. Her stomach lies flaccid, breasts flop enormously, but apart from this there is no change he can observe upon her. The change seems to be *in* her.

He asks, What name have you given him?

—I haven't.

The answer is startling.—Why ever not?

She doesn't speak for a time. Then:—I cannot be bothered.

Adam's thoughts swirl like the wind but he chooses his words with care.—This is most unusual.

—Nonetheless it's true.

He is speechless for a time. Eve brings him some stew, simmered long over the fire, the thick mash easy for his wracked body to swallow and digest. As he chews, his glance rests upon the infant, prone on the dirt, kicking at nothing, slapping the ground. A strange little pink thing it's true and none too appealing to look at, but no less deserving of a name for all that. Not for the first time, he wonders if his wife is as different from him as are the fish and the birds.—We shall call him Cain.

—As you wish.

He sets aside the empty bowl. His body craves more but he must be careful. Eve goes back to the child, who gropes for her and gurgles. She lifts him to her and holds him against her blue-veined teat. Adam watches with a mixture of wonder and envy.

—How does that feel? he asks.

—It hurts.

Her manner is that of someone confronted with a creature who has already caused great pain, and cannot yet be trusted.

—And the birth, says Adam, was difficult?

Her look answers him before her words do.—*Difficult* is a mild way of putting it.

—Tell me what happened. Please.

She takes a long while to collect her thoughts but when she speaks her words are brief.—There was another.

He absorbs this for some moments. Outside warbles the ringing call of an unfamiliar bird.—Another child?

She nods.—This one's twin.

—Which died soon after, Adam guesses.

—Which was dead inside me, she corrects. She holds aloft the infant Cain so Adam can better see him in the light of the entryway.—This one, I believe, killed it.

Adam absorbs this silently for a time.

•

—You are saying that this one is born evil, Adam says at length.

—All the evidence points that way.

—What evidence, exactly?

—Bruises, says Eve.—Here. She points to her own neck.—The imprints of hands and fingers that had squeezed its little throat shut. And this one here? His fingers fit exactly.

Adam wrestles with this. Coincidence surely . . . —You're saying the other was choked to death?

—It looked so to me.

—But in your belly, they could not have breathed. So, what harm in stopping its breath?

She frowns, considering.—I hadn't thought of that. I've been so tired.

Praise God, Adam thinks. But whether he is happy that his son might not be a murderer, or only that his wife might believe the child innocent, Adam could not have rightly said.

Eve presses, I only know that when the time came for the little one to breathe, he could not.

—And so he died.

—He was born dead, I told you.

—But—

—Enough! snaps Eve, and the child—Cain—desists from her nipple long enough to stare up at her, wide-eyed. Adam stares too, as Eve visibly calms herself.—I don't know for certain what happened inside me. Everything pained, that's all I know. I felt a great deal, but I only *saw* what came later, when you were—indisposed.

Adam mulls this over. Somehow he hadn't expected such a somber mood on the occasion of his first child's birth.—Where is the twin then?

—In the ground.

It makes a brutal kind of sense, he admits to himself.

—You were still raving, she says, so I dug a hole in the yard and buried it so the ants wouldn't get it. There was a great deal of . . . other material as well. Liquids, and flesh that was not quite flesh.

She shudders with the memory.—The sleeping mat was a mess. I burned it.

Now Adam does notice a meaty, bloody tang in the air. He had thought it to be the child's smell.

—Imagine, Eve sighs, strangling your brother before you are even born.

Her voice is quiet but Adam can hear the strength of feeling beneath it. He says, I don't believe that human beings are born evil. It makes a mockery of God's commands.

—I wish I could believe you, Eve says sadly.—But how to explain the other child? You didn't see the bruises and welts, they matched perfectly.

—Doubtless arms and legs kick and roll in the womb, unguided by any intelligence or malice.

Eve shrugs.—Maybe.

Adam scuttles across the hut. The child watches him approach with sky-blue eyes. Where *does* that color come from, Adam wonders, and pokes a finger at the infant's hand, not knowing what will happen. Hoping something does. Miraculously, the child grips his finger in its diminutive palm, clutching with ferocity.—As you said yourself: a grip like an eagle's.

Eve's eyes are hooded.—This proves nothing.

—It proves the child has the urge to grasp and clutch. Who knows, in the darkness of your womb, what the two brothers may have felt? Bumping one against the other, gripping this one's foot or that one's neck. Not to murder, just to, to hold.

—It seems most unlikely.

—No more unlikely than God's sending us into the world with our whole character decided for us. No more unlikely than an infant committing murder.

Silence swells between them.

—Perhaps it is as you say, Eve sighs at length.—I'd like it to be. But I have little reason to think it any truer than my own intuition. All we know for sure is that the brother is murdered.

A little desperately Adam tells her, We must give the child a chance. We can't assume he is some bad seed sprung up from between us.

—Suppose not, Eve concedes. She jiggles the infant, who responds with an inquisitive gurgle.—But on the day of his birth, his father was struck down by a scorpion, and his twin was born dead. It is not an auspicious beginning.

—Do we even know what an auspicious beginning is? He is the first child, after all.

—The first of two.

She has him tongue-tied again. But then she says, You're right. He may be perfectly normal, as you would have it. But I'll watch him closely, all the same.

Adam says nothing, but nods worriedly. What else can he do?

# 11 *the arrival*

In the morning Eve cries out, It's coming! I can feel it.

She has been like this, on and off, for days. But no child as yet. Adam crouches beside her and is unsure she sees him. Her breath is ragged and fluttery.—Get me something to eat, she commands.— I'm ravenous.

Her appetite has been erratic, disappearing entirely only to return doubly strong. As if her belly isn't full enough already.

At the hut's entrance he turns to squint at her in the shadows. She has lain back on the reed mat but even from here he can smell her fear.—I will return as soon as I can.

She doesn't answer.

Adam thinks to himself, Everything will change now.

Again.

**book four** *the fall*

# 10 *the arrival*


In Eve's nightmare she is rent like an egg. The child clambers from her broken shell into the world, an ugly fledgling or baby lizard, dribbling yolky fluids. Eve wakes from these visions cloaked in sweat, with pounding heart and twitching eyelids. Her feet are bruised from sole to ankle, their once-shapely flesh swollen and chapped. Her misshapen body hangs before her when she walks, like a premonition of something horrible. Her head throbs incessantly and she grows forgetful, which leaves her more reliant on her husband, who is above all the man responsible for getting her into this state to begin with.

Eve is not happy.

Nor is this all. When she stoops to pick up her bone needle from the floor, the world blurs alarmingly. Arresting herself in midmotion, she shuts her eyes and straightens. Slowly, very slowly. What most enrages her about this confinement is the way it impedes her mobility. She can't be spontaneous anymore; can't just *do* things. The only thing making it bearable is her sense that the situation is nearing its end and will soon be resolved. A few days more, a week or two at most.

Praise God, as her husband would declare. If she has anything to say about it, this first child will be the last.

•

Eve sits and falls into a daydream and loses track of time: another habit of childbearing that she can't abide. When Adam approaches the hut, she rouses herself. His steps are tentative, and she sighs. He went off hunting this morning and has killed nothing, or his stride

**185**

would be loud and confident. She will have to play the ungrateful wench again and send him back out, or else eat whatever pathetic handful of flowers and berries he has brought this time.

He is at the doorway.—Wife?

—Still here.

He surveys her and she looks back in turn. The loincloth of gazelle skin that she fashioned him some years ago is an improvement over the earlier attempts with leaves and vines, none of which lasted more than a few days and some of which gifted them diabolical stinging rashes, swirling pimples like constellations across their loins. But the loincloth is wrinkled and filthy now. Her sewing has improved; perhaps she should make him another garment when she gets the chance. If she gets the chance. If she ever recovers from this current episode, and if Adam ever happens across another injured gazelle that the wolves haven't gotten to yet.

She feels herself sliding into self-pity and shakes it off. Eve must admit: Adam is bearing up well under the pregnancy. Ha ha. Better than she is anyway. These last few years of strenuous living have added a shapeliness to him that was lacking in the Garden. Shoulders have broadened, gut has tightened, calves and thighs bulge appealingly. Despite her impatience, Eve allows her gaze to linger on her husband. If only, she thinks, he had a little more . . . *something*.

For example:—How are you feeling? he asks. Always the same question.

—No different, she tells him. Always the same answer.

—And the child?

She clutches her belly reflexively.—Still reluctant to make his way into the world.

By common consent they refer to the unborn child as *he*. What should happen if it turns out to be a girl, Eve cannot guess.

—He will come. He will. How long has it been?

This too he asks every day.—Months. Eight months or more, nearly nine in fact. Time enough for him to tire of my company.

As if in response to this the child in her belly kicks against her, hard. Eve trembles a little.—Oh . . . Eve thinks, It's as if he hears what I say and wants to punish me for it.

—What is it?

She hesitates.—Sometimes it feels like a tempest going on in there.

—Maybe there is more than one. With some of the lesser animals it is so.

—Don't say such things. My God. Don't even think them.

She sees the confusion on his face and knows he wants to ask, Why not? The more the better, isn't that so? Easy for him to say with his flat stomach and jaunty loins. What does he know of the nightmares that plague her, the acid bowels, the endless headaches? Eve glares at him, silently daring him to speak. He doesn't.

Her foul temper can only be worsened by the fact that he carries no spoils of the hunt.—You found me no meat, she sighs.

—I found you these, Adam says uncertainly, and holds both arms out to her. She peers across the dim hut but whatever he carries is no more than a mouthful.—I can't see.

He steps closer.—Look.

In one hand he holds a mushroom, in the other a limp frog. Eve fights back vomit, then wonders why she bothers.—Do you mock me, husband?

Adam's smile, uncertain at best, vanishes.—You know I would never do that.

—Then why bring me vermin and fungus?

—They are good. At least the mushroom is. I saw a deer eating one and chased it away and tried it. It has an unusual flavor but not unwholesome. The frog, Adam adds with less confidence, is I admit an experiment.

Eve closes her eyes. Her voice is calm but carries granite underneath.—Go experiment by yourself. Go someplace far away and eat your frogs. Mushrooms too, and sticks and rocks and grass and insects and anything else you may find. When you've eaten your fill of such trash I hope you're strong and quick and clever enough to hunt me one of the many animals that share this land with us, that I might eat and grow strong enough myself to bear you your heir.

Adam stands silent.

—Otherwise, Eve continues ruthlessly, I'm unlikely to survive my immediate future and can only assume your heir will die as well. Unless you sprout breasts and nurse him yourself.

Two tiny vertical lines can just be seen between Adam's brows. Good, thinks Eve. Let him earn a few more wrinkles on his face if that's what it takes. She says, And another thing. The next time you see a deer eating a fungus, don't chase away the deer to take the fungus. Kill the animal and leave the fungus for the worms.

He mumbles something.

—I'm not convinced you understand.

—I understand, he says. Clears his throat. Then straightens up to meet her gaze, lifting his chin, and for a moment looks almost like a figure to be reckoned with: tall and lean, hands spatulate and strong, his wiry torso wrapped in animal skins. Lord of the wilderness, dominator of beasts. But when he speaks again the illusion is shattered and once more he is a scared youth who has disobeyed his father and hopes the consequences won't be too heinous.—I'll try my best, he says.—With luck and Providence I should be able to bring you something.

She tries not to hock up sputum and spit it on the ground between them. The habit is an unpleasant one and she knows she should resist it.—Forget about luck and Providence, she says.— What have they done for us lately? Trust your skills instead, and your strength and cunning.

She speaks as if to a child, only there are no children and never have been, not yet. But her words are simple and slow and lead from one place to another like the well-worn path between the river and the hut.—Take the stone that I use for scraping skins. The same that I use to cut fish. You know it? Flat and gray with a sharp edge.

—I know it. Maybe I should try to catch some fish. . . .

—The fish are gone. Stop talking and listen to me. Wrap one end of the stone in skins so you can hold it. Find some animal in its burrow, some rabbit or weasel or something, and club it with a stick and slice its throat. Better yet something large, like a deer or one of those rams on the grasslands. They seem stupid and there are many.

—They run fast.

—Then find a *tired* one, she snaps.—Find one that's sick or old or just born. Yes—find an infant and bring it here and tie it up. Let it eat all the grass it wants. Then when it grows large and fat you can slaughter it with no struggle. Having meat would be no more strenuous than plucking those grapes you're so fond of.

Adam's face betrays his interest in the idea.—It is possible?

—Why not?

He has no answer for this, but stares out the entryway. Eve can almost see the pictures flashing through his imagination. Until now, meat has been an inconsistent luxury, and the thought of so much of it—of eating flesh whenever they want—leaves Adam lost in his fantasies.

Eve, however, cannot afford this inertia. She is carrying a child and needs to keep it fed off the fat of her own bones, of which she has precious little left. She and Adam have subsisted largely on river fish, berries, and peas this past year, but the fish have vanished, the berries are gone by, and all the peas in creation are not adequate to keep body and soul together.

Adam is still staring outside and Eve feels the temptation of hope. It is dangerous to expect too much, she knows, because her husband is a man slow to try new things and quick to fail at many of those. But she knows the look on his face, the distant dreaminess: he is mulling some plan, and may soon throw himself into one project or another. If her sheep idea works, then praise God. But it will take time, and time she doesn't have.

The child kicks again, or perhaps just shifts, seeking greater comfort in his watery world. Something slides from right to left inside her; something else, from left to right. Maybe Adam is correct, and there are two. Or three, or ten. Maybe she'll discharge a string of mewling sticky things still wet with her own fluids, or a pile of oval eggs that will demand all her attention and warmth till they hatch.

She wishes she knew; and she wishes, more than anything, that she never had to find out.

Suddenly she is so tired.—Husband.

He faces her.

—It grows restless, I can feel it. The boy will be here soon. Within days perhaps. I need more strength than I've got.

—All right, he nods.

She remembers the she-cat from two years past, its sore-pocked neck and gummy eyes. The way she could barely totter away from the thrashing litter she had borne: and the way they had died, all of them.—I'm exhausted already, and after the birth I expect to be more so. The food you've grown is good and I appreciate your work in planting and gathering it, but I need more. Flesh is necessary to create more flesh. You must hunt, and find me more meat.

He straightens up and stands a little taller, looking every bit the protector, the provider. The man of the house. For a moment he appears capable of anything.—If flesh is what you need, then I shall get it for you. Whatever you want is yours.

And he smiles at her.

She smiles back and allows herself to believe him.

At nightfall he returns with nothing.

# 9 *the son*

She believes it will be a boy. More than this: she knows it. The child will be a miniature of her husband, not of herself. And how can she be so sure? She couldn't say. Perhaps she senses some logic in all the other important figures in her life being male—God, Adam, even the serpent, though it carried her face—which suggests that her child will be too.

In idle moments she allows herself the luxury of wondering what the child will be like, physically. She has no idea, never having seen one before. But judging from the birds of the field and the lambs that bleat after their dams, the mewling kittens and the donkey colts out on the plain, barely able even to stagger upright—judging from all this, she expects the thing to be small, loud, and bothersome.

So most of the time she puts it out of her mind as best she can, which is not very well in between the nausea and the cramps and the strange lethargy that possesses her at random moments. But she tries. She has only been carrying the child three months as yet, and has begun to think that there may be much more to come. This is something else she is unsure of. Different animals, she has observed, carry their young for different periods. The rule seems to be the larger the animal, the longer it takes. She might be stuck like this all summer, through the fall, even into winter. This is not a joyous train of thought and Eve sees little point in dwelling on it. What's done is, most assuredly, done. Never to be rescinded, repealed, or renegotiated.

That's one lesson learned long ago.

•

Again she wonders what the boy will be like. If like his father, then how much? One sheep is placid and dull, while another betrays curiosity; one sparrow rustles in the same tree all afternoon while the next flits off and returns a hundred times; some donkeys are skittish and high-strung while others are bold and domineering. Could a husband like Adam plant the seed of a confident offspring, one who would take command without dithering and fuss? She hopes so. Eve is about ready for some company who doesn't second-guess himself all the time. Sometimes she wonders what it would be like to have a conversation with a man who said *Yes I'm sure* instead of *That might be so*.

She's being unfair, she knows. Perhaps her pregnancy is making her shrewish. More than once, Adam has shown his ability to change with circumstances. It's just that his adaptability comes in fits and starts, while she craves a steadier, more reliable kind of confidence.

At least he can catch fish. During that first horrid winter outside the Garden, when they truly had come close to starving, she taught herself the art of weaving nets. Inspired by a spider's web hanging rain-speckled in the afternoon sun, catching insects as she watched, she had thought, If only catching fish were so easy. And then, Well why not?

And though she had proven more skilled at weaving, Adam had demonstrated his own mastery at casting them, selecting his spots in the river with care, the narrow cataracts where the fish were unable to escape the current; his net weighted with stones to fall before their hurtling bodies in an impenetrable mesh. He and Eve ate well that spring and summer, foraging and catching what they could. But when autumn grew heavy in the air and foraging turned poor, they needed to devise some alternate plan. They had grown reliant on the fish—overly so, Eve knows. A bad couple of weeks would have left them starving. Luckily there were no bad weeks . . . *that* year.

By the following winter they had settled in this place. Adam tried some experiments, most of which had failed but a few of which worked. The grapes, for example, had taken nicely, and now sprawled in lush exuberance across a rapidly expanding patch. So their second year was better, and last year was better still, despite the long dismal winter. They wrapped themselves up in their new sleeping hut, built of hand-fashioned bricks of burnt river clay, and lay together to keep away the chill. The bricks lay flat one against the next and didn't allow the winter wind to howl through any open chinks or wide cracks. And lying snug in their new brick shelter, Eve grew heavy with Adam's child and her own.

With that everything changed. Eve understands this; knows that more than ever, it's imperative to survive the years ahead of them. Indulging in the luxury of failure—of death—would be worse now than it would have been in previous years. Then, it might have been a crime to give up, to quit struggling and give in to extinction. It would have been suicide. But now?

Now the crime would be magnified. Suicide no more: now it would be murder.

•

Adam returns from a day culling wheat berries and storing them in a pair of big clay pots Eve has fashioned from river mud and baked to hardness in the cookfire's coals. She hears him approaching with lively steps, a sign that he is pleased with recent developments. Eve busies herself stitching the last two pieces of goatskin into a skirt for her distending midriff, and begins singing. She doesn't realize she is doing it until she notices Adam in the entryway, staring at her queerly. Then the sound of her own voice strikes her ear and she abruptly halts.

—What is that? he asks.

She's confused, embarrassed.—I don't know. I'll stop.

—Don't. It's nice.

Self-consciously she hums a little, then trails off, then starts again. Before long she is back nearly as loud as before. It is a made-up song with no words but *lahh tahh yahh* and a melody that floats across the air like a breeze. For a time Eve concentrates on the singing more than the stitching, until at length she forgets it and turns her attention back to the needle.

When she looks up Adam is squatting against the wall, watching her again. She realizes she has fallen silent again.—That was lovely, he says.

It is the first time he has used the word to describe her.—Thank you.

—I hope it becomes a habit. I hope, he adds shyly, it is an indication of your happiness.

—Of course it is, she says lightly. Is this true? She doesn't know. Happiness isn't something she spends much time thinking about. Survival, discomfort, hunger . . . These are the concerns that fill her days. That have filled the past several years.

His smile is a little mischievous.—I am quite jealous.

She blinks, confused.

—You have never sung for me but you are singing for our child before it even takes a breath.

—He, not it. I'm quite sure it is a he.

—Oh really? And no doubt, *he* will grow up well fed on his mother's songs.

A foolish thought of course. Eve has been anything but thrilled about her condition ever since it became obvious some weeks ago. Still . . . was she singing to her child? Or because of her child? In spite of her child? Who could say. Certainly not her.

To mask her doubts she says something that has been much on her mind.—I hope our child is born virtuous.

Adam's face is comically puzzled.—Hem?

—Born good. You know, not evil or drawn toward mischief.

—Yes yes, I understand the words. It is your reasoning that confuses me.

Eve lowers her eyes to her stitching. Maybe she should've stayed silent, but there is too much she hasn't been saying lately.—Suppose our offspring is unkind or unholy in some way. As a, a punishment to us.

—I would think we have been punished enough, says Adam quietly.—But I take your point. In any case we will teach him to be kind and holy and—what did you say before—virtuous. Such is our duty.

—We can try. But some virtues are beyond teaching, don't you think?

His eyes narrow.—Are you thinking of something in particular?

—I'm thinking, she says softly, of myself.

Crows and mynas squabble outside.

—I had no reason to do what I did in the Garden, says Eve.—But I did it anyway.

—You were tricked.

She shakes her head.—I was told the truth, and acted on it. There's no trick in that except the one played by expectations.

—There is no point dwelling on this.

—I think there's no point avoiding it, she retorts.—No one taught me to disobey: I chose to do it on my own. You didn't. Now tell me, isn't that an indication of some basic difference between us?

He refuses to meet her eye.—It might be.

She has her hands on her belly now.—And this child of ours, it's part you and part me. Which way will it turn? Will he be obedient like you, or ungrateful like me?

There is no answer of course, but Eve has been needled by these questions for weeks now, and feels it only fair that Adam labor under them too. From the look on his face, he has indeed taken the question to heart.

—Anyway, she says, there's no telling till the child is born. Then we'll see.

—So we will, Adam nods.

—In the meantime, look at all this.

*All this* refers to the grain Adam had brought into the hut.— You've been busy.

For a moment Adam doesn't answer, as if still troubled by their conversation. Then he comes back to her.—It's those new seeds, the ones I showed you before. They don't drop off the stems, they just sit and wait and we lose nothing.

—Will there be more?

—Certainly. I'll need to keep some for next year's planting, but I expect to have at least as much as last winter.

Eve frowns inwardly. Last year was—though easier than previous winters—not exactly luxurious. But she forces away her reservations and says, It's good you found that grain. I should've been more appreciative when you told me.

—Think nothing of it. Your mind is elsewhere, he smiles.

Truer than you know, Eve thinks, but she says, There's quite a lot for now. I'll grind some up for porridge, maybe bake it into some kind of flat bread so it won't rot. Do you think you'll harvest enough to last the winter?

She longs to hear him say Yes I'm sure, but instead he frowns.—It might be so. We must trust in the will of God.

—Because we're responsible for more than just ourselves, she reminds him.

—So we are. We are responsible both for ourselves, and for God.

This isn't exactly what she meant, but a wave of fatigue curdles across her and she lacks the strength to explain herself. Anyway she suspects she and Adam would not see eye to eye on this question. She can't shake the suspicion that, despite what her husband might aver, it isn't they who are responsible to God. Rather it seems to her that, ever since their departure from the Garden to fight their way through this deathtrap called Creation, it is in fact the other way around.

# 8 *two years previous*

The rainy season comes, bringing with it long gray afternoons and lingering twilight as the sun pokes its fingers through the cloud's spent tatters, filling the landscape with ghostly golden pyramids. At such times there is little to do but watch the rain wash down in curtains and wonder if their tentative crops will die. Grain lies scattered in handfuls and berry bushes sprawl, thickly abundant, in the desolate patch where they relieve themselves. Eve finds this odd in the extreme but so be it: God's sense of humor can be inscrutable at times.

Rain falls hard, tapers, stops. Pauses as if for breath. Begins again.

Overall, their new home has suited them well. They have planted some modest patches of wheat around the house, more as an experiment than in any great hopes of success. Peas grow wild in abundance so they leave them to it. Rams and goats dot the distant hillside bluffs but are averse to coming too close.

—What are you thinking? she asks him. They are sitting in the shelter, watching the rain. The pile of rocks in which they live is too rude to be called a house, or even a hut. Now is midday; the shower started some time after breakfast. A dozen little rivulets trickle into their chamber through various chinks in the roof and walls. They have survived worse, Eve reflects stonily. But that's about as far as optimism could take them.

Adam's gloom is palpable, so she repeats, What's on your mind?

Although this is their day of rest, the expression on Adam's face is far from restful. He gestures at the weather.—I'm hoping all this water doesn't drown our crops. I've no idea how much they require.

—I'm sure they'll flourish, Eve says, though she is ignorant too.

—God willing.

—Yes.

Apparently He is, for eventually the rain subsides. The days grow warm and summery, and in the following weeks the wheat bursts forth and strains for the sun. Eve, who tossed a few handfuls of hoarded seed at Adam's urging but with indifferent hope for success, is startled to find herself standing amid a profusion of knee-high green stalks.

—Next year we shall plant more, says Adam.

Eve nods dumbly.

—And some peas too. Why not? It shouldn't be difficult, just throw them on the ground. If we plant them in regular rows near the shelter, we can do a better job of keeping the birds off.

Birds are a problem with the wild peas that grow by the river.

Eve finds her voice.—With your spear I can punch some furrows in the grass and get them started.

—Might be better to clear away the other plants first. There would be more room for the ones we want.

She raises an eyebrow.—I'll see what I can do. That's a job for a strong back, but we've only got one of those.

—Easier to burn it off, he suggests mildly.

She digests this. More than once they have seen a burnt area where the new growth is vigorous.—That's a fine idea.

—I shall leave you to get started then.

He bustles off to catch more fish, and when that is done he turns to digging out clay from the riverbank. She watches as he slaps it between his palms to form flat, square slices, which he then lays out in the sun to dry.—What are you doing? she asks that evening, as they eat. Although she has an idea, she wants him to think he is surprising her.

Which, in many other ways, he is.

—You'll see, he says.

When the sun has dried the slabs he sets them around the fire to bake to rock-hardness. He does this day after day throughout the long summer, and the pile of makeshift bricks slowly grows.

The days lengthen, pause, then begin to grow shorter again. Still the bricks accumulate.

—I assume you have a purpose for all this activity, she says one afternoon over a little half smile. They are eating lunch by the pit where he is digging out blocks of clay.

—I plan to rebuild the shelter, he says between swallows.—Or build a new one rather. It's been good enough but will be cold to spend the winter in. We need something larger with a waterproof ceiling and a stone floor to keep the damp out, and a proper chimney. And no holes in the walls, he adds with a grimace.

—I'm fond of the holes, she says lightly.—And the lizards who live in them.

—Very funny.

—And the spiders, she goes on.—And the mosquitoes and dragonflies and centipedes and—

—That's enough, he growls, but smiling to show his big square teeth.

Their autumn is taken up with preparations to survive the winter. Eve suspects that this is how life will be from now on. She finds that if she cooks the fish slowly over the fire and lays it in a bed of salt, it will keep for months. Peas can be dried on stones in the sun and stored as well, though she must be vigilant for birds who will happily carry off their whole crop. She weaves baskets to hold their supplies and hangs them from the ceiling to discourage insects. When the wheat comes in she collects that too, and crafts many large clay urns to contain the harvest.

Adam busies himself with the new hut. In her idle moments, which are not many, Eve watches him. Adam seems to have no idle moments at all and she is struck by this, and by his strong back, stringy biceps, and flat stomach. His hair is growing into a rangy cloud that messily frames his head. When he sweats, highlights play across taut muscles. He is pleasing to look upon at such times. Not at all the man she woke to in the Garden. The two years—or is it three?—of their exile have changed him. Even more than his body, his temperament has altered. He has become a man who focuses on a task and doesn't rest until it's done; a man who can juggle several vital operations—building a hut, fishing, collecting peas, scavenging for fruit—at once. True, he is still prone to indecision before starting something new, but once his mind is made up there's no turning him aside.

Animals remain his weakness. Apart from fish, he is plainly afraid of just about everything that walks this earth.

Ah well, Eve says to herself. God has fashioned each of us with weaknesses. She tries for a moment to remember what hers might be, but quickly gives up. Well, even God slips up sometimes. Ha ha.

•

When complete, the new hut is far superior to the old. Adam presents it to her one autumn afternoon like a new groom taking away his bride.

—Someday we'll have a whole compound of buildings, he says shyly.—And this will be at its heart.

—That'll be a lot of work.

—Maybe I'll have help, he says. He is suddenly bashful, and Eve is grateful for him all over again.

This new structure could never be mistaken for a mere heap of rocks: its regular walls denote an unmistakably artificial structure. Adam had stood atop stones to build the walls higher than his head: inside he and Eve can easily stand upright. The roof is built of overlapping layers of flat clay shingles, and the threshold at the entryway is as high as her ankle. There is even a window opposite to let in light, and a chimney in one corner above a flat cooking stone. The floor is constructed of flat slabs of shale.

—It's wonderful, Eve acknowledges.

He seems concerned that she approve.—Of course it could be better. We'll make beds of hay like we have in the other hut, and the window can be covered with animal skins once the weather turns. I can even plug it up if you prefer.

She stops him with a kiss.—It's perfect.

—I wouldn't go that far, he says, but kisses her back anyway. Then once more, with vigor. She breaks free.—I would.

Eve steps inside the new hut and straightens up. He has taken care to fit the bricks one against the next; river clay fills the chinks. But the chinks are few and small, as the bricks lie against each other like lovers.

—You know what you've done? You've built a cave for us. Our very own cave, out here in the open.

—You approve then?

She smiles coyly through the doorway.—I love it. Let's try it out and see if it works.

Confusion swims across his face.—Try it out?

She lies back on the floor. The stone is hard against her rump as she hikes up the gazelle hide girdling her hips.

—Oh, he says.

•

Afterward, while he naps, she lies awake and remembers things she has never told him:

Morning sun hazing through the trees, flowers all around flashing orange-yellow against her eyeballs. No clouds but then there never were; just this early mist that would burn off soon. Stream bubbling gaily, peacocks strutting nearby, bees humming a contented air as they piled into the day's labors. All Creation alive, docile, at her feet and pretty happy to be there. She twining her hair round her fingers, her only garment the locks that tumbled to her waist. She'd never missed clothing: with the sun so mild against her flesh, what need for her to cover herself?

Eve with no particular goal that day, waking refreshed but a trifle restless. If she were completely honest, she'd have to admit a little boredom. Walking helped to fill the space that yawned inside her.

Her stroll carried her past the stream and into an area of thick tangled growth, shrubby trees heavy with fruit, leafy ferns slapping her calves, mushrooms clogging the shadows. Something familiar about this place . . . Yes. Just ahead, a small clearing, perfectly circular, and in it the Tree that was forbidden to her and Adam both. It wasn't a particularly imposing tree, but its abundant leaves were fleshy and its boughs were weighed down with a heavy load of yellowish fruits. Not a fruit that Eve recognized. Of their own accord Eve's footsteps stopped, and she stood and wondered at the tree as if she had stumbled across her parents doing something unspeakable. Which was of course impossible.

The tree said, Hello, Eve.

Her shock was profound. No tree in the Garden had ever spoken to her before. Maybe that was why this one was off-limits?

—Come closer, my child, coaxed the tree.

Eve blinked, then squinted, and caught a slithery movement among the branches. Something in there was sliding from branch to branch—and talking to her, she realized. A long breath escaped her. Beasts of the wood speaking her name was strange indeed, she would admit, but not half so strange as trees of the wood doing the same.

The creature in the branches looked something like a serpent but different from any she'd ever seen before. For one thing it was as thick as her thigh but shorter than she was, lending it a truncated sluglike aspect. Its flesh was dull red and it lacked the lithe grace of a true serpent. Most of all though it lacked a snake's head. The creature's face was pale and fleshy and red-haired. It was a human face. It was Eve's own face.

But the voice was male to her ears.

Eve waited a few paces from this thing. She felt calm enough to remark to herself how calm she was feeling. And why not? Strange as this moment was, she was still in a place where nothing hurtful had ever happened, or could. So Eve said to the fat snake sporting her face:—What do you want?

—I want you to eat the fruit from this tree, said the serpent with no hesitation whatsoever.

Eve frowned.—That's been prohibited.

—By whom?

—By God.

—Ahh. And you know why that is, I suppose?

Eve had no answer.

The serpent wrapped its stubby tail around the tree's trunk and cantilevered itself toward Eve, who stood staring at her own face swaying in the air just before her. A forked snake-tongue flashed from the mouth of Eve's doppelgänger, then she—he, it—spoke.— Your God's power comes from this tree. Did you know that? It's why he protects it so. Eat it, eat *this*, here—and you'll become just like Him. What do you think of that?

Eve didn't know what to think, so she said, I don't know.

Nobody had ever lied to her, so it didn't occur to her to say:— That's not true!

Instead she said, Why wouldn't He want me to be like Him?

The snake's laugh, spilling from Eve's own mouth, was entirely without mirth.—It's not part of the plan, believe me.

Well, so be it.—But I'm perfectly happy with the way things are.

—Are you? Are you really?

Eve hesitated.

—What did you do yesterday? demanded the serpent.

She frowned.—I . . . walked along the river. I was looking for— yes, I was collecting mushrooms, which we ate. Also berries.

—Fascinating.

Eve bridled.—There's nothing wrong with staying alive.

—Certainly not. And the day before?

The day before yesterday was identical to the one that followed, as they both knew. And the one before that . . .

The snake watched her mockingly and Eve felt herself growing defensive.—We have all we need here.

—Oh sure, murmured the snake. Somehow, sans shoulders, it still managed a shrug.—There's a great appeal to being *comfortable*. If that's what you want, I won't argue. Go on then. Keep it up. Off with you! There's a lovely patch of berries just behind this clearing.

Eve didn't move.

—Better get them before the bunnies do.

Eve didn't move.

Suddenly the serpent's voice modulated. It no longer mocked, but spoke in gentle earnest tones.—The power of creation will lie within you, woman. That's what your God fears. What He doesn't want you to know.

Eve didn't move.

—Wouldn't that be preferable to wandering naked all day, plucking fruit and shitting by the river?

She had to admit, the creature had a point.—But it is forbidden.

—Only because of fear. Your God is afraid to treat you as an equal. Who knows what His plans are for you here? Or maybe there is no plan other than your remaining forever just as you are.

The serpent's voice drops to a whisper.—Day after day after day after day.

Admittedly Eve had felt such misgivings before.—The power of creation you say?

—Oh yes, purred the serpent.—You will carry it about with you and it will spring forth from your belly at your command.

Which, in a manner of speaking, would turn out to be the case.

●

She found Adam where she had left him. He looked up from the grass where he lay, his expression of serenity morphing into startlement.—You look different.

—I feel different, she answered. It was true: her heart pounded, her face burned hot, she could barely keep herself from trembling. Whether this was due to the fruit itself, or the knowledge of what she'd done, she couldn't say. She shoved the fruit at Adam.—Here. Eat this.

He eyed it warily. It lay in her hand, pulpy and torn and pink inside like a dead animal.—That's from the Tree, said Adam.

—Yes it is and I've eaten it.

His face went blank with shock.—But it's not allowed!

—I've eaten it, she repeated, and I'm still here.

Adam glanced behind him furtively.—I don't know.

—I do, she said.

Suddenly Eve was overwhelmed by a feeling she had never known before, a desire to lie alongside Adam and twine herself in his arms and legs and—and—and she didn't know what else. But that something would suggest itself she was sure. Was this knowledge? Was this the power of creation?

She jabbed the fruit at his face.—Are you really content to just sit and stare all day, like a leaf? Don't you want to *do* something?

Adam managed to look simultaneously sheepish, mischievous, fearful, and ashamed.—Yes, he said at length.—Sometimes I do. But only sometimes—

She shoved the fruit at him again, a half-eaten offering. Yellow fleshy pulp trickled from his chin as he ripped into it. Moments later it was gone and they were left staring at each other. Eve's excited frenzy of moments earlier evaporated, leaving only the dull ache of trepidation.

—I guess we should try to—

—We'd better do something about—

—What's happening to—?

—Oh . . .

—*Oh.*

And even as she cast about for something to fashion into a covering for her privates, she couldn't take her eyes off of *his*.

# 7 *the gifts*

One morning Adam runs excitedly back to their little makeshift shelter, calling, Look what I have found!

Eve looks, but sees nothing remarkable. Adam carries in his hand a small sheaf of grassy stalks, topped with bundles of pale brown seeds. It's the sort of wheat they've been eating ever since their exile began.—Yes? she says politely.

He is out of breath.—Ran . . . all the way from the river. The far side . . .

He's never shown any inclination to cross the river before. Eve grows more curious about what might have lured him there. Adam thrusts his hand toward her as if the grass is a holy treasure. A fat bundle of grains wavers on the tip of each stalk, like a thumb.—Do you not recognize what is unusual about them? he asks.

—No, she says.

—Look. These seeds are good to eat, as we have discovered. Raw, they are difficult, but cooked a little, they become tasty and nourishing.

She knows all this: she's been eating them as well as he. But as if in illustration he twists a few of the grains off the stalk and into his hand. They sit there like small insects and Eve is unsure of his point.—All right, she says.—What's so odd about them?

—Usually they drop off the stalks to plant themselves in the ground. When that happens, they are of no use to us. These have not done so, for some reason. Do you not see? God has caused them to wait for us. If we save them till spring and sow them into the earth, then by summer we'll have a steady supply. We'll be able to pluck them as we need, and can eat them every night.

Eve smiles weakly at the thought of eating seeds every night.

—I've found a big patch of this, he goes on.—It has lain dormant all winter. If we can grow enough, we won't half starve as in winters past.

Adam is right of course: a steady diet, no matter how monotonous, is far preferable to going hungry. Eve chides herself: she is long since quit of the Garden, she has no right to expect anything better than the bare necessities to live. She should be grateful for anything that lessens that burden.

When Adam has gone, she permits herself a quiet sigh. She doesn't mean to be peevish, but if only. If only he'd discovered a honey tree . . . Or a spring running with milk. Or a waterproof shelter that didn't bleed rain upon them both every time the skies opened up. Or even just a couple of deer, tame enough to eat from her hand while Adam sliced their throats with his flint. Then she'd show gratitude all right.

•

These things don't materialize. But there are other gifts.

Eve leaves a clay dish of milk in the sun, then gets distracted and forgets it. When she finds it next it has thickened and soured and, surprisingly, tastes good to eat. Adding a little of this yogurt to further dishes of milk results in more yogurt, like some living thing that endlessly reproduces itself.

When she adds some to simmering milk—reckoning that the higher temperature will hasten fermentation—she is confronted with soft coagulated chunks of curdled white floating in suddenly clarified water. When drained and left to cool, this soft cheese is mild, but pleasing in texture and taste.

Adam likes it too.—Maybe a little salt next time, he suggests.

She finds that olives pressed between stones secrete a tasty oil that improves the flavor of just about everything else.

She discovers that grapes and dates and apricots grow sweeter if left in the sun to shrivel and crystallize; but still, honey is sweetest of all. The best time to rob the hives is at night, while the bees sleep.

Otherwise they can be anesthetized with a smoldering taper, but this is riskier.

One evening Adam complains of the effort of spearing fish and she remembers her first weaving attempt by the cave, the net that hung useless in her hands, and she says, I have an idea.

And she learns to loosely cover the fire each night with a thin layer of ash, so the coals are preserved until the following morning. She already understands that the fire must never, ever be allowed to die.

In this way life goes on.

•

And in other ways too. One afternoon Eve is startled by a demonic shrieking, and hurries to the door to find a pair of scruffy gray cats rutting with violence not ten steps from her threshold. First she is flustered, then mirthful: the male's resolute expression bears an uncanny resemblance to her own husband's while similarly occupied, though the female in this case appears none too pleased.

This keeps on for some days. Then the male—or males, there seem to be a gaggle of them—disappear, leaving only the increasingly battered female to linger around the woodpile. Eve leaves table scraps for it but the animal has little taste for grains or legumes, and meat is far too rare to give to an animal.

Weeks pass. The cat's body swells as if infected while Eve watches and ponders.

There follows a burst of activity as the she-cat burrows into the woodpile, then an abandoned rabbit warren, then a dry hollow beneath some boulders; in search of the ideal spot, apparently, to bring her offspring into the world. The longer this goes on, the more alarmingly her belly swells, the weaker and more haggard the rest of her becomes. And the more Eve's own belly rolls in acid unease.

The male cat resembled Adam, planting his little red root in her. Is it her lot, then, to resemble this female and bear the consequences?

It's a matter for serious thought, but when Eve thinks on it, her mind seems to spin in pointless circles, never arriving at any useful insight.

Adam is no help. When she mentions her concerns, his brow furrows and he tells her, It is only a cat.

So she says nothing more. She doesn't say, No it's not just a cat. It's me. It's every female that must carry new life into the world. Or die trying. It's the best method, evidently, that God could come up with, and it looks none too promising.

No, Eve doesn't say this.

The mother drops out of sight for a time. Eve notices at first, then forgets.

One cold morning she hears the squeaks and immediately knows what they are. She jogs to the rocky hollow and finds the kittens there, squirming downy bits of flesh. None too pleasing to look upon, nor yet to hear. They are, she thinks, several days old already, but only recently have they begun squalling.

There is one nearby that is still.

The mother looks two steps from death herself: thin, patchy, runny-eyed. She spies Eve and musters a weak hiss, but from where she lies on her side—swollen teats exposed to her offspring's relentless appetite—the threat carries more pathos than menace. She tries to glare with what Eve supposes in malevolence, but halfway through is overwhelmed by exhaustion, and her eyes shut of their own accord. The kittens, oblivious of their mother's parlous condition, claw and clamor with intensity.

That night Eve tells Adam the story. He listens stoically, then shrugs.—I would not take too much from this, he advises. We are unlike the other creatures. Our minds and spirits operate at a higher level, and we are not so subject to the arbitrary whims of our physical nature.

Eve has her doubts.

—Anyway, God does not expect of us any more than we can manage. I find it likely that for us, childbirth will be a simple enough process.

She cannot resist arching her eyebrow.—For *us*?

—Ah—for you, naturally.

—A simple process. Something like defecation, perhaps.

Adam rolls his eyes.—I would not choose that exact comparison. But yes, nothing more strenuous.

Eve considers. The sun has slid past the horizon and the twilit air is blowing cool across her forehead. Nonetheless she feels flushed.— I'm in no hurry to find out, in any case, she says with conviction, and chooses to ignore Adam's disapproving frown.

•

Some days later the mewling ceases. Eve hopes for the best: maybe the mother has moved the kittens to a new hiding place. But after another silent morning, she hurries down to the boulders.

The kittens lie dead on the ground, stiff and covered in fuzz like little bits of moldy meat. Insects have lost little time in taking away what bits they find useful. Of the mother there is no sign until later that day, when Eve is on her way to the river. The cat's scrawny corpse lies half-masked in a thicket of long grass, her lip curled in a permanent, pointless sneer.

Eve stares at the she-cat for a long time before going on to the river to bathe.

She doesn't mention the cat or its kittens again. Instead she waits for Adam to remember, to bring up the subject. To ask her one night, with a little sunburst of recollection on his face, So whatever happened to those kittens and their mother, the one you were so concerned about?

He never does.

# 6 *the years*


The sun rises and sets and does not change. That much, at least, can be relied upon.

So too does the moon rise and set; but it grows fat and thin, full and crescent in turn. Eve watches and counts the nights from one cycle to the next: twenty-eight usually, less often twenty-nine. Once she counts thirty and thinks she must have got it wrong. What odd numbers, she thinks. Why didn't God see fit to make it the same each time? What point is there to this irregularity?

She is assuming, she knows, that there is a point. She is assuming—she knows this too—that such a point is comprehensible to anyone besides God.

In those twenty-eight or twenty-nine days the sun alters not at all: it remains too bright to stare at and its size is unchanging. But often it is possible to detect some shift in the climate during this span. A bit of cooling from late summer to autumn. A slight thaw from the depths of winter to its softer, warmer periphery. A shift from the humid lassitude of late spring to the torrential downpours of midsummer. Eve notices that if she makes a point of remembering the weather at the time of one full moon, it has often elided into something different by the next.

And something more: the points on the horizon at which the sun inters itself each night, and from which it resurrects itself every morning, shift as the days pass. Too subtly to notice from one day to another, but over time, the variation is unmistakable. Eve tries not to dwell on this, as it seems to suggest that even the sunrise itself is a sometimes thing, not to be wholly counted on.

So she begins speaking about time using these terms of reference:

days, weeks, months. Weeks are familiar because that is how long God required to create the world.

Adam looks confused when she talks this way at first, but soon follows her example. They need some way to speak of time, after all, and her words work as well as any.

Keeping up the family tradition, he rests every seventh day.

Eve notices that thirteen months brings the weather around to more or less the same spot it was before. She begins thinking about her life in terms of years. For example: The first year we were out of the Garden, death walked beside us like a companion. If it wasn't wild animals threatening us, it was rock slides. If not fever, poison berries. The only thing worse than the cold at night was the cold in the mornings. We had no fire. We ate food raw or not at all.

For example: We followed the river month after month and lived on fish and fruit until we discovered peas growing wild and realized we could eat them. They didn't taste like much but neither did they leave us vomiting. Later we found berries and date trees; that was about the time I chipped a stone into a sharp knife edge and tied it onto Adam's fishing spear. He discovered he could kill more than fish that way than with a bare stick, which was fine until the fish vanished and we were left to eat whatever we could.

For example: The whole of that first winter, we never stopped being hungry. For three months we wondered if each day would be the last one. We ate dead grass by the handful and vomited it back up, until God bent down and dropped a dying gazelle at our feet. When spring finally came we found two kid goats lost and bleating. If we had any sense we'd have kept them alive to tame and fatten up. But we didn't have any sense. We were too famished to do anything but devour what was before us. At least we had a fire going by then, so we didn't have to eat them raw. Filthy beasts, they were. Who knows what would have happened to us.

•

Things get better when they decide on a place to settle. Or if not better exactly, then at least bad in a different way. When they wandered forth from the Garden, seeking refuge and a land to call their own, their great fear was always: What if the next place is worse than this one? Once they have decided on a home, the great fear becomes: What if this place never gets better?

Deciding on a place was difficult, and the situation had not been helped by Adam's indecision. Eve sympathized at first: she didn't know what to do either. But she nonetheless grew short with her husband's constant second-guessing. No place, it seemed, was good enough. Compared to what they had known, of course, no place ever would be.

—What about here? she asked one afternoon in late winter. They stood beside a lake, with dry hills to the north and east. The day was still and the lake lay unmoving, like a dead dropped thing.

—No trees, said Adam. He rubbed his jaw and squinted at the water.—We'll need trees. And anyway the water looks none too promising, hmm?

She sighed and spoke with heavy irony.—We've known better.

Some weeks later—late spring now—they chanced upon a rocky valley filled with plenty of trees and a thin, muddy creek. But before they could even pause to discuss it, a band of lean wild dogs burst from the surrounding underbrush and formed a loose U shape behind them. Though small, the dogs looked shifty and cunning and worked together with an almost supernatural purpose.

The valley was soon left behind, never to be spoken of again.

•

Then one morning in midsummer Eve simply halts. They have been walking since late winter and she is sick with traveling. Eve tosses her tumbling red hair down her back and says, What about here?

Adam surveys the area. There is grassland and bluffs and a river, and the spot is as welcoming as any they've seen these past months.—Might be good, he concedes.—Then again, there could be predators in those bluffs over there.

—Predators?

—Likely spot for caves. Could be bears, lions, anything.

Since teaching himself the names of all the animals, Adam has learned also to fear them like nothing else on earth.

—Listen, she tells him.—The only thing I see is fresh water and fish in the river, fruit trees in the groves, berries everywhere you look, and a great abundance of small harmless-looking animals. Not a predator in sight.

He nods and tugs on his chin.—You might be right.

—From the way things are growing, the land seems fertile enough and the climate can't be worse than what we've already been through. There's wild wheat across the river and peas along this side, and I think those were olives we just walked past. Didn't you see them?

—I saw.

—My advice is, start collecting rocks to make us some sort of shelter, and I'll go gather up some supper.

He isn't sure, she can see that. But neither does he argue, and this too is because he isn't sure.

That autumn is long and mild and the wild peas give them something to nibble on during the long dark months. The fish dwindle but do not disappear entirely. There is the occasional injured or decrepit animal that they can carve up for hides and meat: Eve isn't so sure it's a good idea to eat another animal's diseased flesh, but they have little choice.

Adam finishes the hut, a modest room of stones roofed with tree limbs and palm branches. From a distance it looks like a heap of rocks, but it will keep the rain off. Most of it anyway. Although too stunted to let them do anything but squat or lie down, the hut ensures that the fire stays lit, and there are plenty of chinks in the walls to suck away the smoke. The floor tends to dampness, so Eve piles in thick beds of prairie grass. A low threshold lies across the doorway to discourage snakes. It is not luxurious, not compared to the Garden; but it is not quite Hell, either.

One winter morning Adam makes a circle of stones pulled from the river to contain the fire inside the hut. The stones are sticky with red river clay, and when the fire burns down, he notices that this clay has dried into a reddish substance as hard as stone.—Look at this, he says wonderingly.—The mud has been transformed into something else.

Eve's attention is on the fish she's gutting.

Adam speaks deliberately, as if afraid of scaring off a newly arrived idea.—We could cut bricks out of this clay and then bake them to hardness. Imagine how straight and square and waterproof our dwellings would be.

The look on his face is a mixture of wonder and determination. Eve squints up at him. She remembers the day he brought home the burning tree, and remembers that his face looked much the same on that occasion. Determination, she thinks now, is a vital ingredient in this stew called survival. She will happily encourage it any way she can.—Then do it, she suggests.

—I believe I shall, Adam answers.

# 5 *the previous spring*

The question is never far from her thoughts. That miserable winter has left plenty of time for idle wondering; plenty of empty afternoons staring out at the cold, a surfeit of unsatisfied nights lying half awake, listening to their protesting intestines. No shortage of days and weeks to endlessly mull the matter of her own culpability. For this is what consumes her.

Why did she do it?

She has no clear answer, even for herself. When the serpent offered the fruit, it seemed . . . easy. Easy to take it, easy to bite and swallow the sweetness that seemed to race down her throat as if possessed of an intelligence of its own. And in the moments following, many things became clear that had been murky, and she ran to find Adam, fruit in hand, the serpent forgotten. When she looked upon Adam and saw his nakedness, she grew flushed, her breathing quickened. Well does she remember that moment: when she wished also for Adam to look upon her own nakedness, and see her—really *see* her—for the first time.

Later of course things got complicated. God showed up with His endless supply of guilt and rage and vitriol. God the merciful withheld mercy. God the forgiving refused to forgive. God the compassionate condemned Eve and her husband to a life of never-ending toil and pain, succored at its conclusion with a dusty grave and hungry maggots.

It doesn't make much sense to Eve. But she figures it doesn't have to make sense: it just *is*. What confuses her more these days is her own role in this drama. When she bit that fruit, was she some passive creature with no more initiative than a honeybee buzzing among the blossoms? Or was she an active—and so actively evil—partner in the serpent's plan?

This is what keeps her up nights. No matter how many times she goes around with it, it never quite coalesces into anything logical.

If she had been taught to sin, who then taught her? God and Adam were her only companions. As for the serpent, she had seen him only the one time. And besides, if the serpent was evil, what was it doing in the Garden in the first place?

Far more likely, then, that Eve was born a sinner; or if not born exactly, then created with some flaw that led her astray as surely as a snake, born legless, will crawl on the ground. But in that case, how can she be held accountable for her acts? It's as mad as blaming the snake for its lack of legs.

Eve is disturbed by these ruminations: she can't shake the fact that she has erred in some way that will mark humanity for the rest of its days. So that winter she prays to God to ease her burden. She prays for enlightenment and understanding. She gets no response, so she tries praying for peace of mind, and when that fails, for acceptance.

At last she prays for forgetfulness. If the matter can't be understood, she resolves to stop worrying about it. And little by little— whether by God's design or some other, less divine method—these prayers start to take effect.

•

One night over supper Adam says, We'd best move on.

Eve has been waiting for this. The goats they chanced upon some weeks ago are now bones and hides, and the gazelle that delivered them from midwinter is a memory. Winter is past and they have survived. Now Eve and Adam wear girdles of animal skin instead of leaves, and some of their tools and weapons (knife, fishing spear, needle) are made of splintered horn and bone instead of stone and wood.

It has been difficult but Eve fears worse ahead.—Must we leave? I've grown used to this place, though it holds painful memories.

Adam chews thoughtfully on a sliver of fish, bones crackling between his teeth—It's true there are fish here and some fruit, but I'd not trust them to hold out forever.

—There are a few animals from time to time. Plus the cave makes a good shelter.

Adam frowns.—I cannot help feeling it isn't right for human beings to be squatting in caves like animals.

She fights to keep herself from bursting into laughter, sensing that this would be an unproductive response.—What are we then, if not animals in this world? You said as much yourself when you killed the gazelle.

—When I said that I was in despair, he says heavily.—I have remembered myself since then. Above all, we are God's children.

Eve says nothing but she thinks many things. She thinks: This might be true, but it hasn't done us much good so far.

She thinks: Judging from the other fathers I've seen in the animals that surround us, He is singular in His attentions.

She thinks: You, husband, seem to put more importance on our parentage than God Himself does.

She thinks: If we're God's children, and I think we are, then what does that make all the other creatures inhabiting this world? The Devil's children? God's mistakes?

Instead she says, I'm glad that butchering animals is something you've grown comfortable with.

He shrugs.—It is only one of the trials that face us.

—Wherever we move to next, Eve continues, I think we should make sure that it has plenty of food already, just like there was when we arrived here. More if possible.

He nods.—So it should. I feel those peas are quite fortifying, and if we can find something more, some grain or such, that would be well for us.

—And fresh water. A river with fish in it.

—And those red berries, Adam nods.—I admit to a fondness for those, though there were few enough of them here. Plus fruit trees while we're at it, and grapes. We still have those seeds, we can try sowing them. Though I doubt they survived the winter.

—We can try. Maybe we'll be surprised.

—Perhaps we shall, he says, all solemnity.

—Beehives, Eve says suddenly.—I want honey. And not too high off the ground either, so we can collect it easily.

—And with lazy bees, he smiles.

—And in the grasslands nearby, a few even lazier gazelles. Or sheep would do just as well.

—But not so many as to eat the plants. Just enough to get us some meat occasionally.

—How about some birds roosting on the ground? Their eggs might be tasty, and their flesh too. What are you calling them, night-jars?

Finally Adam laughs aloud.—That's quite a list. Anything we forgot?

—Tall trees for shade and firewood. Plenty of stones to construct a shelter, since you're suddenly too fussy for caves anymore.

—And a more open landscape than this one, Adam says with a glance around.—With hills not so close, so we can see anything approaching us from a distance, storms or wild animals.

She nods.—I hadn't thought of that.

Adam sits back with his arms crossed and gives Eve a jaded look.—Might as well just say you want the Garden again and be done with it.

She winces. They are nearly a year banished but the memory still burns. Though Adam, to his credit, mentions it only rarely, the memory of it lingers with them always. Like the faint odor of a long-dead flower; like the remembered scent of a lover.

—It's fair enough to decide what we're looking for, she counters.—Though I admit there's little enough chance of finding it all in one place.

But miraculously, after another four months' hiking, find it they do.

# 4 *the murder*

The gazelle is hurt but it's not dead yet. It stares at them with brown eyes full of terror and understanding as Adam stands uncertain. Rock in his hand, chipped along one edge. Arms like twigs and the whole construct of the man looking like something about to topple. Some poorly planned idea with only two legs that could never work.

—Kill it, Eve croaks. She's well past the toppling point herself, can't even manage to haul her body past the mouth of the cave.

Adam sways.

—Kill it, repeats Eve.

The gazelle is as mute as Adam. It has slipped from an icy outcrop hanging above the mouth of their cave and fallen to the stony earth immediately below. As if delivered to them by God Himself in His limitless munificence. Such thoughts are far from Eve's mind at the moment, however.

She just wants her husband to kill the damn thing.

The animal has broken both forelegs and a hip; blood trickles from its nose. It is too young for antlers and in all probably weighs little more than Eve. Still Adam is wary. He circles the animal slowly, seeing how its rear is wedged between two stones so it can't turn. With its forelegs broken it can barely lift its head off the ground. It carries an air of menace nonetheless.

—Be careful, Eve warns.—But kill it.

Adam says nothing.

She smells the fear on it, even from this height above its broken body, thick as the flies that swarm around its head and anus. Or is it Adam's fear she's smelling? Some instinct tells her that this injured animal is unpredictable. A lunging bite or chance kick from its good rear leg could leave Adam with wounds to fester for weeks until, eventually, he'd be no better off than this gazelle. But there is no choice: he must kill it and they both must eat it. They've eaten not enough for two months and nothing at all for a week. They are bones lashed together with skin. Their hair is falling out, their teeth ache, and lately she has been prone to nosebleeds. It is all they can do to stagger to the river and chip away ice so they don't die from thirst.

Adam holds a stick in one hand and a sharp stone in the other. Neither seems adequate to rend the life from this animal. He takes a step forward, halts, retreats. Every time he moves close the deer bucks its head frantically and chuffs through blood-filled nostrils.

—For God's sake *kill* it, Eve moans.

Adam hesitates again, then steels himself with visible effort. He lunges at the beast almost too quickly for Eve to follow.

A clean slice across its neck would be the quickest way to kill the thing, but that is made difficult by its lurching head. Adam attacks from the side, clubbing it uselessly with the stick and driving the sharp rock into the stomach. The gazelle shrieks—a sound Eve hopes never to hear again—and kicks maniacally with its one good leg. Adam yells something too, an incomprehensible bellow, as his arms thrash. Club and blade slap against the hide of the animal and the hole in its side becomes a rip, then a gash, then a massive open rending of flesh and fur. Adam's arms flap like bird wings, blade and club whirling in furious tandem to hack and pummel until life is snuffed out.

The animal lurches like the sea in a storm, causing its blood to burst forth in ever thicker runnels that stain the snowy mud and turn it to slush underfoot. Adam, spattered with bowels and blood and tripe, lashes out in escalating fury. The sounds issuing from his mouth sound no more human than the gazelle's pathetic bleats.

The gazelle's kicks grow feeble. Adam doesn't let up: the animal's fading strength seems to bolster his own. He has dropped the knife now and uses the club with two hands to batter the animal's head where it lies limp in the dirt. Up and down, up and down, up and down. The gazelle has quit the fight but Adam doesn't seem to notice. Eve wonders how long her husband will continue this if he is not stopped. Till he collapses seems most likely.

With strength she thought had left her, Eve rouses herself enough to slide down the path from the cave to the gazelle. Adam frightens her to look upon; he is sheened in sweat and his eyes have gone manic. He has beaten the animal's head to paste and even the club he is using has splintered beyond use. Nonetheless he continues beating on the thing's dead hide with the limp remains of the stick. Little scraps of bone and flesh and wood scatter with each impact.

—You can stop, she tells him.

He doesn't respond so she hollers at him and grabs his shoulder.

—Heh?

—Stop now. It's dead.

Adam's eyes focus on the corpse and he drops the club. Staggering back he slips and skids on wet earth.

—Careful, Eve mutters. She picks up the stone knife and runs it under the pelt of the gazelle. It pulls through with surprising ease: organs and muscle flop out and stink. Steam rises from them like exhaled breath, amid an expanding pool of snowmelt.

Behind her she hears Adam getting up.—Come here and have some of this, she tells him.

There's no response. Wet entrails slide from the animal's belly to slosh around her feet. Its blood is warm against her icy flesh, and Eve feels her own blood surge in response. She calls over her shoulder, You must be famished after all that exertion. I'm famished just watching you. Come eat.

Still no answer. She looks behind her. Adam squats, staring at the gazelle. Tears course down his face to lose themselves in his beard. Though he has eaten nothing for a week, he finds the ability within himself, amazingly, to vomit.

Eve stands with the knife in her hand, her attention torn between two tableaux: the dead deer, the crying husband. She can't help herself: she tears away a rubbery shred of flesh, grinds it between tender canines, chokes it down. Carefully she says, You seem upset, husband.

—Uhh, says Adam.

—I would think you'd be pleased. We'll not starve to death, at least not for a while longer.

He hiccups to catch his breath, then laughs bitterly.—We're well and truly out of the Garden now, aren't we? Killing others to keep ourselves alive. No better than animals, ourselves. And we thought eating of the fruit would make us like gods . . .

Eve inhales sharply. She isn't ready for this conversation, not now. Maybe not ever.—We've been eating fish for months, she points out.

—Not the same, he says, shaking his head weakly. He lifts an arm as if to shield his eyes from what he has done.—It bleeds as we do, it—its flesh is warm, as ours is. This isn't the same as killing a fish, not at all.

No it's not, Eve thinks ruefully. The flesh peels off beneath her knife in thick layers, curling into her hands like an offering. It's different all right. And that's what makes me happy.

•

That night violent wind and raucous thunder slam out of the heavens, and lightning cackles as if the sky is an eggshell hatching some new terror. Eve and Adam huddle in their cave, the deer's raw flesh heavy in their bellies and giving them just enough strength to worry that a previously unrevealed awfulness is on the cusp of making itself known. Molten rock raining down in sheets of fire, perhaps, or locusts the size of foxes jostling to fill the cave and devour them. But nothing materializes worse than the storm itself, raging blackly outside, lit by a glaring chiaroscuro of lightning bolts. Inside the cave they crouch together against the body of the gazelle. Eve has dragged it up the slope to keep scavengers from getting at it. Adam watched, ashen-faced, without offering to help, although he did accept a few morsels from Eve's fingers.—No sense in starving, she'd said, and he nodded wordlessly.

In the morning they find that the rain has thawed the ground and washed away the river's veil of ice. They drink their fill for the first time in weeks. Some distance off a thin finger of smoke trails into

the sky. Adam stands squinting at it, then says, Collect some brushwood and bring it to the cave.

—Where are you going?

—Not far. I'll be back soon.

—Won't you eat first?

—I'll eat when I get back.

Eve is grateful for the meat so she does as she is told, although the
wood she collects is damp and she knows not the purpose of her labor. They have no more need of baskets, that much is certain. Her
husband can be secretive at times but this morning it's not a vice that
annoys her overmuch.

By midday Adam returns, bearing a tree branch over his shoulder
as thick as his arm and twice as long.

Eve stares. One end of the branch smolders. When Adam blows
upon it, little flames flicker out and scamper in and out of the wood
like lizards.

Adam grins at her speechlessness and hurls the log to the ground.
His face carries an expression of surprise and pride, of wonder and
determination.—This should make living easier.

Eve nods. She thinks, One end of that branch is aflame.

—I'll have that meal now, says Adam.

As if dreaming, Eve points to the pile of wood she has
collected.—I don't know if this is suitable. It's a bit wet.

Adam shrugs.—Wood is wood, no?

Apparently not: wet wood burns only reluctantly, they learn that
day. The log spits and crackles like an ill-tempered serpent, while
white smoke from the damp kindling quickly chokes the little cave
and slinks away through the entrance grudgingly. Nonetheless, to
Eve it is the sweetest smell in the world. With a great deal of fussing
and attention, Adam coaxes a little fire to bubble up through the
wood. Eve hacks thick slabs of flesh off the gazelle and impales them
on twigs that she then holds over the flames. The flesh roasts quickly,
growing tender, while the smell of burning blood mixes with the
cloying smoke. To Eve the aromas are sweeter than a garden full of
jasmine and roses. Or even a Garden full of jasmine and roses.

Adam still keeps his distance from the gazelle's corpse. Eve notices that he doesn't look at the animal, and leaves to her the chores of butchering and cooking. So be it, she thinks. It's enough that he bring himself to kill one from time to time.

# 3 *the conversation*

—We can't keep on like this, she tells him.

Adam stares at her with flat eyes and she is reminded of the fish they've been subsisting on without letup. Cold and uncooked and vaguely—she fancies—resentful.

He says nothing. He is good at this, she is learning: silence is one of his most effective tools. It masks so many things: uncertainty, fear, ignorance, resentment. Also, she suspects, fondness, affection, charity. After a time he drops his gaze to his feet, leathery and hard, and to the ground beneath them—gritty, hard. Eve sighs. Everything is unpleasant in this place. In these places. The Garden is a memory and fading fast except at those half-awake times in early morning when she groggily paddles to awareness and hasn't yet remembered that she has left it behind forever.

At such moments there is none of the delicious exhilaration of the fruit left in her mouth or blood. There is only dread and hopelessness, the empty sadness of God's voice when He said *You have until dusk.*

—To do what?

—*To leave.*

Memories catch her unawares at any time, but mornings are the worst. She is groggily unprepared, day after day, for the sullen realization that she is *here*, not *there*. She squeezes her eyes tight to keep back the fury and tears, to hold off the vacant despair that rises each morning like the sun. It usually works.

They have been walking now a month but nothing seems to change except to get unexpectedly, surprisingly, inventively worse. There is no rain unless a downpour. There is no warmth, only

scorching heat. There is no water that isn't clogged with silt and tadpoles that wriggle in her throat as she chokes them down. Insects
sting them or bite; snakes hiss. Distant shaggy predators dog their
steps, heavy with threat. Her bowels are either plugged as with pebbles or gushing like a cataract. Their skin is dappled with sores, pink
with rash. Her desire for her husband is timed in perfect antipathy to
his desire for her: whenever they engage in conjugality, one of them
is always grudging.

They walk from sunup to dusk unless their path brings them to
a grove of olives or a patch of wild peas or date palms, which it
does only rarely. Adam has more or less perfected his spearfishing
technique to the point where he can pull a fat-bellied specimen
from the water almost every day. Sometimes two. Eve knows she
should be grateful for this but has a hard time mustering up the energy while she is busy washing her own dried blood off her feet
each evening. Instead she allows her annoyance to fester inside,
growing like a fetus, till she births it with the words:—We can't
keep on like this.

He says nothing.

She will not allow Adam's silence to prevent her own speech.—
We need to choose one spot and stay there, she says.—This endless
roving about has no point.

—Where would you have us stay? Here?

*Here* is patchy yellow arid grass, the river petering to shallows that
bubble across a bed of pink stones, a few stunted trees and not much
more. Withered hills in the distance, behind which the sun has hidden as if ashamed. The sky a sickly blue, pale and weak. Eve considers: if she had been asked to imagine a landscape as antithetical to
the Garden as was possible, as hellish and desolate and unkind, she
might have come up with something like this.

—Not here, she says.—But someplace, and soon. Maybe we'll see
something tomorrow.

—Tomorrow we rest, Adam counters.

—We just rested, what, three days ago? Four?

—Six, Adam tells her.—And on every seventh day we shall rest, just as God did after creating this world, and we shall do so out of deference to Him.

—To what purpose, may I ask?

—I've just explained the purpose, wife.

Her stomach tightens. She hates it when he calls her *wife*: she has a name after all. Now annoyance loosens her tongue.—Well, *husband,* your purpose seems less than clear to me. If you want to give glory to God, it seems logical that you should keep yourself alive. And that means hunting and collecting food and moving on to find some better place to live.

She might as well talk to the wind. Once Adam has made up his mind there is nothing to do but accept the decision or ignore it. Tomorrow he will lounge by the river and brood, watching the fish amble by but not stirring himself to catch one. Maybe this evening he'll have a bit of luck and will pull something extra from the water to save for tomorrow. Then again maybe not. Beyond this, Eve knows, anything she wants to eat she'll have to find herself.

•

Two days further on, the river deepens and trails into a valley, angling toward the direction of the rising sun. Clusters of rigid river grass and reed grow thick along its banks. Low hills rise up on each side, growing day by day with barely perceptible stealth, until another week has passed and they are suddenly in a shallow valley with grasslands all around them. Cottonwoods line the river and birds prattle among their leaves while vines entwine themselves round their thick gray trunks. Eve spies a spider's web glimmering with dew, and then squints at the trailing morning glory. An idea forms. Her hands reach for a length of the stringy vine.

Enormous patches of wild peas stain the valley floor, and stands of yellowing wheat drop thick heads of seed to the earth. Their world has gotten, suddenly, very lush.

And very cold. Steady wind blows through the valley like a malevolent breath, and the pathetic leaf girdles worn by Eve and Adam do nothing to keep the chill off. Each morning dawns cooler than the last, and soon Eve feels a constant pain in her throat as if some sharp-cornered growth has taken root there. Suppers of raw fish and foraged seeds do little to fight it off.

Both she and Adam continue to lose weight alarmingly. Their ribs are quite visible beneath their hides.

—We need to keep moving, she tells him.

—You were the one so keen to find a spot, and settle there.

She nods.—But I'm not convinced that this is the place I had in mind.

—Look around. Those plants will keep us alive for weeks.

—If we don't die of the cold, Eve replies. Some part of her is annoyed at this role she has grown into: Why must she always be the complainer? She nags while he carries on stoically: this is no good at all. Maybe she should learn Adam's trick of silence.

Too late now. He is stalking away, toward the hills. God alone knows what he is up to. Eve goes to collect some wheat berries and peas, since it looks as though Adam isn't doing any fishing today. While gathering the food into piles, she notices some small red fruit growing on flat bushes. The taste is not so sweet as a grape but it is sweet enough. She devours them by the handful.

The sky darkens. Adam returns to tell her, I have found a cave.

—Oh?

—Yes. It's as good a shelter as any we've had since we were—ahh—

—Sent away?

It is a topic they dread to touch upon too often: the night of their banishment. When it comes up in conversation they both grow discomfited. Maybe one day, many years from now, they'll speak of it more easily. Even share a quiet chuckle about these, their early trials.

Then again maybe not.

—It will keep us dry at least, says Adam, speaking of the cave.—And somewhat warm.

—That sounds pleasant. How far?

—Just in the hills there.

She surveys her little harvest, piles of peas and grains and a few tiny berries.—If we could keep this with us there, we'd not have to fish every day.

—What's the point?

She arches an eyebrow at him.—We don't know how cold it will get. There may be days you won't want to stand in the river. Or there may be storms.

—True enough, he frowns.—But I see no way of carrying such tiny things to the cave without making so many trips and getting so hungry in the doing that the effort is pointless.

—But it's just as stupid to leave it for the insects and the birds.

He grunts.

—Let me show you something, she says.

•

He proves surprisingly adept at weaving: he grasps the basic principle immediately, and his fingers possess a quite unexpected nimbleness. Eve's mistake is in attempting to weave the vines. Seeing the morning glories twining round the cottonwoods had given her the idea of trying to make them into a platter or basket, but she ends up with only a loose floppy net. Disgusted, she casts it aside, only to find that Adam has fallen upon a pile of straight stiff reeds. As she watches, he forms an X with two of them and binds them together with vines, then starts weaving thinner, supple reeds between them. He catches her watching and winks.—They bend more easily when they've been softened by the water.

She winks back.—I have the cleverest husband in all Creation.

—That is no more than the truth, he nods.

By sunset they have each woven a large shallow platter wide enough to require two hands to carry. Eve lines them with flat palm leaves, and they pile them high with as much food as they can forage. By the time they get to the cave it is nearly dark and they can only place the platters inside the entrance and set themselves elsewhere for fear of disturbing their work.

The cave is damp and smells sharply of urine but appears uninhabited. Eve feels peculiarly elated, as if the food stores and solid roof above have awakened some primal impulse. She murmurs, It was good you found this place.

—It was good you thought to weave those baskets, he says.—Even that net of vines you made might prove useful in some way.

She considers this.—For catching fish, maybe. Just as a spider catches insects.

He turns to face her.—That's an idea.

—Tomorrow is your day of rest, is it not?

—So it is.

Around them the crickets start up.—I may join you in your observation.

—Praise God.

For the first time since leaving the Garden, Eve feels almost content. Paradise this is not, but she has a snug shelter and a pile of food nearby, and part of her feels a certain confidence that these things will allow her and her husband to survive whatever the coming cold weather brings. Even, perhaps, while enjoying a degree of comfort.

In the event, this is not the case. They work through their stored food in a week and go to collect more and that is gone in a week and they go to collect more but by then the wheat grains have fallen from the stalks to root themselves in the earth, and the peas that are left are barely larger than the grains of wheat, and the fruit has gone by completely. Adam tries fishing with the net and this holds them for a time until the net falls to pieces. The weather grows even colder. It is the cold of fury, of ruthlessness, of rage. Eve sits at the mouth of the cave, a strange lassitude overwhelming her: she plays at chipping the flat gray shale that makes up the floor of the cave, knocking stone against stone; and unexpectedly she begins fashioning blades and knives and points. She binds one to Adam's spear and his fishing again improves for a time. Then one night the wind howls through the valley like all the angels falling into Hell at once, and in the morning the river has iced over. Adam knocks against it feebly with the butt of his spear but he is too enervated to keep it up. Anyway the wood has cracked and split.

—What's happening? Eve calls to him.

His voice holds wonder mixed with terror.—The water has turned to stone.

Sure, thinks Eve. Why not? What next?

On the ice his feet turn first red then blue, finally translucent. Watching from the riverbank, Eve calls out, Forget this. Come back inside, we must get out of this cold.

She is freezing herself: her nipples stand out like berries and her flesh is bumpy.

—What will we eat? Adam calls after her.

She shrugs.—God will provide.

He stares as if searching for mockery but she means none. Turning her back on him, she staggers toward the cave. Her legs are barely thicker than her arms. The ground underfoot is limned with frost like mold on a dead thing. Eve wonders what they will do now. She wonders why she is going back to the cave, then figures it is because they have nowhere else to go. She wonders if God will provide, really, or if He is enjoying Himself too much to stop now. She wonders, not for the first time, just what the Hell God is up to, anyway.

# 2 *that first morning*

They wake up into their first morning of—exile? Banishment? Liberation, freedom? Self-reliance? No, certainly not that—huddled mere steps from where God abandoned them the night before. The Garden is just over that hill, there. Or is it that one? Hidden as it is, they might as well be in another world.

Maybe we are, thinks Eve.

Last night rain had lashed down from a bruised sky, not the gentle showers of the Garden, but angry torrents intent on drowning everything that couldn't be broken apart by main force. Eve huddled next to her husband and he huddled right back. There was no question of protector and protected: they were both terrified.

This morning the rain has stopped, but dawn is limited to a paling of sky from black to dark gray to light gray. Only a hot silver spot in the clouds suggests the presence of the sun.

Eve squats beneath the tree that had sheltered them, staring at the dawn. It's a dreary scene. Low mist and rocky hills, thorny straggling scrub and the sky like a dead eel. She feels like a dead eel herself, as damp and limp and vacant.

—How does it look? comes Adam's voice from behind her.

—See for yourself.

There is no response. She looks over her shoulder to see him hunched on his side, eyes screwed shut.—Rise, and say hello to your world.

—No.

—What?

—I am not moving this day.

She blinks. Blinks again, and thinks about this for a time as the sky lightens.

They are faced with many inconveniences, doubtless even many dangers. It will be necessary to struggle and fight and overcome, and any rest will be fleeting and vaporous. She understands this well enough: God made it clear yesterday. But it had not occurred to her to just give up. Indeed the impulse is quite outside her ken. Perhaps she is fashioned with that particular bone lacking. She has few illusions—the fight ahead will tax her and age her and probably kill her. Fair enough, but she isn't dead yet.

Adam hasn't stirred, though his eyes are now open. She squats beside him and leans close.—Rouse yourself.

He says nothing, just stares at the heavy bark scaling the tree trunk, while the earth's grit grinds into his flesh. Doesn't she know what that feels like? She does indeed . . . and despite herself, she smiles fleetingly.

The smile vanishes fast. Adam is weeping. Well, all right: Eve wept through the duration of last night's storm too. But it is morning now and the rain has stopped, it's time for the tears to dry up as well.

—Come on now. Be a man. She leans forward further and her breast swells out, brushes his hip. A tremor runs through her loins.—You were one last night.

He scowls.—Licentious woman. Can you think of nothing else?

Anger flares through her then, O yes it does, flashing through her marrow like the lightning they'd witnessed for the first time last night, after God had left them and Adam had known her and the Heavens howled their fury as if in divine retribution. Anger gives Eve the energy to stand and leave the tree behind as she strides off.—I can think of much else, she snaps.—Breakfast for example, and securing shelter more comfortable than the bare earth, and finding something to wear—here she shakes the pathetic fistful of leaves girdling her hips—in place of *this*.

She has taken barely ten steps when he appears beside her.—No reason to be unpleasant, he pants.

—I can think of many.

He holds up his hands as if to say, Yes, all right, I understand.

—Being called licentious is one of them, she goes on without pause, when it is you who gorge on my flesh all night long.

—We both gorged, he begins.

—You needed no encouragement.

He walks silent for a time.—You are right, I'm sorry. I'll not say that again.

They plod on, step by joyless step beneath the sun's silver boil.

—Blame me for many things, she spits.—Blame me, if you must, for transgressing in the Garden and bringing ruin down upon us both. But never—*never*—blame me for your own lusts.

It's necessary to concentrate on their footing as they walk, step-ping gingerly, their feet soft as a pair of newborn's. Jagged pebbles and splintered shards torment them with every step.

They walk. And walk. And when that is done they walk some more without cease. For her part, Eve walks in the hope—even the expectation—that things will improve at some point. That the land-scape around them will soften, grow more colorful and lush and Garden-like. But this does not happen that first day.

After some time they bind their feet with broad tough leaves tied with vine. This protects them for a while, until the leaves wear through and fall to pieces. Then they find more. This helps relieve their bruised soles but does nothing to ease their cramped thighs, their clenched calves, their stomachs growling with emptiness or tongues thick and dry.

—Where are we, anyway? pants Adam.

Eve has no answer. There is no answer. No place has, as yet, any name to call it by.

They have been planted in some desolate landscape inspired by dust and bones, fashioned it would seem by a madman. Behind them, the patch of ground where they spent the night is long since swallowed up by a low line of rocky outcrops. The tree that gave them shelter disappears first to a speck, then nothing. Ahead lies a wide patch of half-naked loneliness, stretching to every horizon, pocked with scrub grass and low thorny bushes and stones. Lizards scuttle by; birds of prey hang motionless over their heads like curses. The only blessing is the thick cloud blanket: beneath the full force of the sun, this landscape would crush them with little effort.

Eve and Adam trudge onward. They do so because they have no choice, because staying in this place would be suicidal.

They have seen no sign of the Garden since waking. Eve remarks the oddness of this. It should have at least been visible as a green smear in the distance; the tree where they spent the night was only a few hurried footsteps away. But there is no hint of it anywhere. The Garden has vanished as thoroughly as any dream.

Eve is grateful for her exhaustion then. If she had any strength at all she would shatter into tears. Banished or no, some small part of her had clung all night to the irrational hope that, come morning, they might be allowed to return. That the awful night was just a warning. But with each heavy step she grows more certain: it wasn't a warning. This isn't a lesson. This is life.

•

Morning shifts and shuffles into an endless, staggering rhythm, sand crunching underfoot, shabby bushes watching silently as they pass. A squally wind kicks up, tangles their hair, strips their leaf girdles nearly off. They squint against the wind and dust, leaning into the air as into a wall. Time seems mutable; at moments Eve feels as though she has been walking all day, at other moments she is sure they've barely started. But no, her feet ache too much for that.

She stops, apropos of nothing, and looks behind her. The rocky outcrops are gone. So is everything else. Vaguely she wonders how far they have walked, but distances mean little to her. Leagues at least, anyway.

Adam squints ahead, pointing.—There are trees, tall ones. Perhaps a spring or a river.

—I'm hungry, she says needlessly. They are both ravenous, but apart from lizards they have seen no animals, nor any edible plant either.

—There will be animals if there is water, Adam asserts. They move off with fractionally more energy than before.—Maybe fruit.

Some distance from the trees they spy a small fat pig.—Wait here, Adam says, and trots toward it. But as he draws near the animal stiffens, then bolts into the underbrush. Adam returns empty-handed.— Now that's odd.

A small circle of worry is expanding in Eve's stomach.

—I wonder what's wrong with it? Adam ponders.—It ran from me as if afraid.

As they approach the treeline they encounter more of the same. Fat geese fly off honking at their intrusion. Bees hum a warning around their hive and whirl menacingly around Adam's head, stinging suicidally until he runs off. Deer and sheep bound away instead of settling at their feet and cooperatively expiring. The circle in Eve's belly expands into three dimensions and becomes a hard, heavy stone.

—Look, says Adam, there is a stream after all.

They collapse on its grassy banks. The sky is starting to clear, and now the shade is a balm that succors them. The water is clear and slow-moving, but even here the fish fail to hurl themselves out onto the bank. Instead they glide past as if oblivious to their need. Eve makes up her mind that something must be done about this.

—I don't understand, cries Adam. He rubs the sores left by the bees, little red eruptions dotting his arms and chest.—The way these animals ignore our presence or flee or even attack us, it is most unnatural.

—Husband, do you remember when God told us we would labor and toil all the rest of our lives?

—I do.

—I believe this is what he meant.

Adam sits back on his heels as if considering.—It bodes poorly for us if even food and shelter and fire are to be denied.

Eve has taken hold of a long straight branch and is fiddling with it.—Poorly or no, I believe that's the case. Not denied exactly. But not provided either.

Adam sighs.—It is difficult to contemplate such a thing.

—We'd best get used to it.

She strips bark from the branch, nearly as long as her arm. Now she is intent upon one end, where the wood has split and left a pointed sliver. Adam asks, What are you doing?

—The fish aren't moving very fast, she tells him.—Since they're not coming to us voluntarily, maybe we can coerce one.

Adam's distaste is palpable.—A bit barbaric, wouldn't you say?

Her eyes flicker at him, then away.—You don't have to eat it. Myself, I'm hungry.

The water is cold around her calves but soothing against the tortured soles of her feet. The river bottom is soft with decaying leaves. Well-fed fish amble past her, around or between her legs. She watches carefully, spear upraised, choosing her victim, waiting for the moment. She closes her eyes, remembers the herons of the garden with their golden plumes and silent, watchful grace. Like a heron she strikes, the spear stabbing into the water with a great splash and fury. She misses everything. She strikes two more times, missing again.

Adam splashes into the water.—Let me.

She wants to say, Make your own damn spear, but she is tired and so hungry she's afraid she'll start sobbing at any moment. So she relinquishes her weapon, saying only, The current is stronger than you think. The fish swim with it while the spear fights it.

Adam jabs downward once and retrieves an empty stick.—I see what you mean.

But on his second try he succeeds in stunning one of the fish and then, moving faster than Eve has ever seen him, uses the spear to jab sideways through the gills and hurl it onto shore. Without a word they clamber from the water and kneel on each side of it. The question hangs unasked: Now what?

—We should have a fire, says Adam.

—All right, says Eve. She is giddy with lack of food and the promise of it.—Go ahead and make it then.

Adam licks his lips.—I don't know where to find it. In the Garden it was always just *there*.

—We're not in the Garden anymore, Eve giggles. She is aware in some part of her mind that giggling is inappropriate. But then, what isn't?—In case you hadn't noticed.

He has begun tugging at the fish.

—Here, the animals run away from us, Eve goes on. She feels only a few steps away from hysteria, and wonders what it would be like to give in. Comfortable, in a way: like a warm fleece around her shoulders.—It's almost as if they don't wish to be eaten. How uncooperative of them.

Adam says nothing. The fish's fins tear off in his hands, which are coated with scales and blood. Giving up on the fins, he inserts his fingers into the gills, ragged and misshapen where the spear entered them, and pulls. The fish, though dead, resists: its flesh is unwilling to be rent in this unexpected fashion. The gills stretch but do not rip. Adam is sweating. He is faint with lack of food and lack of sleep and a full day's anxiety and fear.

—Use the spear, Eve says. Her giddiness has fled.—It has a sharp point, we could use it to cut. Where did it go?

Adam hesitates, then confesses, I think I, hem, dropped it.

—Where?

—In the river.

She stares at him, then snorts, then starts laughing.

—Don't be like that. Once I had the fish it's all I could think about. Same as you.

—Yes, but I wasn't holding the spear, was I? Never mind, I'll get another. Eve totters off among the nearby trees, where she finds any number of likely twigs and branches littering the ground. She returns with several.—One of these should do.

They set to peeling the sticks, and Adam discovers a split along one of them that reveals a long, smooth-edged blade. He jabs this like a lever into the gills and suddenly flesh snaps, guts unglue, and a long ugly gash opens the length of the animal. Vile-colored intestines leak onto the ground between them. Eve feels her appetite evaporate, then rush back a moment later, stronger than ever.

—My God, Adam mutters.

The thing is a mess of bones and guts. The skin, once broken, peels back easily enough, but Eve rejects it as anything to eat. Then comes a thin layer of flesh, chewy but mild in flavor and quite pleasant if one could only ignore the putrid mess oozing beneath it. Eve finds, if she closes her eyes, that she is able to do this. With every mouthful she feels herself growing stronger, calmer, clearer in the head.

Unfortunately there are too few mouthfuls. She notices that Adam eats faster and so gets more. Maybe this is fair because he killed the fish. Maybe it's fair because he is bigger and needs more food. Or maybe it's not fair.

Soon only entrails are left. She shuts her eyes. Some of the bits taste foul and she spits them out. Some bits have no flavor at all and she swallows these. None of them tastes as good as the flesh.

She opens her eyes to see bones on the earth. Adam smiles at her, blood and bile on his teeth, fingers, lips. He looks a savage, but no doubt she is much the same.

—Our first meal, wife.

—Indeed . . . husband.

He eyes the river.—Are you satisfied?

—I wouldn't turn down another morsel, she admits, if one were to be had.

—Nor would I.

She leaves him knee-deep in water, a new spear cocked overhead. She doesn't expect immediate success, and anyway there is something she remembers from before, when she came this way to gather sticks to cut open the fish. At that time she had been too addled to notice properly, but in retrospect—ah yes. There they are. The leaves are fat and pointed like thick stars, the vines clamber around the bare boles of taller, branchless trees, and the clusters of fat green grapes hang down like breasts, like testicles, like anything that promises life, continuation, eternity.

Eve stuffs her mouth with handful after greedy handful, seeds and all, deciding only after several bunches that she should rinse away the dust and insects and bird shit. So she twists off a half dozen of the largest clusters and carries them to the water and submerges them briefly, then eats two more bunches straightaway before bringing the rest to her husband.

The fruit seems to dance inside her. Even more than the fish, or probably in combination with the fish, her heart pounds with new vigor and her eyes take in the world with a clarity of detail she has never known before.

Behold, for example, her husband. Adam still wades in the river, but two fish lie dead on the bank beside him. Both are larger than the first he caught. Adam's barrel chest tends to softness in his belly, Eve sees, but his arms are rangy and attached by wiry cords of muscle to wide, well-set shoulders. His legs are slightly bowed and well turned, his buttocks as molded and firm as his biceps. As for the rest, well, Eve has no basis for comparison, but from what she knows already, no basis for complaint either. She stands there at the river's edge, watching her husband catch her dinner while she herself holds bundles of fruit against her belly, and for a moment she can almost, if not quite, admit to feeling happy. If she squints her eyes she can almost pretend she's in the Garden again. Except of course that in the Garden, Adam never needed to wade knee-deep in the river with a pointed stick in his hand. His lips and fingers were never smeared with blood. And he never looked on God's creation with the intent to rip its life away by force.

He turns and sees her. She arches an eyebrow at him and says, Look what I found.

•

They stay in that place for many days until the weather begins to turn cold. At the same time the fish mysteriously dwindle and the grapes are in the main consumed. Adam has the idea of using the seeds to plant further vines elsewhere, so they have collected a great quantity of them.

—We'd best continue on, Adam suggests one morning.

Eve had been thinking the same.—Shall we follow the river and see where it leads?

—I have no better suggestion.

—Let's take the last of the fruit then, and that fish you caught this morning.

—No.

—What?

Adam won't meet her eye but she can see from the set of his shoulders that he has made up his mind about something.—We need to leave it behind. As an offering to God, he adds before she can ask.—He has given us so many blessings.

—And taken away a few, she retorts.—Lest you forget, He has banished us from Paradise for all time.

—And we both know why.

Eve scowls at the ground.—Am I to be reminded of that every day?

—No. But listen: He has not abandoned us. We have enjoyed of his bounty, and it is meet that we should show our gratitude.

Eve eyes the grapes. The *last* clusters of grapes, fat and green and freshly washed.—Uh huh.

—He has given so much, Adam persists. In his eyes glitters a fire that Eve has never observed before. She seems to be noticing many sides to her husband that she has never seen before.—To show ingratitude would be churlish.

—We know not where we are going, Eve counters.—It would be sensible to take along what little food we have.

—Sensible perhaps, but not faithful. We must have faith.

—And sense.

He shrugs, conceding.—And sense.

Eve can tell she's not going to win this battle. She goes into the thicket to relieve herself and when she returns, Adam has piled the grapes into a little mound and set the fish on top.—It would be better to burn it as a holocaust, but we know not the secret of creating fire.

Eve thinks, That rather proves my point.

—Still, this is better than nothing, Adam says. He bows his head and holds his hands apart.—Lord, look upon your children with compassion and mercy. We admit our transgression and beg forgiveness. Accept this offering as a sign of our love and our understanding that all good things flow from you.

And not a few bad ones, thinks Eve.

Adam stands silent then. Eve wonders if he expects God to make His presence known and engage him in a conversation there and then. About free will perhaps, or predestination or original sin. But nothing happens. Eve, unable to resist needling her husband, observes, Maybe you should speak a little louder. I'm not sure He heard you.

Adam glances upward uneasily, but there are only the willows shouldering out the sky, and the birds dancing among them. Redstarts, waxwings, martins.—You don't need to shout to get God's attention, he says.—A sincere heart is all that is needed. Don't worry, wife, God has heard us this day.

Eve says nothing. Let him believe what he wants, she thinks. For her part, the time of certainty is over with, and she is not so sure of anything anymore.

# 1 *the old man*

God leaves them then.

Eve is glad for that. She's had about enough of His scorn and derision and threats, but Adam trembles with apprehension.

—What will we do now? he gabbles.—We have nothing.

—Things will get better, Eve tells him, stripping off her girdle of leaves.—In time.

She has her doubts about this, but it's pointless to voice them now. Overhead the sky keens and the trees shudder from side to side, as if seized by fits.

Adam stares at her. Eve yanks away his girdle as well and is heartened to see that, frightened or not, he stands ready to know her as a husband should.

—What are you doing?

The ground beneath her is hard when she lies back. There is no plush grass here; the earth is riddled with pebbles. Ants crawl into her ears. But it will have to do. She pulls her husband on top of her and opens for him.

—This is no substitute for Paradise, he gasps.

Eve shuts her eyes and tries to keep the sadness from her voice. More than anything, she is sure that things are going to get worse.— It's what we've got, she says.